Wristband Diaries

LADY IN WAITING

LADY VICTORIA HERVEY

Lady in Waiting
ISBN # 978-1-78651-859-0
©Copyright Lady Victoria Hervey 2016
Cover Art by Posh Gosh ©Copyright May 2016
Interior text design by Claire Siemaszkiewicz
Finch Books

Published in 2016 by Finch Books Newland House, The Point, Weaver Road, Lincoln, LN6 3QN, United Kingdom.

LADY IN WAITING

Dedication

To those that inspired this work of fiction. Thank you.
This book is dedicated to everybody that helped me
become the person I am today, especially to my
Yorkshire nanny June Rawlings who taught me I
could accomplish anything I put my mind to—
I love you.
Since I spent most of my childhood at boarding school
(age 8-18) I thought I'd give you an insider's view of a
teenage girl growing up in the mid 80s/90s.
Thank you also to my mother for giving me this life
adventure.
I'm still to this day in touch with many friends I first
shared dorms with and whose characters helped
shape this book.
All names have been changed.
Guess at your own peril.

The sunlight streamed into the room, warming my outstretched foot where I'd kicked the sheet off in the night. Blowing thick strands of long blonde hair out of my face, I burrowed deeper into the plush, soft pillow and tried to slip back into the delicious dream starring Leonardo DiCaprio I'd reluctantly been pulled out of.

A soft breeze stirred the gossamer thin curtains, a heady scent drifting into the room — a mixture of fresh sea air and vibrant floral perfume that I always associated with home in Monaco. Inhaling another deep, relaxing breath, I snuggled further down into the mattress, trying to make myself boneless and languid.

A sharp crack sounded through the house.

My eyelids flew open. Disappearing back into that dream — that I really wanted to know the ending to — was no longer an option.

"Daddy," I whispered before flinging off the sheets and leaping from the bed. My feet met the blue-carpeted floor and I skidded on the yellow sundress I'd left discarded in a heap the night before. I launched myself out of the room then rushed down the corridors.

All around, the house was abuzz with activity. Aimee pottered around in the kitchen, which was her domain — the usual sounds of dishes chinking and conversation with the gardener, M. Vincent, drifted out into the hallway. Somewhere out of sight, Mummy scolded Louisa for staining yet another pristine white dress with sticky fingers coated in jam.

Rounding a corner, I collided with a body and crashed into the sideboard. My elbow smarted from the impact.

Augustus steadied himself and flashed me a glare. "Freddie! Watch where you're going, will you?" Only last year Augustus would have been knocked to the floor at such a collision. But age combined with a mammoth growth spurt over the summer had made my younger brother catch up with me in height. He was starting to fill out, his young body maturing into the man it would one day become. The ladies had better watch out when that day came—at fourteen Augustus already showed the signs of a face that had the potential to break hearts.

Augustus resembled our father, with dark hair and tall build, unlike Louisa who took after our mother, with a slim, willowy figure and glossy blonde hair that we both possessed. Mummy had gifted all her children with her ocean grey-green eyes. I was an even mixture of both my parents. Mummy had given me her slim build and Daddy had blessed me, his oldest daughter, with his great height. At sixteen I was already five feet eight and expected to continue shooting up for another few years yet.

"Sorry," I said on a breath as I turned to continue my original course. "Daddy's at it with the air rifle again."

Augustus' eyebrows shot up into his dark hairline. "Does Samantha know?"

I grimaced. "I don't know. Better go fetch her, just in case. He's going to end up getting one of them accidentally sooner or later."

Augustus nodded, and I hurried off in the opposite direction, rushing down the marble staircase.

Outside my father's office door, I took a deep breath and steeled myself for what I might find on entering. Unable to put off the inevitable forever, I tapped on the door before turning the handle and slipping inside.

Daddy sat in his usual blue satin chair at his desk, his eyes pinned on the garden beyond the wide, open French doors that led outside. He twisted in my direction at the sound of my bare feet on the floor and placed his rifle back in its usual spot under his desk. "Another pest got in again."

Letting out a reproachful breath, I said, "Oh, Daddy."

Daddy waved my young concern away with a flick of his hand. "Don't 'oh, Daddy,' me, Frederica. If the dratted things stopped coming into my garden then I'd simply stop shooting at them."

I nodded, knowing it would be another useless conversation to beg him to stop. We'd had it countless times and his conviction never changed. Walking towards the garden, I squeezed his shoulder as I passed. With my feet on the warm patio stone, I froze to the spot and covered my mouth with my hand as a shocked gasp escaped me.

Instead of seeing a skittish, frightened cat, I saw a dead one.

The body was just in front of the hedgerow that the unfortunate soul had climbed over, not knowing that in doing so it had sealed its fate at the hands of my father and that rifle.

A lump formed in my throat and my eyes stung. The poor creature…

Squatting beside it, I didn't need to touch it to check if it was still alive. The glassy, vacant look in its eyes and unfurled, hanging tongue told me that it was as dead as it could be.

Poor cat.

I wished our neighbour would either stop breeding them — because they inevitably got curious and decided to check out our little patch of the world — or that my father would stop shooting at them for invading his garden. It wasn't that he had set out to kill the poor thing. Daddy shot at the cats to warn them off, to frighten them enough that they wouldn't come back.

But I suppose this time the cat had moved, as they are often wont to do, and put itself right in the firing line.

Daddy, clearly, had not even realised that he had hit this one — knowing Daddy he would have fretted over my reaction, been worried over how upset I would be and he made no mention of it when I was in the room.

Swiping away a stray tear, I released a heavy sigh and checked under the hedge. The trap my father had concocted was thankfully empty. On more than one occasion I'd fashioned a jailbreak before Daddy had noticed that a cat had become trapped and set about scaring it away.

I headed back inside the house. My father had returned to his usual position, hunched over the papers on his desk. He wasn't the sort of man to rest on his laurels. As well as being a member of several important leagues and clubs, he adored being in the thick of things and fighting for a cause he believed in with all his heart. His cheerful and dedicated personality made him a perfect character for the important positions he held.

I loved my father dearly, even if our views on animals couldn't have been more different. Where my siblings and I adored all creatures great and small, Daddy couldn't stand them. Which was why he had no idea about Duke, the cocker spaniel that we had had for two years. It paid to live in a more-than-spacious home like ours.

He paid me no notice as I passed by him on my way back through into the main house. Augustus and Samantha met me in the corridor outside Daddy's office.

Samantha, our nanny, took one look at my crestfallen expression and shook her head, a resigned look on her face. "I'll get the shovel."

Later, once the body had been taken care of, I was shoving everything I'd need for the morning into a canvas shoulder bag—towel, comb, magazine and enough francs to keep me stocked with pop and ice cream.

"Come on, Freddie!" Louisa cried from somewhere outside my bedroom.

I rolled my eyes at her whiny voice as I bent down to fasten my white sandals. Louisa, five and a half years my junior, was impatient like most eleven year olds were. Except I was fairly certain she set the bar to which all impatient adolescents were measured. Louisa was wilful and headstrong—like me, but unlike me, she could be a brat about it. *And* she stole my things. "I'm coming, Louisa!"

She poked her blonde head into the room, a scowl marring her tanned face. "Well hurry up about it. I need all the practise I can get before the competition this afternoon." Louisa pushed open my door fully and folded her wiry arms across her chest.

We wore matching outfits—pretty neon pink shorts with embroidered blouses that matched the swimwear we both had on under our clothes. Augustus would also be dressed similarly in shorts and a smart shirt, so that we all matched. At the MC Beach Club, appearance was everything. Mummy was *in* with all the heads at the club, and therefore we always had a member's tent where we could change and store our things.

Fighting back a sigh, I picked up my bag and swung it onto my shoulder. "You're the best swimmer in the MC Beach Club. You already know you're going to win most of the events." My lips twitched with amusement as I peered down at my younger sister. "Except the diving competition."

Louisa's face turned puce as she held her breath in frustration. She threw me a filthy scowl and marched from the room in a cloud of contempt.

It wasn't fair of me to tease her about diving—her greatest phobia. Well, it was her own fault, really. The little minx had followed me up to the high board a few summers before and it had taken us hours to get her back down once she'd frozen with fear at the top.

On my way out to meet the others on the drive, I paused at the nineteenth century French antique console table in the hall by the front door. Atop its thick verde antico marble top was a collection of family photographs. As always, my eyes were drawn to one in particular—a shot of me, Mummy and Daddy in our family home at Heyworth House. We stood in front of one of the many huge portraits with a gilt frame. Mummy smiled for the camera, looking as perfectly put together as she always did in a stylish matching skirt and jacket with not a hair out of place and her face exquisitely made up. She held me in her arms, a wriggling toddler with wispy blonde curls wearing a black velvet dress and white tights that my dressmaker, Jackie, had flown over with the fabric from England to make for me. My father was beside us, smiling down at me while I squeezed my little fist around his index finger.

I adored it because the love rose out of the photograph in a way that couldn't be forced or faked. We looked like a happy family, because we were. To the outside world they were the Lord Beaumont, and Lady Beaumont. But to me…they were Mummy and Daddy.

Augustus was leaning against Samantha's beat up old blue VW Golf when I made it outside. Louisa was already strapped in the front passenger seat, a look of defiance in her eyes. As the oldest I always sat next to Samantha, but something told me Louisa would draw blood if I dared attempt to move her.

"Where's Samantha?" I asked my brother.

Augustus scrubbed a hand over his dark hair. He needed a haircut, it was becoming a wavy, unruly mess. "Your guess is as good as mine."

"I'm here, I'm here," Samantha called as she rushed out of the house and towards the car. She'd freshened up her makeup since I'd seen her last, accentuating her hazel eyes, and had changed her blouse to one that flattered her tall figure and showed off her lovely olive skin. Her thick, brown hair was pulled into a sleek ponytail.

"You're looking nice, Samantha," I said, climbing into the back seat after Augustus. "Making the effort for anyone in particular?"

Samantha's eyes flickered to mine in the rear-view mirror. A blush stained her cheeks. "No, of course not. Why would you think that?"

Pursing my lips, I gave a shrug and gazed out of the window. "No reason."

It was a short drive to the MC Beach Club—situated in a swollen curve beside a white sandy beach and the cerulean blue sea. The club was utter luxury and only the finest would do. It was where I spent a lot of my time, playing ping-pong with Augustus and cooling myself in the pool.

Once we'd arrived, Louisa scarpered off in the direction of the children's pool. We followed after her, and Samantha smoothed down her blouse and checked her hair. Louisa's swimming instructor stood by the poolside wearing tight speedos with a pale blue and white T-shirt. His head was covered by a swimming cap and goggles hung around his neck.

"Freddie, Augustus," he said with a nod as we approached. His gaze softened as it fell on our pretty nanny. "Samantha."

"Hello, Andre," she said, a wide smile stretching across her lips.

Augustus elbowed me in the side. "Let's go, Freddie. I want to practise my back dive before this afternoon."

I nodded and bade farewell to my sister and nanny somewhat reluctantly. Samantha and Andre had been acting differently lately—coy and flirty, and I wanted to stay and watch the romance that they thought they were keeping hidden.

The Olympic pool at the beach club was a sight to behold. Sparkling, crystal clear blue water twinkled in the sunlight and a high, proud diving board stretched into the sky. Sun loungers surrounded all sides of the pool, large and comfortable with umbrellas between each one, the area enclosed by the red-bricked buildings of the Beach Club. Tall palm trees swayed in the warm breeze, their leafy green prongs creating a soft whisper. The hills of Monaco were the backdrop to the pool, luxury homes dotted along the hillside, none more beautiful than Karl Lagerfeld's white fairy-tale house. Further above were jagged, rocky cliff faces that stretched up to the pristine, cloudless sky.

Augustus and I made a beeline for our member's tent and after changing we snagged the loungers in front of the tent and draped our towels across them to claim ownership. Wasting no time, Augustus was straight up the ladder of the diving board to get in as much practise as he could before the events that afternoon.

Every year, the Beach Club put on a fun day of sporting competitions for the children. Ranging from swimming and diving to beach volleyball and football, the activities were endless. All three of us enjoyed taking part—competing with our own age set as well as with each other. Whoever won the most events always got a treat of a curly ice cream cone from Mummy.

I'd always been sporty and athletic and I took the competitions seriously. This year I was only taking part in the swimming events, leaving more opportunity for Augustus and Louisa to win.

"Freddie!"

I turned at the sound of Cornelia's voice and saw my best friend rush towards me, a gleeful smile stretching across her face. "Morning! What's going on?"

I adored Cornelia, my beautiful friend. She had the palest blonde hair—it was practically silver in certain light—and the clearest blue eyes I had ever seen. We had been friends forever—well, since we'd been two and my family had moved to the warmer climate of the south of France. Cornelia was Dutch and I loved going to her house so we could explore the hills that surrounded her house in Eze.

Cornelia slowed to a stop beside me. She grasped my forearms and practically hopped on the spot. "You won't believe what has happened!" Cornelia took a deep breath, and I prepared for what seemed to be explosive news. "Okay, so, you know how I've sort of had a thing for Rupert?" she asked in a rush.

My eyebrows shot up. Saying Cornelia 'sort of' had a thing for Rupert was like saying the planet 'sort of' had gravity. Rupert was tanned with sandy-blond hair and so handsome he had all the girls acting like blithering idiots when he was in the vicinity. I could appreciate his good looks, but I didn't drool over him like Cornelia and our other friends. My taste in guys was pretty simple—tall, or the same height as me at the very least. Rupert was a good three inches shorter than me and therefore didn't make it onto the list of guys I was interested in.

"Oh, do you? I hadn't noticed," I teased my friend.

Cornelia huffed and rolled her eyes. "Okay, so maybe I like him a little bit more than that. Anyway, that's not the point. The point is…he asked me if I wanted to take a walk along the beach this evening! Oh, Freddie, doesn't it sound so romantic? Do you think he will try to kiss me?"

I couldn't help but smile at Cornelia's enthusiasm. "Very. What are you going to wear?"

"I was thinking about my new pink bikini and white cover-up. What do you think?"

"I think you'll look gorgeous no matter what you wear."

My answer must have been the right one, as Cornelia's smile widened even more. She dropped down onto my lounger and hugged her knees. It seemed swimming was going to be postponed for a while.

"The only trouble is, if we really hit things off, it's the end of summer and we won't see each other for such a long time. Do you think he'll write to me while we're off at school?"

"He had better, or he'll have me to answer to," I said.

Cornelia sighed and leaned back against the lounger. "I can picture us now—staying up late and writing letters by torchlight under the sheets so we don't get caught."

Smothering a giggle with my hand, I sat beside her. "You're such a romantic."

She laughed and nudged me with her foot. "You will be too once you meet someone. Will you help me get ready later? I'm so nervous already, I'll never be able to put my makeup on with shaking hands."

"Of course, what are best friends for?" I asked.

"Freddie, you are the absolute best." Cornelia jumped to her feet, startling me. "But now I need to be distracted for the rest of the day. Last one to finish five lengths buys the ice cream?"

"Hmm…" I pondered, tapping my chin. At the last second I vaulted to my feet and darted towards the pool. "You're on!"

"Frederica, you cheat!" Cornelia cursed as she started after me.

The cool water sluiced over my body as I dived into the pool. I cut through the water like I was born to it, or was, at the very least, part-mermaid. My height, along with slim build and athletic body, made me unbeatable in the water. Cornelia knew it, but she didn't care. We raced all the time for fun and her goal in life was to truly beat me in a race.

After the first few lengths, I slowed my pace and allowed Cornelia to begin to catch me up. On the last length I faked a cramp and let her zoom past me and tap the edge of the pool, declaring herself the winner.

Cornelia hoisted herself out of the pool and stood dripping wet. "You can make mine a double cone for the un-sportsmanlike conduct!"

I threw my head back and laughed before climbing out of the water. Slinging my arm around Cornelia's shoulders, I steered her towards the vendor. "I'll even spring for a Snickers, too."

She giggled and wrapped her arm around my waist. "This is why we're friends."

For the rest of the morning, I alternated between lazing on the loungers with Cornelia and dipping in and out of the pool to cool off. We watched Augustus practise his dives and cheered him when he landed a perfect one.

Samantha came with Louisa to collect Augustus and me for lunch. After getting changed, we met Mummy at the Oasis Restaurant where we had hamburgers and French fries dripping in sauce. Louisa couldn't stop talking about how well she had done with her instructor that morning, and bragged about all the events she would win that afternoon.

As soon as we were finished eating, Augustus and I left the others to play a few games of ping-pong and escape the afternoon heat. He beat me five games to three! Our peace didn't last long, and we were soon discovered by Louisa and subsequently ordered to the poolside to watch her race.

The rest of the day was a blur of swimming races, dives, beach games and a little bit of healthy competition. When we weren't competing, Augustus and I would join Mummy and Samantha in cheering on our little sister.

We waited for her front crawl race to start, and one particularly nasty girl — whose older sister had always had it in for me too — distracted Louisa right before the horn sounded to start the race. Louisa stumbled on her starting block before sloppily diving into the water.

A hot rush of anger coursed through my veins. *Stupid girl…who does she think she is?* This was all meant to be harmless fun, with a dose of friendly competition, but still harmless fun. I hated anyone picking on my little sister, even if she did drive me to distraction with regular occurrence. But God help anyone who tried to pick on her…wrath of Big Sister and all that. Poor Lou…she'd spit feathers if she lost.

She tried her best, but that rocky start ruined the race for her, and she came in fifth place. Louisa walked over to us, her narrow shoulders slumped and her forehead wrinkled in a disgruntled frown.

But I knew my sister, and not only was she angry at having lost—she was hurt at having been sabotaged. Her eyes were downcast as she wrapped her towel around herself.

"Never mind, Lou," I said. "Girls like that never really win."

Louisa nodded but didn't seem cheered up by my reassurance. Carefully, so she didn't get her clothes soaked, Mummy hugged her wet little body and kissed her damp cheek. Louisa's age group were finished in the pool, and it was time for the older boys' diving event. We moved closer to the diving boards, and watched as Augustus climbed up to the middle one.

I bent down to put myself at Louisa's ear level. "Do you want to borrow my new eye shadow? I'll help you do your makeup before we go out for dinner tomorrow night?"

Louisa eyed me cautiously, as though I could be trying to trick her. "What about your green top, too? The one with the little stitched on daisies?"

Oh, she was an opportunistic little madam. But at least she was asking. Usually she just stole my clothes and pleaded ignorance when I questioned where they had gone. "Sure."

Her sullen face brightened and a wide smile took over her lips. "Thanks, Freddie!"

It made me wonder if she'd been faking being so upset. Like I said, opportunistic.

We trudged back to Samantha's car, all of our movements sluggish. It had been a long but fantastic day. Without an argument, Louisa took her place in the back seat. She had cheered up immensely after she'd swindled me.

Augustus had won most of his events and recapped them all for us, as though we hadn't all been there. Nevertheless, it had been great fun to cheer our friends and family on, and the air was alive with excitement.

After dinner, I showered and changed into fresh shorts and a vest top then rode my bicycle to Cornelia's house. It only took me around ten minutes, and I had travelled the route so often I could probably have done it blindfolded. The housekeeper showed me into the house and I made my way to Cornelia's bedroom. Cornelia and I had grown up in each other's house and knew them like the backs of our hands.

I found Cornelia amongst such a mess I honestly thought for a moment that their house had been burgled. She whirled around as I entered her room, a pair of shorts clenched in one hand, a sundress in the other.

"Are you all right?" I asked, swallowing a laugh.

"Don't laugh at me, Freddie!" Cornelia cried. "I'm lost— I don't know what to wear. What if I dress up and I look silly? What if I *don't* and I look silly? What if we go swimming and I haven't worn my swimsuit under my clothes? What if we *don't* go swimming and I look silly that I've worn my swimsuit under my clothes?"

Stepping forward, I clasped Cornelia's arms. "Cornelia, firstly, breathe. Secondly, why are you getting so worked up? How long have we both lived here? You know what to wear to go to the beach."

Cornelia searched my eyes for a long second. "You're right. You're absolutely right. I should wear what I'd always wear to the beach. And I should definitely have my swimsuit on underneath. Right?"

"Right. But because it's a date, maybe a little more effort than you would usually put in?" I suggested.

Cornelia nodded frantically. "Yes, of course. Will you help me pick some things out?"

I dropped my eyes to the catastrophic mess of clothes on the floor. "Sure. How long do we have until you're meeting Rupert?"

Cornelia checked her watch. "An hour."

God… "Okay. We'd best get cracking then!"

We sorted through the clothes explosion on Cornelia's floor and found the perfect outfit for her, consisting of a pink bikini with multi-coloured geometric shapes and a form-fitting black cover-up. She wore new jewelled sandals and kept her makeup light. I helped Cornelia style her hair in loose, relaxed waves to give the impression that she hadn't gone to *too* much effort. Fashion had always come easily to me. I was naturally good at picking outfits and I adored dressing my friends and myself up.

The overall effect had Cornelia looking like a knockout — Rupert wouldn't know what had hit him!

I walked Cornelia towards the beach, pushing my bicycle along beside us. We parted ways before we got too close — heaven forbid Rupert should see that Cornelia had brought reinforcements, or was nervous enough to need her friend to escort her to her date.

Cornelia released a shaky breath then flashed me a smile that wobbled at the edges.

My heart went out to my friend and I wrapped my arms around her in a fierce hug. "Have a brilliant time."

Cornelia nodded and hugged me back. "I will. Thanks for your help, Freddie."

"Anytime," I said, pulling away. "I'll see you tomorrow. I can't wait to hear all about it."

She nodded again then turned around to walk to the beach.

I took my time cycling home. The sun had begun to set, still casting rays of warmth, the breeze coming off the ocean carrying with it that salty fresh scent. The day was drawing to a close but that didn't mean that life was slowing down. The impressive vocal range of Whitney Houston danced through the air from the Sporting Club and the rich and famous residents of Monaco were beginning to hit the nightlife.

Aston Martins, Rolls Royces and Jaguars were just a selection of the cars that passed me, taking their occupants to the Monte Carlo Casino for a night of decadence and gambling. I had read somewhere that our avenue was the most expensive street in the entire world, and it was easy to see why just by the cars that drove along it.

It wouldn't be long before I had to bid farewell to my home here again. It was a bittersweet feeling, like it always was. School this year would be extra exciting, but it never got easier saying goodbye to my family. Not to mention the sun. Swapping the south of France for Kent took some getting used to.

During my last days in Monaco, I always tried to soak every last piece of it in. The warmth, the floral and coastal scents, the ice cream...the shopping. I wouldn't return for many months, maybe not even until the following summer. I wanted to absorb all that I could while I still could, enough that would last me during the long separation, and to warm me during cold, rainy nights in England.

One of my neighbour's cats sunned itself on the wall surrounding the enormous apartment building we lived in. Our home was a house within the building, and we occupied the entire first two floors including the gardens.

I slowed to a stop in front of the cat. I stroked its glossy ginger fur, smiling as it pushed into my touch and rubbed its face against my hand.

I scratched the cat's cheeks. "Keep out of the garden, all right? I won't be around much longer to check the traps."

The cat, oblivious to my concern, purred.

I could only hope the message would somehow translate. Or that Daddy's next warning shot was a good distance away from my furry friends.

2

The next morning I awoke, thankfully not to the dulcet tones of an air rifle, but to Duke pushing his wet nose into my hand. I rolled over to peer into the big brown eyes of the spaniel. He whined low in his throat and shuffled closer to me on the bed. I stroked his silky soft head, and his tail thumped against the mattress in response.

"Morning, Duke," I said through a yawn.

Duke gave a yip of excitement, happy that I was now officially awake, and stood up on his short legs.

I yawned again, but so wide it almost split my face in half. "All right, all right. I'm getting up."

Usually Samantha or Aimee walked Duke in the mornings, but every so often he chose me, my brother or sister to do the honours. Perhaps he sensed our imminent departure and wanted as much attention from us as he could get.

After rolling out of bed, I pulled on my shorts and vest top from the night before and shoved my feet into a pair of flip flops. Duke barked at my ankles as I tied my long hair up into a messy ponytail.

I scrubbed the last of the sleep dust out of my eyes when Duke and I left the house to stroll down Avenue Princesse Grace. It seemed the rest of the world was still in bed. The air was tranquil, already holding the promise of another hot day in paradise. Birdsong broke the silence. A gentle breeze carried the sweet scent of honeysuckle from a nearby garden and the refreshing aroma of the ocean.

A couple whizzed past me on their bicycles. They trilled their bicycle bells and waved. Duke yipped at the noise and pulled on his lead to give chase. Little dog syndrome at play once again. Heaven forbid the small creature didn't defend me from the dangers of cyclists.

When we returned to the house, my stomach grumbled for my breakfast and luckily for me, Aimee was in the kitchen. She was slicing a grapefruit and arranging it on a plate. The kitchen was filled with the scent of fresh fruit and pancakes. It was a Felton tradition to have a special breakfast before we all went our separate ways. We were leaving first thing the next morning, so there would be no time for a heavy breakfast then.

I unclipped Duke's lead and he made a beeline for Aimee's feet. He stood up on his hind legs to beg her for a piece of whatever she was preparing. The dog was too clever for his own good—he knew Aimee was *always* preparing something.

Aimee flashed me a look. "That dog will get himself discovered one of these days."

With a smile I reached for a handful of fresh blueberries. Popping one into my mouth, I bit down to release a flood of tangy sweetness onto my taste buds. "He hasn't been discovered for two years. Perks of having a wing just for us kids."

And wasn't that the truth. Our house was big enough that we really did have a children's wing. When we were younger, it served to contain the mess that could be created by three children. Because Augustus and I had been inclined to disappear for most of the day and

23

get into all sorts of mischief, it wasn't uncommon for us to return hot, sweaty and filthy. Our nannies were always ordered to make sure we were clean and presentable before being set loose on the rest of the house.

We even had our own kitchen and thus, plenty of room to hide a small dog from Daddy.

Aimee sighed and swatted my hand when I reached for more blueberries. "Those are for the muffins!"

I groaned and slumped down into a chair at the table, "Aimee, I'm *starving*!"

Her lips twitched in amusement as she scanned me from head to toe. "Yes, you're positively wasting away before my very eyes. You may not see your seventeenth birthday." She laughed. "I'll grab you a plate, the pancakes are warming in the Aga."

"Aimee, you are absolutely my favourite person," I said. My mouth watered as she dished me up a loaded plate full of pancakes. Aimee placed a jug of maple syrup and plates of fresh fruit on the table, before returning again a few moments later with a rack of toast and a pitcher of juice. Now this I would most definitely miss. I was never this well fed at school and I mourned the loss of Aimee's cooking for months when I left Monaco. But she always ensured I had plenty of her meringues and hot cross buns to take back, and Mummy would make each of us one of her delicious chocolate cakes.

Every girl at Mapleton Manor had a tuck box filled with goodies and treats to last the terms, or at the very least, until the next exeat when we could refill it. As my years in boarding school had passed, I'd grown more and more savvy when it came to packing a successful tuck box.

As a First Former, it had been stuffed full of Skittles, Kool-Aid, bars and bars of chocolate and bottles of fizzy pop. Now it was still full of sweets, but also cereal bars which were great for shoving in my sports bag, squash that lasted much longer than fizzy drinks, jars of Nutella and Marmite and packets of crisps.

This year there was also pasta and a few jars of sauces. Going back to Mapleton Manor as a Sixth Former brought with it a new sense of freedom and liberation. I would be living in Masters, in Thornbury House with a handful of my best friends. No more dormitory life, this year we would be in single room accommodation. I couldn't wait!

The week before, Samantha had taken all of us to buy the stock for our tuck boxes. We had filled the cart with Wagon Wheels, Hartleys jelly, chocolate mini rolls, Monster Munch, Boost Bars, Skips, Crunchies, Ritz Mini Crackers, Curly Wurlys, Dip Dabs, Pot Noodles, Jelly Tots, Jaffa Cakes, Hobnobs and chocolate marshmallows. Not to mention – Tang. I could only get it in Monaco and it was my absolute favourite. Tang was orange sherbet that I would dip my fingers in and it dyed the tips orange.

And that had just been *my* cart.

Watching Louisa throw items into the cart made me smile – it was like flashing back to myself five years earlier. Louisa's box was stuffed to the brim with sugary treats and I honestly had to wonder how any of us had any teeth left. Good genes were nothing to be laughed at, I supposed.

I was digging in to the mountain of pancakes that Aimee had dished me up when Augustus sloped into the kitchen. He ran a hand over his unruly, unkempt hair as he yawned.

"Just in time," Aimee said as she reached for another plate. "Sit down and I'll fetch your breakfast."

Augustus grunted something in response that I didn't catch as he sat down opposite me at the table. I let him dig into his breakfast for a few minutes before attempting to engage him in conversation. I wasn't fluent in caveman, which was my brother's mother tongue first thing in the morning.

"Do you have any plans for today?" I asked him once his pile of pancakes had diminished. Usually the last day of summer was spent at a lazy, relaxed pace. Mummy hated leaving things to the last minute, so our trunks were already packed. It meant we got to enjoy our final days and we weren't rushing around like headless chickens.

I despised headless chickens.

Aimee had a peculiar sense of humour. I'd been chased around the kitchen table my fair share of times with a little chicken head while Aimee had prepared the bird for dinner.

Augustus shrugged as he threw half his glass of freshly squeezed orange juice down his throat. "I don't think so. Why?"

"Just curious."

Augustus chuckled under his breath. "A few years ago all we would have been interested in was getting out on the water with our little dinghy to earn as much money as we could for ice cream."

I grinned as I remembered all the hours and hours Augustus and I had spent fishing and catching crabs. Mummy had paid us for our spoils — two francs per fish and one franc per crab. We would stay out as long as we could, hoping to earn enough to keep us stocked in ice cream for the holidays. "I loved fishing! We got so good, too."

Aimee chortled. She had her back to us as she made the batter for the blueberry muffins. "*Too* good, I seem to recall. Don't either of you remember how long it would take to get the smell of dead crab out of the house when the ones you caught inevitably wandered off?"

Augustus clutched his belly as he roared with laughter. "I'd forgotten about that! Do you remember the one that got stuck behind your dresser, Freddie?"

I wrinkled my nose at the memory. Lord, it had taken us *weeks* to discover the source of the smell. "Remember? I'm sure it still smells a bit iffy behind there."

"That's what we should do today—go fishing. What do you say?"

There would be no better way to spend our last day in Monaco. Reliving our childhood hobby sounded idyllic. "Sounds perfect. Should we ask Lou?"

Augustus snorted. "And have you push her overboard when she annoys you?"

I gasped and folded my arms across my chest. "I would never do that!" Though, I did have to admit, the idea was tempting. Especially because we all knew she couldn't help herself when it came to annoying me. The girl had it down to an art form. "Okay, just us then?"

Augustus nodded. "Shall we leave in about an hour?"

"Yes. And shall we make it interesting? Loser buys the ice cream?"

"It would be fitting. You'd better get your wallet out, Freddie, I'm feeling lucky."

I grinned over the rim of my glass. "We'll see about that."

Augustus was waiting for me outside just over an hour later. He scowled briefly when I appeared—my brother wasn't known for his patience either. I wore my favourite green swimsuit and a pair of flip flops and had tied my hair up into a high ponytail.

"All our old gear should still be at the Beach Club," Augustus said.

We headed there at a leisurely pace, with no rush to get anywhere. And sure enough, all our stuff was still in the storage place with piles of fishing supplies stacked against the wall. And most importantly, our little dinghy still looked seaworthy. All our old nets and buckets and crab baits were exactly as I remembered them, and just seeing them brought back a rush of childhood memories.

We also used to fish whilst on our yacht, the *Poseidon*. The captain, Felix, had taught us to catch fish by sprinkling breadcrumbs over the side of the boat into the water and scooping them up with our nets. When I wasn't fishing, I was tanning myself on the top deck as we sailed the seas. Sometimes we would head to St Tropez and stop for some lunch.

That afternoon was nothing short of blissful. Being out on the water with my brother, laughing as we grew more and more competitive over the number of catches, was one of the best feelings in the world.

Monaco was laid out before us, the view from the ocean was one that took my breath away. Our home rose into the sky, dominating the line of houses. People were spread out across the white sandy beach sunning themselves, ice cream shops were bustling with families and children. The faint sounds of music came from boats behind us, carrying holidaymakers and year-long residents who populated this incredible city.

Further out to sea, sunbathing on a floating raft was Robert Redford. Samantha would be sad to have missed him in his red Speedos again. She was never fortunate enough to catch a glimpse of him wearing them.

My brother and I had spent half our childhoods fishing these waters, and it all came flooding back to me. We baited our lines and waited patiently for the fish to bite.

After a while, I resorted to my favourite method — and therefore laziest — of catching fish...dropping crumbs of bread into the water.

But even with my mad fishing skills, after a few hours, there was a clear winner in the form of Augustus. He put my meagre collection to shame and bragged the whole way to the ice cream shop about what a skilled fisherman he was.

We swung our legs off the rickety wooden jetty to enjoy our treats. As we sat in near silence eating the ice creams as quickly as we could to avoid them melting and dripping down our wrists, a few men who had been sitting on the deck at the Beach Club dived into the water.

Augustus and I shared a mischievous look and scoffed down the rest of the ice cream. Amongst our fishing gear was our snorkels and masks and we pulled them on in a hurry. The seabed beneath the jetty was a treasure trove of notes and coins. One of our favourite pastimes was to scour the sandy bottom beneath the jetty, and also under the diving board at the Olympic pool. Members of the beach club would enjoy long, liquid lunches, polishing off a few drinks. More often than not, when they dived into the sea, or the pool, they inevitably forgot their pockets were full of money and lost it all to the bottom.

It was safe to say Augustus and I had cottoned on to this pretty quickly, and armed with our snorkels and masks, collected all the money we could find. We would dry the notes out on the jetty and a good day's haul could also be added to our ice cream fund that would last us for most of the summer.

It *was* all about the ice cream, after all.

We carried everything back to the storage at the Beach Club and as soon as everything was tidied away, I hopped on my bicycle and rode the short distance to Cornelia's house.

Cornelia was stretched out on a lounger in her garden when I arrived, a collection of teen and fashion magazines littering the grass beside her. She pushed her sunglasses atop her head when she saw me approach, a wide smile pulling at her lips.

"Should I take that gloating grin to mean last night went well then?" I asked as I took the empty lounger beside her.

Cornelia sighed—the noise a purely girlish and smitten sound. "Freddie, it was amazing. We talked for hours and just walked along the beach. It was *so* romantic. We shared a milkshake and when he kissed me he tasted of chocolate."

I giggled, pleased my friend was so happy. "Where do you stand with the separation?"

"We're going to write. And hopefully see each other again at half term."

"I'm happy for you, Cornelia."

She sighed again. "Me, too. What have you been up to today then?"

"I went fishing with Augustus. He out-fished me and I had to buy him an ice cream." I held up my finger for Cornelia to see. "And one crab didn't take too kindly to being plucked out of the water. I thought he was never going to let go."

Cornelia wrinkled her nose. "Ouch."

"What did you do this morning?"

"Mummy and I took a trip into Nice. I got the most gorgeous new handbag to take back to school."

I flopped back against the lounger. "Sounds amazing. I wish I had time for another trip before I have to leave."

Cornelia flashed me a grin and reached for a magazine. She tossed me the next one in the pile. "Well, you will disappear off on your boat for hours, Freddie, otherwise you could have come too."

Rolling my eyes, I opened the magazine. "Yeah, yeah." When I wasn't competing with my brother in fishing, one of my other favourite pastimes was devouring fashion magazines from cover to cover. Living in Monaco, I got to see the best-dressed people in the world. High fashion, hot new trends—it was a little bit like living in a permanent runway show.

Cornelia and I used to scan the beautiful people in restaurants and pick out our favourite outfits. As children we'd argued over the best clothes for our Barbies—especially shoes as we inevitably lost at least one and barely had a pair between us.

"Are you all packed?" I asked Cornelia as I idly flicked through the magazine.

"Almost. I have another few days before I leave."

"I can't believe summer is almost over again," I said, a hint of sadness creeping into my voice.

"Remember when we were little and they seemed to last forever? Now they're over in the blink of an eye," Cornelia said.

She was right. As a child on the first day of the summer holidays, it had felt like I was poised on the brink of a never-ending adventure and autumn was decades away. And now as a teen, they hardly seemed long enough. Just as they were beginning, they were over and I was once again saying goodbye to my friends and family.

"I can't think of a better way to spend our last afternoon together," I said, slipping on my sunglasses and settling back more comfortably on the lounger.

Cornelia smiled and tilted her face into the sun. "Absolutely."

The housekeeper came out to us in the garden a short while later, bringing with her a pitcher of lemonade and a plate of freshly baked chocolate chip cookies. Cornelia set up her portable CD player and blasted her latest Wet, Wet, Wet disc. We spent the rest of the afternoon listening to music, giggling and flicking through magazines…and chatting about writing romantic letters to Rupert, of course.

It was nothing short of perfect.

Before I left, Cornelia dashed inside. She returned a few moments later with her hand hidden behind her back.

"What are you up to?" I asked her with a smile.

"I have a surprise for you. Close your eyes and hold out your arm," she demanded.

I did as I was told, and resisted the urge to peek.

Something was slid onto my wrist. "Okay, you can look now," Cornelia said.

A rubber wristband now hung from my wrist bearing the emblem of the Beach Club. I grinned and a laugh escaped me. I threw my arms around my friend and hugged her tightly. "Thank you, it's perfect."

"Just another one to add to your collection," she said, hugging me back.

"You can never have too many wristbands!"

I had dallied at Cornelia's house longer than I'd intended, and it was late in the afternoon before I arrived back home. Samantha shot me a warning look as I strolled down the corridor towards my bedroom.

"What's the matter?" I asked her.

"Your mother will be on the warpath if you're late for dinner tonight. Hop in the shower right away or else there will be hell to pay," Samantha said, shooing me away with a flick of her hand. Samantha had a deep, no-nonsense Yorkshire accent. I don't think any of us had argued with her or talked back. Ever.

"Yes, yes," I said, as though it was a great injustice. I darted to the side to avoid her warning cuff aimed for my backside.

In all fairness, I hadn't realised just how late it was, and got a shock when I saw the time in my bedroom. Samantha was right, and there would indeed be hell to pay if I was late. Family dinners were always important, but this one was extra so as it was our last of the summer.

I rushed through my shower, giving myself a nasty gash on the leg with my razor in the process. It was still hot enough that I could leave my hair to dry naturally, letting it take on a natural wave.

As I finished zipping up my white shift dress with a floral lace overlay that showed off my deep tan nicely, Louisa poked her head around my bedroom door.

"Are you almost finished?" she asked, a timid tone in her voice I didn't hear very often.

"Almost, why?" I asked, crouching to peer under the bed for my sandals. My room was so big I was forever losing things.

A few years ago I had found out just how deceptively big my room was. My English friend Caroline had come over for tea and we'd been messing around in my room. We'd decided to try and jump from my dresser onto the bed. I'd gone first because I was the tallest and used that as logic to mean I would be more likely to cross the distance.

I hadn't made it, and I'd broken my leg in the process.

Mummy had been in London on business, and when I'd spoken to her I'd had to reassure her that I had taken my shoes off before climbing on the furniture.

"You said you would help me with my makeup," Louisa said, stepping more fully into the room. I saw she was already wearing my green top with the little stitched on daisies—apparently my permission was all she'd needed to come and pilfer it herself, she hadn't waited for me to actually give it to her. Louisa was as ballsy as they came.

I finally located the sandals I was looking for and I fastened them onto my feet. "Have a sit down and I'll help you."

Louisa took a seat at my dressing table and waited for me as patiently as she was as capable of. She picked up little pots and lipsticks, holding them up to her face to see if they suited her. Louisa trailed her fingers over the colourful wristbands hanging from the bracelet holder.

Collecting wristbands was one of my favourite things in the world, and I almost always picked one up when visiting a new place. I had quite a few now, ranging from leather, or rubber ones, like Cornelia had given me that afternoon, to paper ones that I had to carefully peel off my wrists in case they ripped.

Some days I would wear lots and they would pile half way up my arm.

It made me smile to see my sister curious in my things. It only seemed like yesterday that all she'd been interested in were her dolls. And animals — that was one passion we shared. When I was little, I'd devised new ways to smuggle pets into the house. Augustus and I had had an assortment of animals and were known for adopting any and all stray animals we came into contact with.

Louisa had soon followed our example and had picked up all the tricks we'd learnt. We'd even had three tortoises once, one for each of us, called Charles, William and Harry. I'd loved the wrinkly little things, but M. Vincent had hated them as they'd dug up his flowers and made a mess of the garden.

Sitting beside Louisa on the bench at the dressing table, I picked up a few of my subtle pieces of makeup that wouldn't be too over the top on her young face.

Louisa was a more patient model than I had expected her to be, and didn't question a single one of my choices. Perhaps she had been watching me for long enough that she trusted I knew what I was doing. It was a rare moment shared between us sisters—the elder taking the gentle lead of the younger and bringing her into the grown-up world of clothes and makeup. I had to wonder why we didn't do things like this very often. I should be patient with Louisa—she was only young, after all. It was easy to forget that had been me a few years ago. And I hadn't had anyone to show me, no wise older sister to teach me. Mummy and Samantha were fantastic, but I didn't think it was the same.

I should, no, I *would* make more of an effort with Lou. *Look at this! We're having a lovely time together and —*

"God, how long are you going to take? I should have known you'd take forever. You had better not be making me look stupid," Louisa whined, her forehead wrinkling in a scowl.

Ah yes. That's why we don't do things like this more often.

"Almost done," I said through gritted teeth, somehow resisting the urge to purposely mess up her makeup.

When we were finished, Louisa darted off without bothering to thank me or even toss me a grateful smile. Not that I should have been surprised. I quickly finished getting myself ready then left my bedroom.

Mummy was in the hall by the front door, checking her hair in the large mirror. She looked exquisite in her designer dress, the latest fashion, as always. At my approach, Mummy turned. She slid her eyes down me and a warm smile touched her lips.

"You look wonderful, darling." Mummy reached up to press a featherlight kiss to my cheek, taking care not to smudge her lipstick. "Is that the dress we bought last week?"

I touched the hem of my new dress and nodded. "I love it. Do you think it looks nice?"

"It looks fabulous," Mummy assured me with a smile. "Where is Louisa? Have you seen her?"

"She should be ready, I helped her with her makeup. Do you want me to go and find her?"

Mummy shook her head and turned back to the mirror, giving her reflection another once-over. "She'll be along in a moment, I expect."

Sure enough, Louisa then Augustus appeared shortly after. Mummy collected Daddy from his office and the five of us trooped outside. Mr Bateman stood tall and proud in his uniform beside the Rolls Royce Phantom. The black paintwork gleamed in the early evening sunlight, the car polished to perfection. Our family crest was emblazoned on the side, proud and bright, and the special tags of the MC Beach Club were on the front. Mr Bateman tipped his cap and opened the passenger door first for Daddy. They exchanged a few pleasantries before Mr Bateman opened the suicide doors in the back for the rest of us.

The cream leather was cool against the backs of my legs as I slid into my seat. That smell was another that I always associated with home – the heady scent of worn leather from one of Daddy's fleet of luxury cars.

It was cool inside from the air conditioning, and it was a balm to my skin. Louisa sat opposite me so she could swing her feet and kick my shins 'by accident' and play the wounded soul when I eventually got cross and either scolded her...or kicked her back.

"Where are we going, Mummy?" Louisa asked, swinging her legs and cutting a glance my way.

"The African Queen, sweetheart," Mummy answered.

Louisa clasped her hands together under her chin and beamed at our mother. The African Queen was a favourite restaurant of our family's, situated on the Port de Plaisance in Beaulieu sur Mer. It was roughly a twenty minute drive from our house in Monaco. Usually Mummy would drive us, as we frequented the restaurant often, especially when we were all home for the summer. But tonight was a special occasion, the last meal out together before us children returned to school, and Daddy insisted on using his driver.

Mr Bateman opened the doors for us again once we arrived, and we all climbed out of the car and headed inside the restaurant. We were greeted every way we turned. Mummy and Daddy knew practically everyone in the vicinity, and we were familiar faces, especially at the African Queen.

The restaurant was named after the Humphrey Bogart and Katharine Hepburn movie from 1951. Ethnic artwork was scattered across the dining room and movie posters hung from the walls in large gilt frames. We were seated as usual on the terrace overlooking the magnificent cliff faces that stretched up towards the heavens, and below, the scattering of yachts that bobbed in the cerulean Mediterranean Sea.

"Everyone all ready for tomorrow?" Daddy asked no one in particular once we had ordered our usual pizzas that The African Queen was famous for. It was rare we ordered something different.

"I am," Louisa said, sitting up straighter in her chair. "I finished packing a week ago."

"Then why is your bedroom still such a mess?" Mummy asked, smiling over her water glass.

Louisa turned a shade of red and slumped back in her chair. "I was looking for something," she mumbled.

"Frederica?" Daddy asked, glancing in my direction.

I nodded whilst I swallowed a mouthful of water. "All packed and ready. I just want to have one last check to make sure I have everything."

Daddy nodded. "And you, Augustus?"

"Yes, Daddy."

"Looking forward to getting back to your friends at Seaton?"

Augustus nodded. "I am. It's always great to hear about everyone's summers. We all write, of course, but it's not the same."

I often wondered if Augustus felt a certain kind of pressure attending Seaton College. Since birth his name had been down to attend the prestigious school and he carried a lot of weight on his young shoulders to do well. He would more than likely follow in Daddy's footsteps and go to work for him once he had completed university.

Shortly after, our food was brought out. We fell into comfortable silence as we dug into our meals, the chink of silverware against china one of the only sounds to be heard. I enjoyed an enormous banana split for dessert, and Mummy let me have a glass of wine.

It was late when we drove back home, Louisa falling asleep with her head on Mummy's shoulder. She held her hand whilst walking her to her bedroom, Louisa trailing a step behind, her gait slow and drowsy.

"Night, Freddie," Augustus said, squeezing my shoulder on his way past me to his room. "See you in the morning."

I nodded and gave him a smile. Though it was late and I was tired, I wasn't quite ready to say goodbye just yet. Creeping out into the garden, I lay down on the cool grass to peer up at the sprinkling of stars strewn across the sky. A soft breeze stirred the lemon and avocado trees, casting up a delicious aroma of nature's perfume. The hush of the ocean could be heard if I strained my ears hard enough, the lulling whoosh of the tide that had acted as my lullaby for years. Shirley Bassey was singing at the club and every scent and sound mixed together into a recipe that conjured up everything I associated with home.

A part of me couldn't wait for tomorrow — couldn't wait to get back to Mapleton Manor and my friends. But another part would mourn Monaco and my family.

To my left, a quiet mewl of displeasure came from the darkness. I tiptoed over to the hedge that separated our property from the neighbours and discovered a cat stuck in the trap that Daddy had fashioned.

"Shh, shh," I crooned as I unfastened the lock.

The cat crept forward cautiously, as though it didn't trust my motives for releasing it. Once it was clear of the trap, it darted under the hedge and back to its own safe garden.

A disbelieving laugh bubbled in my throat and I rose back up to full height. I had to wonder if other people had fathers like mine, or if Daddy was a remarkable individual.

Daddy's light was on in his office, and I entered the house through there. He was hunched over his desk again, the lamp casting an amber glow over him and his paperwork.

I kissed the top of his head. "Night, Daddy. Don't stay up too late."

He hugged me to him for a moment. "You, too, darling."

Leaving him to his work, I turned to leave.

"The cat got away then, Freddie?" he asked when I was almost at the door.

His voice stopped me in my tracks. I turned, almost expecting to see him spitting mad. Instead, an amused smirk pulled at his lips. I bit down on my cheek to keep from grinning and nodded once.

Daddy sighed and let out a chuckle. "You have a kind heart, my Frederica. Goodnight, dear girl."

"Goodnight, Daddy. I love you."

"I love you, too."

Something told me that Daddy knew full well about my attempts to thwart his cat-trapping schemes, and he didn't overly mind.

My tuck box and trunk were stacked in a corner of my bedroom. I adored my trunk, full of my clothes and uniform for the year. When I first attended boarding school at Bourne Park at the tender age of eight, I had thought it was quite exciting to wear a uniform. Fawn coloured jumpers and socks, grey woollen culottes and pullovers with cardigans had been my staple, though now it was the navy blue of Mapleton Manor. We had got our uniforms at a large department store in Sloane Square, and always had our nametags stitched into everything. If someone lost a jumper, there were four hundred identical ones to choose from. It paid to know for certain which one was your own.

Now I was at secondary school, my trunk and tuck box were both dark navy blue in colour, with my initials embossed in orange for my house on the side. It was almost symbolic of my life, not just at school, but overall. One of my greatest passions was travel, and I adored flitting all over the world and seeing different cultures and hearing different languages. If I had my way, I'd spend the rest of my life being a globetrotter, the world as my residence and my passport crammed full with stamps.

For the next half an hour, I carefully pawed through the trunk and tuck box to triple check I had everything. Except, I was sure I'd packed more than one box of bourbon cream biscuits… I'd definitely had more than three Mars bars…and had I left out the Dip Dabs completely?

Wait a minute—I smelled a rat. *Louisa!*

Sure enough, in my trunk at least two of my favourite blouses were missing, along with Lord only knows how many eye shadows, lipsticks and creams. My makeup bag was half empty!

My annoyance stewed and I quietly tiptoed down the hall to her bedroom. "Louisa? *Louisa!*" I hissed through my teeth into the dark room.

Louisa turned over in her bed, the sheets rustling with her movements. "What?" she mumbled sleepily.

"Have you been in my trunk, you little thief?"

"No," she answered too quickly. "Go away, Freddie, I'm sleeping."

"Louisa—"

"Frederica, it's late, you had better not be keeping your sister up."

I turned to see Mummy come way down the hall, her arms folded across her chest and a less than impressed expression on her face. Cringing, I closed Louisa's door and crossed the hall back to my own bedroom. "Sorry, Mummy. I was just checking to see if Louisa had seen a few of my things."

"You were supposed to have seen to your things by now. Honestly, Frederica, it's as though you've never gone to school before. Why did you leave it until the last minute?"

Oh, I'm going to throttle that girl… "I thought I had everything. I am sorry, Mummy."

"Hmm," my mother said, my apology doing absolutely nothing to pacify her. "Well, if it isn't packed by now it isn't going with you. Now off to bed or you will never be able to get up in the morning."

I nodded, deciding that any more arguments wouldn't end well for me. Before slipping into my bed, I set my alarm clock half an hour earlier than it had been. I'd get my things back from Louisa and her sticky fingers.

And I would *definitely* get my sweets back.

3

There was nothing quite like the bubbly feeling I got in my stomach when the Mapleton Manor gatehouse came into view. The old house was as quirky as they came, with Tudor elements and a curved second-floor bay window. Lattice windows and a tall chimney completed the look. The centuries-old building stood as the first port of call for the school and it almost seemed to symbolise my arrival, welcoming me back.

The girls on the coach tittered as we trundled along, getting louder when they spotted the gatehouse. I had travelled with Augustus and Louisa that day, first flying by helicopter to Nice then boarding our flight to Heathrow. It was there we'd parted ways, with each of us heading to our own schools. I'd caught my school coach at Bressenden Place in Victoria, along with a bunch of other girls.

We passed by the gatehouse and turned onto the long, straight drive that led up to the school. My excitement had reached new limits by the time we slowed to a stop in front of the main building, its beautiful red bricks gleaming in the sun, the white detailing the windows and roofline accentuating the school's beauty.

After today, I would only have one more first day at this school. *Gosh, only one more…* Mapleton Manor had been a huge part of my life, and it was a peculiar notion that it wouldn't always be.

Today was a special day, another *first* to look forward to. A smile touched my lips as I peered out of the window. The excitement I felt was not unfamiliar. It was, after all, what I had been feeling on the beginning of my boarding school career when I was just eight years old.

The exterior of Mapleton Manor softened, faded, until it was a different school altogether that I saw.

I looked up at Mummy, then around to Daddy. I was sandwiched between them, a bit squashed, but I didn't care because it wouldn't be long until they were awfully far away.

The Range Rover was parked and the driver opened the door for Daddy. A flutter of nerves began in my belly, shadowing the excitement I had harboured since learning that I would be attending a school in England. I peered up at the tall, old house – my new home for a long time.

Bourne Park.

It sounded like something out of a novel. An exciting novel. I wanted to rush to the end so I knew what to expect.

Mummy squeezed my shoulder and ushered me forward as the front door opened and an older woman stepped outside.

She smiled at Mummy and Daddy before dropping her eyes to me. "Hello," she said. "You must be Frederica. I'm Mrs de Pauw and I run this school. Are you excited to come in and have a look around?"

"Yes, I am," I said and found I meant my words.

"Why don't I show you to your dormitory and you can meet some of the other girls? I can have a chat with your mother and father and then we'll come and get you to show you around the school."

I nodded and we all followed Mrs de Pauw inside. She led us up a steep staircase and down numerous hallways. Mrs de

Pauw paused to give me a smile before she opened one of the many closed doors.

There was a gaggle of girls in the room, rows of narrow beds and little porcelain sinks. On our entrance, the girls turned to stare with unabashed curiosity.

"Girls, this is Frederica. She will be joining us here at Bourne Park. Do make sure she feels at home." Mrs de Pauw turned and motioned for my parents to follow her back the way we had come.

Leaving me alone.

With all these girls.

Who were still staring.

"Hello. Which bed is mine?" I asked.

One girl stepped closer with a wide grin on her face. "I'm Fenella. Your bed is that one over there. I like your coat. Where are all your things?"

I liked this girl and her forward nature. "Thank you. I like my coat too. I think my things are downstairs."

"Where are you from?"

"Monaco," I said. It was peculiar to me to be having a conversation entirely in English. French had become my mother tongue.

The girls oohed *at this and I wondered if they had ever been before.*

"My old school was right next door to the Palais Princier. Princess Grace lived there with Prince Rainer before she died."

The room exploded with excited chattering. I was bombarded with dozens of questions and it was almost a challenge to keep up. I shrugged out of my coat and sat down on my new bed, and told the girls all about life in Monaco.

"When we were younger my best friend, Cornelia, and I loved to play silly games where we imagined ourselves living in the palace like royalty. We pretended to wear gorgeous gowns of spectacular fabric." I glanced down at my thick

navy tights that I had to wear because it was so much colder here. They itched. "I think I'll miss playing those games."

Another girl sat on the edge of my bed. "Don't be sad. It's really fun here, too."

Fenella nodded her agreement. "There's the spinney – a forest – on the grounds and it is just the best playground. Everyone loves Mr Fingers – he's a tree – and he is great fun to climb."

"Yes," said the other girl. "And we get to go camping all the time. It's super fun."

"That does sound fun," I said, a bubble of excitement growing in my stomach.

"Do you like pets?" Fenella asked. "We have loads here – you can have whatever you like! Rabbits, guinea pigs, hamsters…not to mention the horses!"

"I would love a horse." I sighed.

Fenella giggled and leaned closer. "We hide our sweeties in the horse jumps. Mrs de Pauw takes away the extras we get given on exeats if we don't hide them first. We tried the attic for a while, but the rats found them." She wrinkled her nose.

"Urgh!" I squealed.

Shortly after, Mrs de Pauw arrived and brought me back downstairs to where Mummy and Daddy waited.

"We have a little surprise for you before we leave." Mummy took my hand and we walked across the grounds to a stable. They stopped in front of a stall where there stood the most beautiful pony I had ever seen

"This is Kitty," Mrs de Pauw said. "She was one of the school ponies, but your parents have arranged for her to be yours. Won't that be lovely? Many of the girls enjoy riding in the afternoons, and there really is no better way to see the Kent countryside than on horseback."

I looked around to Mummy and Daddy. "Really? Do you mean it? She's honestly mine?"

Daddy smiled and touched my cheek. "Of course, darling. We want to hear all about how well you are getting on in your letters home."

I threw my arms around both of my parents and squeezed them as hard as I could. "Thank you," I whispered. "Thank you so much."

Shortly after, it was time for Mummy and Daddy to leave. I stood on the front steps of Bourne Park with a lump lodged in my throat as their Range Rover drove away. Mrs de Pauw escorted me back to my dormitory and I soon forgot all about feeling sad. I stayed up super late with the other girls, giggling into the night. It was like having a sleepover with lots of friends, and I had a feeling every night would be the same…

The coach doors opened, pulling me from my reverie about my past and thrusting me back into the present. I rose to my feet and joined the crush of students all clambering to get off first. First days back were always chaos—everyone wanted to see their friends and get into their rooms. Finally we all disembarked and girls scattered in different directions, heading for the different Houses. I made a beeline for Crosby, the place I had called home for the last four years.

Crosby House was one of three original Houses at Mapleton Manor, named after the Crosby family who had once owned the estate. It used to be in the main building, but it had moved into its own boarding house a few years previously.

In Crosby, I sought out the housemistress to let her know I had arrived, and signed in the register book. But I wasn't staying—I was off to my new dorm.

At the end of last term, my friends and I had requested to room together in Masters. But the best part was that they didn't all have to be from your original house. The friends I'd been separated from in those early years were now my roommates.

Each Masters block had a shared kitchen between eight of us. It would mean we didn't always have to eat in the main dining room with the rest of the school, potentially earning us a few extra minutes in bed each the morning. There were also a few common and lecture rooms, computer rooms and group rooms for hanging out.

The Masters Houses were always alive with activity. There would be lectures, debates, play rehearsals, music and tutorial sessions – not to mention when the younger girls would visit and we would entertain them. I had waited for this for years, and now it finally my turn.

I practically raced across the grounds to get to the Sixth Form Centre, keen to move into my new digs.

As I strolled down the corridor, the sound of a girl singing drifted along to greet me. A smile spread across my cheeks as I recognised the voice, and I hurried along faster.

The door to Fenella's bedroom was flung wide open. She stood on her bed, pinning something to the corkboard above it. Wet, Wet, Wet blasted from her boombox on the desk and I smothered a laugh with my hand at the sight of my friend shaking her hips and tossing her hair around in time to the music.

I cleared my throat, and Fenella whipped around. The moment she laid eyes on me, she leapt from the bed and was in front of me in a heartbeat, wrapping her thin arms around me and squeezing me so tight I feared for my ribs.

"Freddie!" Fenella squealed in excitement. "What took you so long? I've been waiting forever! How was your flight? How was your *summer*? Gosh, didn't it feel like it went on forever?" Fenella released me from her iron-tight hold and her eyes searched mine.

Ah, she was finished then. With Fenella I could never be sure. She could lay one question on you or bombard you with twenty thousand. "I'm sorry, I got here as soon as I could. The flight was good, same as always, really. So was summer — hot, just how I like it!" Already I was feeling the difference in temperature. Back home I would have been lounging around in shorts and a T-shirt or just my bikini if I was sunbathing at the club or in the garden. But back in Kent, I was in jeans, lumberjack shirt, blue jumper and Doc Marten boots.

And I was still feeling a little chilly.

It wouldn't be long before I was going to bed with more layers than could comfortably fit on my body.

"Well?" Fenella asked, throwing out her arms to gesture to the entire room. "What do you think? Bit different from the dorms, isn't it? We've waited four years for this, Freddie."

I turned in a slow circle, drinking in every inch of the room. Releasing a soft sigh, I dropped onto Fenella's bed. "It's fantastic, it really is."

To an outsider, the room was nothing special. Four cream walls, narrow single bed, window, corkboard, wardrobe with matching chest of drawers and a desk that had seen better years.

But to us girls…it was everything.

Fenella followed me to my room where she lounged on my bed after I'd made it up with the duvet set Mummy and I had bought a few weeks before. Throwing open the lid of my trunk, I scanned the contents with a heavy heart.

I hated unpacking.

But it wasn't worth the lecture from the housemistress if my uniform was permanently crumpled. I passed out the collection of magazines I'd brought from home over to Fenella to flick through whilst I began the long, dreary task of sorting out all my clothes.

The halls of the Sixth Form Centre slowly came to life as more and more girls arrived back at school. The chatter rose in volume as they darted down the halls, in and out of each other's rooms. Shrieks and giggles were piercing as friends were reunited after a long summer of separation.

Our friend Alicia arrived an hour or so later. She burst into the room like a tornado of excitement, pulling Fenella and me into a tight hug as we danced around on the spot. And so it went, until we were all together. With all of us coming from vastly different places, the arrival of girls could take all day. Our friend Cassandra, who was coming from LA, wouldn't arrive until almost dinnertime.

Unpacking was a slow process. All I wanted to do was chat and catch up on what everyone had been up to over the summer, but it was better if we all got organised as soon as we could. Our matron was of the strictest and would let nothing slide. It paid to keep her sweet, though, as it was she who decided whether or not to let us have a day off our subjects when we were ill—legitimately or not.

Once all of us were more or less unpacked and our clutter had been cleared away so that the matron didn't complain and scold us, we retired to the common room to hang out.

We laughed for hours until my face hurt and my friends had tears streaming down their cheeks. Fenella was our storyteller, and told her tales of summer with enthusiasm and, I'm sure, a hint of embellishment.

"Any boys this summer, Freddie?" Alicia asked, winking at me from her seat in front of the empty fireplace.

I pulled a face at her and bit into my strawberry laces. "No."

Athena huffed and rolled her eyes. "Come on, Freddie! Haven't you gotten over this silly hang-up of yours yet?"

"I hardly think wanting my boyfriend to be taller than me 'a silly hang-up'," I said with a playful scowl.

"You never know — the boys at Stonebridge could have shot up over the summer," Jemima said from beside me on the couch as she reached into her packet of Doritos. The tuck boxes were getting a hammering tonight. "You might be pleasantly surprised by the time the first dance comes around."

I nudged her and flashed a smile. "Fingers crossed."

"Anyway, who are you to talk, Athena?" Annie asked. "Wasn't the reason you dumped that boy from Upton last year because his hair wasn't the shade of blond you prefer?"

Athena pulled a face at Annie but didn't answer.

My 'hang-up', as Athena had put it, was something that the girls were in equal measures amused and frustrated by. Amused because even half an inch was enough for me to be put off by a perfectly handsome and charming boy…and frustrated because even half an inch was enough for me to be put off by a perfectly handsome and charming boy.

It wasn't as though attending an all-girls school provided exciting dating prospects. But a few times a year our school held dances with Stonebridge, an all-boys school that wasn't too far away and allowed the girls and boys to mix. Usually they were horrifically embarrassing with the girls on one side of the room, boys on the other and no one daring to even glance at each other until the last five minutes where there was a desperate scramble to find someone to dance with.

There were local boys in the village, and some of the girls at school enjoyed sneaking out to meet their boyfriends, but so far none had caught my interest. For the last few years, my friends had returned to school after the summer to tell tales of the summer romances they had enjoyed.

And me?

Not. A. One.

Oh, there'd been awkward kisses and a couple of almost-boyfriends who'd sworn to write once I was back at school, but hardly ever did. Or, if they did, it was only once or twice until it petered out to none.

Fenella was desperate for me to find a proper boyfriend, one who made my heart splutter and turn me into a puddle of girlish mush, but I was sticking to my guns.

I could not get serious about a boy who was shorter than me.

Later, once we'd all been tossed out of the common room and shooed back to our rooms, I sat cross-legged on my bed and carefully pulled out posters from my magazines of boys I liked.

Leonardo DiCaprio got the prime spot right above my bed with Will Smith next to him. It wasn't long before the corkboard was almost full. When I had read a magazine to death, I went through it armed with a pair of scissors to cut out pictures of outfits. Fashion had always been a passion of mine, probably stemming from having my own seamstress who would make Augustus, Louisa and myself our own outfits.

I wanted more than anything to work in the fashion industry, although I hadn't a clue to what degree. I just wanted to be immersed in the world of clothes, the latest looks and hottest trends — see them all before anyone else did.

As I tidied away my things, there was a soft tap on my door. A moment later, Fenella and Athena crept inside my bedroom.

"Hello," I said with a smile. "What are you two up to?"

Athena held up a packet of Camel cigarettes. "Your room is right beside the east wing."

My smile widened into a grin and I shoved my feet into my trusty Dunlop Flash Greens.

I climbed onto the window seat and threw open the window. Peering outside, I glanced around to check the coast was clear and gently eased myself out onto the ledge directly below my window. Taking care, the three of us shuffled along a few yards until the sloping roof of the east wing met the ledge and we scrambled up onto its shingled roof.

There was a little collection of cigarette butts near one of the chimneys where older girls must have sneaked out onto the same spot.

Athena was a genius when it came to figuring out the best spots to sneak up onto the roof. When it came to creeping out of a room, or even the school grounds, she was the girl to know. She knew all the secrets that Mapleton Manor tried to keep hidden.

I shivered in my thin jumper and wrapped my arms around myself. It was only September, I had worse weather to face yet.

Athena passed us a cigarette each and we leaned in to the open flame as she flicked her lighter. It had been ages since I'd had a cigarette, and I tried my best not to cough, as I'd never hear the end of it.

"Have either of you met your shadow yet?" Fenella asked, leaning back onto her elbow.

Athena and I both shook our head.

"I can't *wait* for Polly Pearl night," Athena said before taking a long drag on her cigarette. "Remember the year they got us? I've never been so terrified in my life."

A shiver crept up my spine at the memory. While it was fun to look back on now, at the time it had been like living in a horror film.

Fenella started whispering in a childlike, sing-song voice.

"Stop it, Fenella," Athena scolded, giving Fenella a shove as she chuckled. "You'll end up giving me nightmares."

Fenella laughed. "Sorry. What do you think the shadows will be like?"

As I pondered Fenella's question, I tipped my head back to gaze up at the stars, so much more vibrant here than they'd been at home. Being in the countryside, Mapleton Manor received excellent views of the skies above thanks to barely any unnatural light. "Who knows?"

"Mine had better not be annoying," Athena said, tapping the end of her cigarette.

With a laugh, I leaned my head on her shoulder. "Do you think she'll develop a crush, Athena?"

My friend snorted a laugh and pushed me off her. "There isn't really any doubt, is there? The poor girl is bound to be infatuated with me."

Fenella let out a loud laugh and we shushed her before she got us discovered. "Conceited much, Athena? You'll lead the girl astray."

Athena grinned. "Well, someone has to train the new generation. It would be sacrilege to let Mapleton Manor's secrets die with us."

"She has us there," I said, winking at Fenella.

"What about you, Freddie?" Athena asked. "Will you depart all your worldly wisdom to the younger girls before leaving next year?"

"What wisdom is that?" I asked as a laugh bubbled in my throat.

Fenella stubbed out her cigarette. "Oh, please, Freddie! No one can get their hands on contraband like you can."

I snorted. "*Contraband*? We aren't in prison, Fenella."

She huffed and rolled her eyes. "Fine, you know what I mean. You're always scoring stuff for free. If it wasn't for you, we'd have to wait until exeats before we could refill our tuck boxes. Not to mention you always get tons of magazines sent to school."

It was true. Over the years I'd devised sneaky ways of getting free things from companies. It had all started at Bourne Park when I was nine and I'd opened a Dip Dab to find the lolly was all weird and not at all what I'd come to expect from the sweet. I'd decided to write to Barratt's to let them know how disappointed I'd been to open my favourite sweet to find it was not up to its usual high standards.

They'd sent me a box of fifty Dip Dabs by way of apology.

And thus, the sweetie queen of Bourne Park had been born.

Now I was sixteen and the same trick still worked. We applied it to much more than Dip Dabs, and found we could get anything from Mars bars to *More* magazine.

It had saved many wars when tuck box supplies started to dwindle and girls would start stealing from each other. Older girls were the worst for it, raiding the boxes belonging to the poor new girls who didn't have the sense to hide their spoils.

I, myself, changed my hiding spots on a regular basis and even went so far as to hide my actual tuck box, but on opening it the thief would discover old raisins and a half empty bottle of Robinsons squash.

Deception was the key.

Not even my closest friends realised my best hiding spot was in the ceiling, as a few of the panels could be pushed up. Perhaps if the fashion career didn't pan out, I had a future in espionage.

"It won't be long before girls are coming to you with wish lists of things they want, Freddie," Athena said with a wink.

"And let me guess, you'll be one of the first?" I asked her teasingly.

Athena's eyes widened in mock innocence. "Of course! I've already eaten all of my Shrimps."

Fenella, Athena and I dissolved into giggles at her declaration.

A few minutes after we'd climbed back through my window, my bedroom door opened and the other girls all piled in. Their arms were laden with goodies from their tuck boxes, and Fenella and Athena quickly left to get their own supplies.

We dumped everything in the middle of my bed, each of us helping ourselves to whatever we fancied. It was the age-old problem — a girl could pack the best tuck box in the world, but they would always want something someone else had brought.

Giggling quietly, we swapped holiday stories and tucked into our treats. We kept our voices low so the housemistress didn't come and tell us off. Midnight feasts were a time-honoured tradition, and there was none better than the one on the first night back.

It was wonderful to feel silly and young again, to laugh with my friends.

It was wonderful to be back.

4

A persistent banging on the door ripped me from sleep. This time Johnny Depp was the star, and I was getting increasingly sick of never finding out the ending to my dreams.

I bet Johnny Depp is taller than me...

I burrowed deeper into my duvet and the door flew open.

"Frederica! It's after seven-thirty!" Matron scolded.

Shoving a mass of blonde hair out of my face, I sat up in bed and tried to blink the sleep dust away. "I'm up, I'm up," I mumbled past a wide yawn.

"Hmpf," Matron huffed. "Up properly, if you please. Breakfast then morning prayers in the chapel."

The instant the door was shut, I fell back against the pillows and felt my eyes droop shut again. Chapel wasn't going anywhere. It would still be there in twenty minutes...

The girls and I had ended up staying up until the small hours of the morning, talking and laughing, reminiscing over our summer antics and years of Mapleton Manor past.

It had been great fun at the time, but I was sorely regretting the late bedtime now as I could barely drag myself out of bed. Today was the first official day back at school and as usual, morning chapel was a chore I could gladly see the back of. But at least I didn't have to trudge all the way over to the main dining room for breakfast.

Another bang on the door had me jumping up in fright. "Frederica! I don't hear you moving around in there!"

I pulled a face at the door, quickly smoothing it out into an innocent smile as the door was wrenched open and Matron popped her angry little face into the room.

"I'm awake!"

Matron narrowed her shrewd eyes at me. "See that it stays that way."

I gave her a jaunty salute once her back was turned, and finally crawled out of bed. Grabbing my wash things, I dashed down the hall to the communal bathroom. It was near deserted and I bit back a groan. An empty bathroom could only mean one thing— everyone else had already used it.

No hot water.

After a lightning quick and freezing cold shower, I raced back to my room. I dressed in the traditional Mapleton Manor uniform of navy cords, white blouse, blue jumper and the orange tie unique to Crosby House.

Fenella and Annie were already in the kitchen when I arrived, both looking as bleary-eyed as I felt. We mumbled our good mornings as we moved around each other, making rounds of toast with Nutella.

"We need to figure out a way to sneak a few minutes extra in bed," Fenella said as she scrubbed her eyes.

Annie and I nodded our agreement.

We finished off our quick breakfasts and headed outside before Matron came to chase us again.

It was like taking a trip back in time as I got onto my bicycle. Every Mapleton Manor girl had her own as the grounds were so big and some of the buildings so far apart that it was an everyday necessity. I dreaded to think just how late we would all be if we didn't have them.

"Matron makes it near enough impossible," Annie grumbled as we set off for the chapel. "It's easy enough to stuff a bed to make it look as though there's a body in it, but how do you fake an empty bed and still be in it?"

My friends and I spent half our lives devising new ways to get extra sleep, along with also trying to perfect sneaking out of the school grounds. We would need a serious plan in a few months for Polly Pearl night. Nothing could go wrong and everything had to be executed to the letter.

Athena and Harriet had saved us seats beside them on the pew and we took our spots mere moments before the chapel doors closed and the chaplain began. For the most part, I mumbled my way through the hymns and nearly dropped off to sleep again as I dipped my head in prayer at the end.

Once chapel was finished, it was time for the back to school assembly in the main hall before lessons began.

"What's your timetable like, Freddie?" Athena asked as she pushed her bicycle alongside me and mine.

I handed her the printed out sheet of paper that would dictate my life this term.

"French, history of art, English lit, history, physics... Ugh, you're mad." Athena screwed up her face and passed me the timetable back. "I'm in your physics class but that's it. Why did you choose those subjects?"

I tucked the timetable back into my bag so I didn't lose it. Again. "Most of them have class trips. And I promised Daddy I would take physics." My A-Level timetable was loaded with as many subjects that would take me abroad as possible. Secretly, history of art was the class I was really looking forward to as it had the best trips, but also because I was genuinely interested in art. I mean, our home in Monaco, and the family estate, were full to the gunnels with artwork.

History was also a keen favourite of mine. I adored learning new nuggets of information from the past. It probably came from my parents' rich family history. My mother's father was Russian and his past was a great mystery. He had had to flee his home when he was only seven, and was separated from his parents for safety. He had lived with a family in Switzerland but had kept in touch with a few people from his past. Mummy thought he must have been close to the royal family, as the Tsar Nicholas had gifted him many things including some hunting dogs.

My father's father was an ambassador and had travelled all over the world. He'd been very clever, and at only sixteen he'd passed the Oxford-Cambridge examination.

I had promised myself to one day explore the vast history of my family, as I suspected there would be quite a few interesting surprises to discover.

Athena tipped her head back and laughed. "Anything for a holiday, eh, Freddie?"

"A girl has to have her priorities right," I said, flashing Athena a wink.

The assembly didn't take too long, only about half an hour. It ate into first lessons, so none of us minded. The main objective was for the older girls to meet the new girls who would be shadowing us.

We arranged into our Houses, and the housemistresses went around with their clipboards and a gaggle of frightened looking girls. It was strange to think that that had once been me — once upon a time I'd been a young First Former following my Housemistress around, waiting to be introduced to the older girl who would show me around Mapleton Manor and watch over me.

I'd been a lucky one. My shadow had been a lovely girl called Sophia. She had taken me under her wing and had seemed to genuinely care about me. Even after the first term was over, and shadowing had ended, I knew I could go to her about anything. When I'd struggled with a girl in my form who had teased me mercilessly, it was Sophia who'd listened to me as my young heart had broken and given me a bar of chocolate and a pep talk.

Athena had shadowed a girl who loved to break the rules and had taught Athena most of the tricks she still used to this day. Maybe the girl we shadowed determined the kind of Mapleton Manor girl we would turn into.

"Frederica, this is Jessica," Housemistress said as she stopped in front of me and interrupted my reverie. At her side was a gangly blonde girl who wore her long shiny hair in braided pigtails. Her uniform was too big — it wasn't uncommon for mothers to buy them a size or two too big just in case a girl had a growth spurt during term time and they wanted the uniforms to last.

"Hi, Jessica," I said, opting to pull the girl into a hug instead of a more formal handshake.

"Hi…"

Giving her a wide, reassuring smile, I said, "Frederica. But everyone calls me Freddie."

"Freddie," Jessica said with a breath of relief.

I wondered if she thought I'd be a terrifying older girl who wanted to do nothing but torture her and make her first term hell on earth.

"It's nice to meet you."

"And you. How are enjoying Mapleton Manor so far?" I asked, nodding to Housemistress as she moved on to the next pair of girls.

Jessica's face took on a pink tinge. "It's okay."

I just melted. Was she struggling with boarding school? "Is this the first boarding school you've gone to?"

She nodded and dropped her eyes to her sensible Mary-Jane flat shoes her mother must have insisted on.

I squeezed her arm. "It gets easier, I promise. Are you missing your family?"

When Jessica lifted her big blue eyes to meet mine, they were swimming with tears. Her chin dimpled and her lip quivered.

Oh, well done, Freddie! She's only known you two minutes and you've already made the poor girl cry! Fenella and Athena would love this… I gestured to a few seats and Jessica followed me over. We sat down and I fished a tissue out of my pocket to hand to her. "I know it's hard when you first get here. I was eight, you know, when I went to my first boarding school."

"Eight?" Jessica exclaimed, her eyes widening.

"Yep," I said. "And it was a little scary at first. But do you know what I realised pretty quickly?"

She shook her head.

Gesturing to the room, and all the girls it held, I said, "These girls become your family. I promise you, you will make lifelong friends here. My best friend was with me at prep school and I expect she'll be my best friend for the rest of my life."

"I don't really know anyone yet," Jessica admitted in a quiet voice.

Gosh, she must be painfully shy. "Maybe not yet, but you will. Before you know it, you'll be part of the mischief in the dorms. You'll be up half the night talking and giggling, and won't be able to get out of bed in the morning!"

At this Jessica cracked a smile. "That does sound like fun."

"It's the *best* fun." I patted Jessica's arm. "Give it time. It really will get easier. And there are always tons of things to do at the weekends. Mapleton Manor is really good for organising lots of trips and things. Just wait and see. In one month you'll think you were silly for even feeling like this."

"Do you think so?"

"I know so."

Jessica dabbed the last of her tears away and gave me a shy smile. "Thanks, Freddie."

"Any time, Jessica. It's what I'm here for."

I was going to enjoy shadowing. I felt like an agony aunt in one of my magazines.

Most of the day passed by in a blur. My lessons were good and the teachers weren't horrific. I had at least one of my close friends with me in each class, so that was good. It was dinnertime before I knew it, and I found Fenella and Jemima halfway down a long bench at one of the tables that ran almost the full length of the great hall.

Fenella scooted over to make room for me, but Jemima made no effort to move at all. Maybe she was still grumpy from having to get up early this morning.

"How was your day?" Fenella asked me.

I shrugged as I climbed in beside them, placing the salad I'd served myself from the bar onto the table in front of me. "Can't complain. You?"

Fenella screwed up her face. "Mr Pennington was his usual grumpy-arse self in physics."

"Oh, don't," I groaned. "I have him tomorrow."

"Well, he's even worse than last year. Maybe he got dumped over the summer or something."

Jemima laughed. "Mr Pennington? Dumped? Are you mad, Fenella? I bet the man hasn't seen anything close to resembling a naked woman in decades!"

Our physics teacher was so old he was practically part of the foundations of Mapleton Manor. Each summer that we'd returned back to school he'd seemed to have become even grumpier.

"Freddie!"

I turned at the sound of my name to see a Third Former rush down the hall towards me. I couldn't remember her name, but I knew exactly what she was after.

The girl practically shoved Jemima out of her way as she squeezed herself between us. "Freddie," she said breathlessly.

"God, Amy, will you watch what you're doing?" Jemima said, giving the girl a hard glare.

Amy! That was it.

The girl threw Jemima a filthy look. "It's Xanthe," she said.

Ah...perhaps not Amy then... "What's up, Xanthe?" I asked her before Jemima could respond.

"Am I too late for the first round of shopping lists?" Xanthe asked, her eyes searching mine.

I laughed, my eyes widening in shock. "We've only been back a few days, give a girl a chance!"

"Sorry, sorry. I just know that once term gets going properly that you'll be busy and the lists will be too full," Xanthe said. She pulled a piece of notebook paper out of her pocket. "Can you get me these?"

Giving her list a quick scan, it looked as though everything would be easy enough to obtain. I gave Xanthe a wink. "Leave it with me. I'll be in touch."

Xanthe grinned. "Thanks, Freddie!" She whipped around to leave, smacking Jemima in the face with her ponytail in the process. I wasn't entirely sure it was an accident.

"At it already, Freddie?" Fenella asked with a smile.

I gave my friend a gentle nudge with my elbow. "Oh, like you haven't thought of a few things that you want."

She sighed. "I'm sorry. I just can't survive without my supply of Hubba Bubba."

"Forget Hubba Bubba!" Jemima exclaimed. "When are you getting the good stuff?"

I rolled my eyes at Jemima. "I'll pop into the Ville at the weekend, okay?" The local village, or the Ville to us girls, was our little shopping hotspot to pick up the things that would surely be confiscated if found in our tuckboxes.

At this Jemima softened, probably since she had got what she wanted. "Great stuff, Freddie. It pays to have a friend like you."

Her words made me wonder if that was the only reason she was my friend. There had always been something about Jemima that made me give pause, but

I could never put my finger on what it was. I had to be getting paranoid in my old age. She had never been outwardly rude to me, never deliberately cruel. It was my imagination, that was all, seeing things that weren't really there.

I blamed Fenella, and her mention of Polly Pearl the night before. It was messing with my head.

Somehow, over the summer I had completely forgotten how utterly exhausting the first day back at school was.

I'd had lessons until six o'clock then homework that took me a further two hours to complete. After I'd tidied away all my homework things, I started writing the letters to the sweetie companies. Some were innocent complaints, others were childish and bordered on pleading.

I discovered early on that playing on people's heartstrings worked like a treat, and asking big companies for a donation to supply us with sweets for an upcoming camping trip was one of my more genius ideas. As were the whimsical 'please can we have sweeties for midnight feasts' letters, they usually worked wonders.

When my wrists started aching, I finished up the letter I was writing and promised myself I'd finish the rest I still had to do tomorrow. There were still the magazines to write to, and the video shops. Sometimes people were all too willing to send girls in boarding schools free stuff. And you got sick pretty quickly of watching the same films that were in the common room.

After getting myself a spoonful of Nutella as a pre-bedtime snack, I settled in the common room to chill out with the girls for a while before Matron shooed us out. We chatted about our day and what the new girls were like.

"Mine is super annoying, just like I thought," Athena said, rolling her eyes. "But she has the promise to be an expert mischief-maker, so there's still hope."

"One thing is for sure, Freddie's girl has the biggest crush," Fenella said with a laugh. "She's already told my girl how fantastic you are."

It sounded like Jessica had listened to my words of wisdom and was starting to make friends. I was pleased for her, and couldn't wait until she told me how happy she was at Mapleton Manor, and how wonderful her newfound friends were. "She's a sweet girl."

"Do you just like having someone worship the ground you walk on, Freddie?" Jemima asked.

I frowned. "No. Why?"

Jemima smiled and shrugged. "It must feel nice, that's all. Having someone look up to you like that."

"I just want her to enjoy her time here. I'm hardly going to torture the poor girl, am I?" I shook my head and gave a short laugh. "I think she was struggling a bit."

"Just wait until the eleventh day of the eleventh month," Athena said, waggling her eyebrows. "They won't know what hit them!"

And so that sparked the great Polly Pearl debate, and how to do it bigger and better than all the other girls before us.

I was utterly spent when I finally fell into my bed that night. There would be no room hopping for me and I could only hope that the other girls were just as tired and didn't come knocking on my door. Athena could find a different way of sneaking her cigarettes.

5

There was no better feeling than knowing I only had half a day of school that day. I stretched out in my narrow bed, my feet almost poking out of the end, and snuggled deeper into my duvet.

It was Saturday. We only had lessons for a few hours then the rest of the day was mine...ah, it was heaven.

When I finally finished my lessons a few hours later, most of the girls were in the group room. Fenella had a textbook open on her lap, Athena flicked through a magazine and Jemima was filing her nails.

"Ah, and she rises!" Fenella said with a laugh when she spotted me.

I waved away her teasing with my hand and dropped down beside her on one of the couches.

"All set for today, Freddie?" Athena asked. There was a twinkle in her eyes and I knew exactly what she meant.

"Of course," I said, flashing her a grin. "Would you expect anything less?"

Annie rounded the couch and sat on the floor at my feet. "What are we talking about?" she asked.

"It's Freddie's first trip to the Ville today," Fenella supplied. "We need the supplies for the weekend."

Annie's eyes widened in excitement. "Of course! I'd completely forgotten."

"You're going to get the good stuff, right, Freddie?" Jemima asked.

I snorted a laugh. "I'll get what I'm able to."

"*I* would get—"

"*You* would get nothing, because you can't get served yet," Athena said, throwing Jemima a pointed look. "*Freddie* can. So save your cheek and be bloody grateful."

Ah, Athena.

She and Fenella had always been my champions. Out of all of us, I think we three were the closest. It wasn't uncommon to have cliques inside of cliques, and our group was no different. We were an odd formation of friends. If someone were to examine us all, they would find us wildly different.

Fenella was the clever one—the one who actually studied and worked for her good grades, whereas it was usually Annie and I who stayed up into the wee hours the night before an exam to cram like mad because we'd barely revised at all.

Athena was the rebel of our group. If there was any mischief, you could almost guarantee that she would somehow be at the centre of it. Athena convinced us to do daring things, to sneak out onto the roof for a cigarette.

Jemima was boy mad. She was all about her looks and what other people thought about her. When we went to the Ville, Jemima would be dressed to impress with her hair done and makeup perfect.

Harriet was the sporty one, like me. We were in a lot of the same teams, like lacrosse and netball, and loved anything athletic. Harriet was the latecomer to our group. She had been in a different boarding school until last year when she had joined Mapleton Manor's ranks.

She was half Swedish, and had beautiful golden blonde hair and bright blue eyes.

Cassandra was the glamorous girl in our group. Her dad was a big time movie producer in LA and knew everybody worth knowing. Cassandra had grown up in a mansion in Beverly Hills next door to a famous actor and it wasn't uncommon for her to attend movie premieres and parties.

Alicia was the sweet one. You could always count on Alicia to have a smile on her face and a laugh bubbling out of her. Alicia was everyone's best friend, and was adored by teachers and students alike. She was our Get Out Of Jail Free card whenever we flirted with getting caught on one of our many adventures.

Annie boarded at Mapleton Manor, but her family lived in Sandhurst. Her Dad served as an officer in the military academy there. He was scarily fit and put us athletic girls to shame.

Then there was me.

I was the lady of our group. Literally. Lady Frederica. Sometimes Fenella would tease and address me as 'Her Ladyship', but always in good humour. Aside from the title, I was a fairly down to earth girl — a bit flukey, loyal to my friends and a devoted animal lover.

Not to mention Acquirer of all Things, whether it be sweets and magazines, or cigarettes and alcohol. Perks — or downfalls — of being the tallest girl in the year.

The rest of the morning — what was left of it, anyway — was spent planning out Polly Pearl night. It would be a long wait until it came around. Every Mapleton Manor girl looked forward to the year it was finally their turn to get their revenge, even if it wasn't on the ones who did it to them.

We all cycled over to the dining hall for lunch where we scoffed our food down as fast as we could so we could get on with our trip to the Ville.

The Ville was about a fifteen-minute bike ride away. We were allowed out of the school grounds at weekends and apart from going on long bike rides through the countryside, there wasn't much else to do apart from take a trip in the Ville.

There wasn't much to it—a few clothes shops, a chemist, a couple of cafés, charity shops, a newsagent, a quirky novelty shop, a post office, a few pubs...and an off-licence. But it was our main source of weekend amusement. The off-licence, luckily for us, was at the far end of the Ville, away from the other shops we would be likely to visit, so it meant we didn't really have to worry about being seen together. I daresay it would look a tad suspicious if I was seen with a group of schoolgirls when I was trying to pass myself off as a grown-up.

We whizzed through the country lanes, rushing by long, green fields filled with cows and sheep. Tall hedgerows loomed up from the ground and the breeze stirred the branches of the lines of trees. As much as I loved Monaco, I also adored Britain and her greenery.

The rain, however, I could gladly do without.

Once we arrived at the Ville, we split up. Jemima, Annie, Harriet and Cassandra went to the supermarket to stock up on crisps and other snacks, while Athena, Alicia, Fenella and I hit the off-licence. The other three stayed a good distance away while I went in alone, armed with a fake ID that I had made in the CDT centre with the laminator and made-up tennis club names.

The middle-aged guy behind the till paid me no notice as I wandered up the aisles, pretending to browse the selection of fine wines and beers when really I was waiting for him to wise up to the fact that I was a schoolgirl and toss me out on my behind.

A few minutes passed by, and he hadn't even given me a second glance. Whoever was on page three of his newspaper was occupying too much of his attention.

I picked up a few bottles—mostly whatever was cheapest, as we didn't have much money between us. Vodka was always a good pick as we could pass it off as water and it didn't make your breath smell.

The guy served me without a problem, and didn't bat an eye when I also bought lots of packets of cigarettes.

Fenella and Athena both gave me a thumbs-up when I left the shop laden down with carrier bags, the bottles chinking against each other as I lowered them into my bicycle basket.

We met back up with the other girls, and our shopping list of supplies for Polly Pearl night was complete.

Back at Mapleton Manor, we resembled a slow moving convoy taking careful surveillance of our surroundings. It was one thing to actually buy the alcohol for our fun night, it was quite another to smuggle it into Masters. Any moment a teacher could round a building and see our bicycle baskets full of carrier bags...not to mention the fact that the bottles rattled against each other when I rode over any uneven patch of path.

At the bike shed, we formed a tight huddle and stashed bottles up our jumpers, or tucked them into the waistband of our Levis. The carrier bags full of junk food wouldn't alert too much suspicion, but just in case, we hid a few bags of crisps and packets of sweets too. We tucked cigarettes into our bras and filled our pockets with extras.

We went two at a time into Masters so it didn't look like we were a huge group of girls coming back from an illegal shopping spree. I went last with Fenella and she was a bundle of nerves.

"Oh, I hate this bit," she mumbled as we walked into the building. Her face was a shade paler than normal, as though she was walking into a haunted house rather than the place she slept every night.

I smothered a laugh with the back of my hand. "Why? This is the easy part, Fenella!" It wasn't, not really. It was the part where we were most likely to get caught. Mapleton Manor girls were savvy when it came to smuggling stuff into school, but Housemistresses and Matrons had been confiscating them for far longer. For every trick we had, they had one too.

"I get so nervous, it's so obvious I'm up to no good," Fenella mumbled.

Our feet had just touched the stairs to go up to our floor when there was a voice from behind us. "And what no good is that, Fenella?" Housemistress asked.

Fenella froze like an ice sculpture and her face completely drained of blood. Slowly, as though she was about to face her maker, Fenella turned around. "Um..."

I sighed and turned around also. "We'd better tell her, Fenella. She'll find out sooner or later anyway, I suppose."

Housemistress's eyebrows rose.

Hanging my head, I reached into my jeans pocket and pulled out a packet of itching powder I'd bought at the novelty shop in the Ville. It was a shop kept in business mostly by Mapleton Manor girls who bought copious amounts of stock to play our pranks on each other. I handed the itching powder over to Housemistress. "I'm sorry, we were going to get some of the First Formers."

When I risked a glance at Housemistress, she looked as though she was trying to contain her mirth. "Thank you for being honest, Frederica. Do I need to remind you girls how horrid it was to have your bed coated in itching powder?"

Fenella and I shook our heads.

"Then it should come as no shock when I tell you to leave the younger girls alone." Housemistress waved her hand in dismissal. "Off you go, the pair of you. And no more pranks."

"Yes, Housemistress," we chorused like the good schoolgirls we pretended we were. We darted up the stairs and rushed into my room where we shed ourselves of all the naughty things we shouldn't have had in the first place.

"My gosh!" Fenella said with a breathy laugh. She placed her hand over her chest. "My heart is racing! How do you think on your feet like that, Freddie?"

I shrugged. "It is but one of my many talents."

The bedroom door opened and we jumped about a foot in the air. Athena and Annie came in and shut the door behind them.

"What took you two so long?" Athena asked in a hushed voice.

"We nearly got busted by Housemistress," Fenella said, widening her eyes, making it seem as though she'd narrowly missed the gallows. She crossed the room to where I stood and threw her arm around my shoulders. "Luckily for me, who cannot lie to save myself, I was with Freddie, who can bluff like a poker shark."

Athena and Annie fell into giggles along with us. We finished hiding our loot, covering the bottom of my desk drawers and piling jotters and textbooks on top to hide them.

"Did everyone else get in all right?" I asked Athena once we had finished.

She nodded. "They're probably waiting downstairs by now. We're going for a walk, are you both coming?"

Fenella nodded. "Let me grab a magazine."

"Is Cassandra bringing her ghetto blaster?" I asked.

Annie laughed. "Of course she is. Shall we meet you down there, then, Freddie?"

"Yep, just give me a few minutes!"

The other girls filed out of my room, and I tucked a packet of cigarettes into my pocket and grabbed a handful of the latest magazines that I'd picked up that afternoon in the Ville.

I was the last of our group to arrive a few minutes later, and we all jumped back on our bikes and headed out to the Hemston Forest, the woodlands that surrounded Mapleton Manor.

Our usual stomping ground was a small clearing in the woods that we'd discovered one camping trip. We had moved some smaller fallen tree trunks into a makeshift circle that surrounded where we built a campfire. We'd spent many an afternoon in the clearing, and also many a night, sharing sweets and ghost stories.

Cassandra set up her ghetto blaster that she carted everywhere with her — back to Mapleton Manor and home again every term, camping trips and afternoons out of school like today. She popped in her East 17 CD and sat back against her tree trunk.

The afternoon was like many others that had been before it — a group of girls hanging out, swapping magazines and reading out embarrassing agony-aunt stories. We scoured the fashion pages for inspiration for the event of the year, which was the mixer dance with Stonebridge.

We stayed out there until the light began to fade, our stomachs started to growl and we were forced back to school.

After dinner, I caught up on some homework. I checked on the common rooms in Crosby to make sure everyone was behaving themselves and helped two First Formers with their homework. Jessica seemed to be coming out of her shell more, and I found her playing a board game with another girl in her room. I joined them for a spell, but left after one game when they both kicked my butt.

Back at Masters, I dropped in on Annie in her room, and found her sitting cross-legged on her bed. She gave me an excited smile as I entered her room and took a seat in her desk chair. "Are we still on for tonight?" she asked.

"I think so. Are the others?"

Annie nodded. "They can't wait. Athena and Fenella nabbed a ladder from the maintenance shed and left it propped up against the wall near Fenella's bedroom window. We should be able to get out no problem."

I grinned. "Brilliant."

It felt like time moved backwards as we waited for a good time to sneak out. I had already helped Miriam, the Upper Sixth girl who was House Captain, check the First and Second Formers in Crosby. In Masters, it was both easier and harder to sneak out. Easier because you didn't strictly have a bedtime.

As Sixth Formers we were encouraged to manage our own time and think responsibly, so as long as we were quiet in our rooms, no one bothered enforcing a strict bedtime.

But this also made it harder as there was no guaranteed time when a housemistress or matron could come checking. It was like sneaking out Russian roulette.

At eleven that night we stuffed our beds and crept down the hall to Fenella's bedroom. One by one, we tiptoed down the ladder, cringing at every creak and groan of the metal.

If anyone saw us we would surely resemble a renegade band of female criminals. We hugged the walls of the Sixth Form Centre before darting across the open space and disappearing into the safe coverage of the woods.

Never mind—I was fairly sure I was learning invaluable life skills.

As though by entering the woods all noise was blanketed and we were ensconced in a sound proof bubble, we let out peals of laughter that bounced off the trees and soared into the night.

We rushed through the dark woods, and though we only had the light of the moon to guide us, not one of us tripped or stumbled. We knew these woods backwards, and had been sneaking out since we were young, impressionable First Formers.

By the time we reached the clearing, we were breathless with laughter. Athena and Annie lit the few camping lanterns we had, and Cassandra started handing out cigarettes.

Jemima cracked open a bottle of vodka and after taking a swig for herself, passed it on to Alicia.

"Who wants a Wagon Wheel?" I asked, reaching into my backpack and withdrawing the packet of biscuits.

"Ooh, I'll have one!" Harriet said, reaching for one.

"And me," Fenella said, snatching the entire packet out of my hands. She giggled and handed them to Cassandra.

I accepted the vodka from Annie and settled down onto a log beside her.

"Man, I missed this," Athena said, blowing smoke circles into the air.

"And me," Alicia agreed as she sat on my other side. "I love summer holidays, but I miss you lot something terrible."

"I bet Jemima didn't miss us," Fenella said, giggling. She elbowed Jemima. "Did you, Gem? What was that boy's name? Tony?"

Jemima let out a wistful sigh. "Timothy. And he was dreamy. He kept me busy most of the summer."

We squealed with laughter at this.

"So does that mean no poor Stonebridge boy stands a chance with you at the dance?"

Jemima smiled coyly. "Never say never."

That was our Jemima — heartbreaker.

We stayed out until two in the morning, swapping more stories from the summer holidays and pondering the good looks of several boys from Stonebridge who would be at the dance later in the year. When our vodka bottles were empty and our snacks depleted, we staggered back to the Sixth Form Centre like tipsy little criminals who couldn't stop giggling.

That ladder was awfully more difficult to negotiate the second time around.

It was a chore to force myself out of bed the next morning. On Sundays the entire school attended chapel in the Ville for a special Sunday Service. We all dressed in our finest to give the best impression of Mapleton Manor. Which meant you could guarantee everyone wanted a shower, and hot water wasn't something that lasted long.

There was already a queue when I sloped into the communal bathroom on our floor. Athena and Jemima were dotted in the line, and both gave me sleepy waves as we all waited for our turn.

I had a lukewarm shower, which was wildly preferable over a cold one, then hurried back down the corridor to my room. After taking the time to blow dry my hair properly, I styled it in a neat plait that fell down the middle of my back. I pulled on my smart blue dress, black tights and black shoes and was ready to go.

For the most part, I yawned my way through the service. It made Fenella giggle and there was nothing worse than getting a giggling attack in a quiet church. She clamped a hand over her mouth but it was useless as the laughter had already taken over her.

When it at last broke free, it did so in the form of a most unladylike snort that seemed to reverberate off the old walls. Every head turned our way and I bit my lip to not burst into laughter myself.

Mrs Macpherson pinned us with a glare, and I fought back a groan. Just what I wanted — punishment on a Sunday. Turning to Fenella to glare at her myself, she gave me an apologetic smile and shrugged her shoulders.

My annoyance melted and a giggle of my own bubbled in my throat.

Well, that was it.

There was no coming back from it now, and so I might as well resign myself to it. We were getting punished anyway.

After a stern lecture about decorum and being representatives for the school, Mrs Macpherson sentenced us to scrubbing the red staircase in the main building with toothbrushes. We fought back groans. Scrubbing the steps was backbreaking work. The wide, curved staircase seemed to reach dizzying heights and it would take the pair of us a few hours at least to complete the chore.

When Mrs Macpherson turned her back, I gave Fenella a gentle shove, and she shoved me back. "Thanks a lot, you nuisance. You're worse than Louisa!"

"You shouldn't be so entertaining then, your Ladyship," Fenella said with a grin.

It took us almost three hours to finish scrubbing the staircase. And my back definitely felt like it was broken by the time we were finished. We trudged back to Crosby House like we had just been released from ten years in a workhouse.

"Freddie, your mother called while you were out," Housemistress said on our return. "I think there's a queue now to use the phones."

Of course there was a line! Sunday was the day everyone called home, or parents called their daughters. There were only two phones in the Sixth Form Centre to go between all the girls, so the wait could be agonising sometimes. "Thanks, Housemistress. I'll go get my phone card."

Leaving Fenella to her own devices, I grabbed my phone card from my room and headed back downstairs to begin the long wait. Parents could top up phone cards for their daughters, and with so many of us having families who lived abroad, it was something that had to be done fairly often. Cassandra, in particular, had a fortune spent on her phone card.

Around forty-five minutes later, it was finally my turn to use the phone.

It was Daddy who answered, when the phone had rung for a minute solid. "Christian Beaumont."

"Hi, Daddy, it's Frederica," I said with a smile.

"Hello, darling," Daddy said, his voice softening. "How has everything been?"

"Everything is fine, good, great. Everything." I laughed. "How are you?"

"I'm well, I'm well. Mummy and I went to the African Queen last night. We had a banana split in your honour."

"How kind of you!" I exclaimed.

"We're nothing if not kind, Frederica," Daddy said. "How are your lessons going? Are you finding them harder this year yet?"

"My lessons are fine. Not too hard, not yet, anyway. I'm confident I'll get good A Levels." Well, I hoped I would get good A Levels. Only time would tell. And how well mine and Annie's last minute cramming went. "I have a trip to Paris next month for history of art. It's only for the weekend. I wish I could drop in and see you and Mummy."

"Not to worry, sweetheart. You have a good time while you're away. I'll make sure you have some extra spending money. Ah, here's your mother, I'll hand you over to her. Talk soon, darling girl."

"Bye, Daddy."

"Frederica?" Mummy said as she came on the phone.

"Hello, Mummy. How are you?" I asked.

"Very well, thank you," she answered. "How is school going?"

"School is good. What about Augustus and Louisa? Have you heard from them?"

Mummy sighed. "More often than I'd like. It seems Louisa has taken your knowledge of school pranks and outdone you, darling. I've already had her school on the phone twice and it's only been a week."

I stifled a laugh. *Oh, Louisa...* "She'll keep your hands full, Mummy."

"Hmm," Mummy said, not sounding overly happy at the prospect of having a naughtier daughter than me. "What about Masters then, Frederica? Are you enjoying living with your friends?"

"Yes, it's brilliant," I said with a grin. "I'd forgotten how much I had missed all the girls until I was back. It's wonderful living with them."

"I'm glad to hear it. And is your kitchen well stocked?"

"We get a few staple things delivered every day. It's nice to have breakfast here rather than having to go into the main dining room."

Mummy laughed. "I'd hazard a guess it's because you can enjoy a few extra minutes in bed?"

"Ah, you know me so well, Mummy!"

A girl behind me coughed. I twisted around to see the long line of impatient looking girls. I huffed. "I'd better go, Mummy, there are lots of girls waiting to use the phone." Not only was it annoying that my time talking with my family was limited, it was never a private conversation. There had been a few times I'd wanted to talk to Mummy about a boy, or something embarrassing when I'd been younger, and hadn't been able to because then the rest of the school would find out.

"Of course, darling. We'll talk next Sunday."

"Okay. Give my love to everyone."

"I will. I love you, Frederica."

"I love you too, Mummy." I hung up the phone and stuck my tongue out at the girl waiting next in line who had coughed.

6

After that first week back at school, all us Sixth Formers soon found ourselves bogged down with work. Homework took even longer to complete as it was harder and more in depth. History of art, in particular, took hours. We were expected to know every painting we studied, the artist and the year. It made for a lot of factual information that clogged my brain until it all became a big jumbled mess.

The history of art trip to Paris came and went in a blur as we visited the Louvre and the Palace of Versailles. I loved being around all the art and I was actually quite moved by a few pieces. My friends would have called me a swot, but I had started to enjoy the class for more than the trips abroad. Or perhaps I just enjoyed looking at pretty things.

My birthday came — seventeen!

Mummy flew over from Monaco to take Annie and me on a shopping trip in London and we had a ball. On our return, the other girls had arranged a low-key party in the Sixth Form centre with lots of yummy treats and sugary pop drinks. It was great fun and my friends spoilt me rotten.

As the weeks slipped away and November got closer, older Mapleton Manor girls could be found in whispering huddles in the corridors, plotting and scheming. The First Form girls had no idea what we were up to — but they were soon to get the shock of their lives.

Any boarding school worth its salt had a good ghost story, and Mapleton Manor had a thumping good one.

Polly Pearl was a British courtesan and was one of the first ever 'It' girls. She was famous for simply being famous. People talked about Polly's good looks and charm, which was only amplified by the attention she gained from renowned artists.

She married Frank Norton and came to live at his family home, Hemston — which would later become Mapleton Manor. Polly died a few months after her marriage to Frank, and girls believed her to have drowned in the lake on the school grounds.

Over the years, many people claimed to have seen Polly roaming around Mapleton Manor in her gown and there was a particular legend that went around about spotting Polly's ghost.

And like all good older girls, we used this as an excuse to…welcome the newcomers to Mapleton Manor.

We chanted our Polly Pearl rhyme in low, whispering voices as we crept into the First Formers dorm room. The girls had been in bed for a few hours and were fast asleep as we woke them all up.

One by one, they sat up in their beds, blinking in confusion.

"Everyone up!" Athena commanded in a firm voice that no one would dare to argue with. "Shoes on and follow us."

The girls did as they'd been told without complaint. Some were wide eyed as they followed us out into the dark night in their nightgowns and school shoes, others giggled in nervous excitement. One or two I saw whisper to their friends—no doubt they had an older sister who had spilled the beans on what happened on Polly Pearl night.

Spoilsports. We should have to sign non-disclosure agreements or something.

We older girls were dressed more wisely and had changed out of our nightclothes and into Levis, jumpers and wellies. All the housemistresses knew about Polly Pearl night, and usually let us get away with it. It was never talked about, but someone had to notice a bunch of Upper-Form girls sneaking the First Formers out into the grounds late at night.

The younger girls huddled close together as we led them deeper into the darkness, farther away from the safety of their house and their beds. I spotted Jessica amongst them, looking small and scared as she shivered in her nightdress.

My forehead pinched in concern, and all I wanted to do was to give her a hug and reassure her that tonight was all just a bit of fun.

"Feeling sorry for them, Freddie?" Jemima asked from behind me.

Of course Jemima wouldn't feel sorry for any of them. "I can't help it. Were we ever that small, Gem?"

She chuckled under her breath. "We probably were. You would have been heads above us all."

I rolled my eyes at her slight, but didn't bother to answer back.

We walked for around ten minutes in the dark, until we reached the narrow brick tunnel. No one knew what it had been used for, but we assumed it was an older part of the estate.

Whatever it was for, it provided the perfect creepy prelude to our spooky night.

Ankle-deep muddy water coated the bottom of the tunnel and various shrieks and yelps bounced off the walls as the girls stepped into it.

Wellies — they would remember that one in years to come, I was certain of it.

"Remember our year, Freddie?" Annie asked as she tugged on my hand in the darkness. "A frog jumped on my foot and I almost hit my head on the ceiling I jumped so high."

I let out a giggle at the memory. "I remember. And I remember all too well how disgusting that water felt creeping into my shoes. They stunk for weeks!"

Annie laughed and we continued on through the narrow tunnel, herding the girls along.

"Polly Pearl is the most famous Mapleton Manor girl of all time," Athena said at the front of the group. She was the most dramatic out of all of us, and was the perfect person to lead the night's activities. She lit a candle that she had brought with her. The glow from the flame lit up her face from below, creating an eerie, haunting look. "Young, beautiful, charming…Polly Pearl had it all. Everyone wanted her — wanted to know her, wanted to be friends with her…wanted to be with her. But Polly set her heart on Frank *Norton*!"

Several girls from Norton House tittered, either amused or shaken at the blatant reference to the school and to themselves.

"There she was—a young, beautiful bride to a handsome, wealthy man. As soon as they were married, Frank brought his bride to his family home of Hemston!" Athena declared.

This time it was the Hemston House girls who whispered and clutched each other.

Athena was doing a fantastic job of scaring the girls, gently leading them into the story of the ill-fated Polly Pearl. Our year, I'd been scared senseless. The older girls had been meaner than we were, and had pushed us along, whispering and making spooky noises.

"But," Athena said, dropping her voice to a low murmur.

I could have heard a pin drop in the tunnel. She held every single person's—including all us older girls' who knew the story inside and out—unwavering attention in the palm of her manicured hand. "The young lovers were about to discover that love doesn't last forever, and it doesn't conquer all...especially...*death*. When Frank brought Polly to Mapleton Manor, he sealed her fate! You see," Athena said as she took a few slow steps backwards, almost reaching the end of the tunnel. Beyond her, the swollen full moon that hung in the dark sky was reflected in the still, glassy surface of the lake. "Polly had another passion besides her new husband. Polly enjoyed swimming, and every morning she would walk this very tunnel to swim in this very lake."

Athena glanced over her shoulder at the lake before turning to the girls with a sad, mournful smile on her lips. "She wasn't to know that the very thing she loved most about Mapleton Manor would be the end of her. For one morning, Polly would follow her usual path through this tunnel towards the lake...she would enter the water...but she would never leave it alive."

There was a collection of gasps that echoed around the tunnel.

"No one really knows what happened," Athena said. "But it was known that Polly was a strong swimmer, and she knew this lake well. There wasn't any proof, but around the Ville, it was believed that she was...*murdered*!" Athena shouted the last word, making the girls directly in front of her jump and squeak with fright.

She took another step away, and the older girls at the rear of the tunnel ushered the crowd of frightened First Formers deeper inside like lambs to the slaughter.

"Poor, young Polly's life was cut short while she was in her prime. She was buried in Mapleton Manor churchyard in her very best gown, a symbol to how she lived her life and *always* looked her best." Athena dipped her chin as if in sadness for the demise of Polly Pearl. "They say that once a year Polly Pearl emerges from her watery grave to wander the grounds of Mapleton Manor once more. They say that she can be seen in her very best gown, searching for her way back to her husband, Frank Norton. And the night that she returns...is on the eleventh day of the eleventh month at the eleventh hour...*tonight*!" Athena exclaimed her last word, bringing her candle up slightly so that her breath blew it out, eliminating what little light it had provided.

The girls tittered and huddled closer together, and I could practically smell their fear. My own pulse was hammering—Athena was an exceptionally good storyteller. It was no wonder she excelled at theatre and helped run the drama department.

A good ten seconds passed where nothing happened as we let the tension really amp up before the big finale.

Harriet, dressed in a vintage ball gown we'd found in a charity shop, jumped in front of the mouth of the tunnel and let out a ghostly wail. She moaned and ran at full speed towards the group of girls, rushing past them as they screamed and darted out of her way. She disappeared out of the other end of the tunnel, leaving a bunch of terrified First Formers in her wake.

As their screams died down, we older girls pulled out the torches stashed in our pockets and turned them on, flooding the tunnel with light. Most of us couldn't contain our laughter, but it didn't come from a place of malice.

"Come on girls, this way, this way," Athena said on a laugh as she gestured for them to follow her out. "Well, girls, you have officially survived Polly Pearl night!"

The atmosphere buzzed with excitement. Now that they knew they were no longer face to face with the real Polly Pearl, the First Formers were in tremendous spirits. They laughed in girlish, high-pitched squeaks and hopped around like they had ants in their pants.

All but one.

Jessica stood a ways back from the rest of her peers. She wrapped her arms around her middle and her face was pale. Leaving my friends, I walked over to Jessica and placed my hand on her shoulder.

"Are you all right, Jessica?" I asked her.

Jessica peered up at me with her big blue eyes widened in shock. "I'm not— I didn't…"

My heart just melted for the girl. There had been one or two in my year who'd also got a more serious fright than the rest of us had. And they had been teased mercilessly for it. I shifted around so that I shielded her from everyone else with my body. "Polly Pearl night is like a rite of passage for every Mapleton Manor girl. We don't do it to be horrible...it's more like keeping up tradition as we initiate the newcomers to the school."

Jessica nodded but didn't seem convinced.

"Did you get a really big fright?"

She nodded again. "I don't like scary things like that."

"Not many people do, but it's just a bit of fun. And do you want to know the best bit? The bit that will make the horrible feelings about tonight go away?" I glanced over my shoulder to make sure no one was eavesdropping. "In a few years, it will be *you* leading out the new First Formers for *their* Polly Pearl night. Don't worry, you'll get your turn."

At this Jessica cracked a small smile, which only widened the more she thought on it. "That does sound fun."

"It's brilliant fun." I wrapped my arm around her shoulders and steered her back towards my friends, who were dishing out the sweets and drinks for the rest of the night's festivities. "We'd better hurry before they give out all the good stuff."

"I hope there are some Dip Dabs left," Jessica said, flashing me a timid smile.

I let out a laugh and squeezed her to me. "Oh, Jessica, you will soon discover that I almost inevitably have at least one Dip Dab on me at all times." Reaching into my pocket, I pulled out the sweet and handed it to her.

Jessica giggled and took it with thanks. "You're pretty awesome, Freddie. Thank you. I'm really glad that I'm your shadow."

"No problem," I said, smiling. We reached Fenella and Cassandra, who were dishing out packets of sweets. I took a handful from the bag and gave them to Jessica. "Go give some of these to your friends, you'll be the hero for blagging extra sweets for them."

She nodded and hurried off to a small cluster of First Formers.

"Well, someone definitely has a crush, don't they, Freddie?" Jemima asked as she approached me.

I shrugged. "Maybe a little. Can't be helped sometimes, I suppose."

"Of course not. Everyone loves you, right?" She didn't say it as a question, and she said it with a smile on her face, though I couldn't help but get the impression that she meant it as a slight. Jemima snatched a Mars bar from Fenella and Cassandra's stash and headed off towards the lake.

Once all the First Formers had been supplied with enough sweets to rot a hundred teeth, a few older girls escorted them back to their Houses. The rest of the Sixth Formers made our way to the lake where we had stashed a ton of camping chairs earlier in the day.

Someone had already lit the campfire, and a few girls were clustered around it, warming their hands near the flames. The lake was far enough away from the school that no one would be able to spot the campfire, and the Housemistresses would assume that we had sneaked back into our own rooms along with the First Formers. Our beds were stuffed too, just in case any of them felt the need to check.

We passed around the alcohol and cigarettes and settled into our chairs. The others soon returned, and our party began.

It wasn't long before the truth or dare games started, and they only grew more outrageous the more alcohol we drank. The dares ranged from silly—a tongue twister rhyme or hold a handstand for twenty seconds—to the traditional humiliating ones— streaking, get caught picking your nose in class and being the first girl to ask a boy to dance at the end of the year dance. No girl ever asked a boy to dance. Ever. It just wasn't the done thing.

There were never any dares involving the lake. Instead of being a smooth, crystalline clear expanse of water, it was murky, stodgy and disgusting. And it always had a weird greenish film on the surface of it. No girl would ever use it in a dare for another girl. It was bad taste, and the only rule agreed by everyone.

The alcohol started to take effect and someone had the idea to break out the ghost stories. Of course, being at boarding school together, many of us going back to prep school days, we'd heard every possible ghost story at least a hundred times.

It didn't matter, and we didn't care that we knew the stories backwards. It was about the atmosphere, and the bonding of friendships as we tried to scare the other girls silly. Plus, a few girls, Athena included, made the telling of the story scary, not the story itself. They had a rare gift of pulling in their audiences and having them eating out of the palm of their hand.

I had no idea what time it was when we crept back into the Sixth Form Centre. All I knew was that I had to keep one eye shut so I could see the steps of the ladder properly, and I was far too tired to undress for bed.

Somehow, in my tipsy state, I had the good sense to take off my wellies before climbing into my bed.

7

Time seemed to disappear like water down the drain. After Polly Pearl night, it felt like I had only blinked and the term was over. As well as crazy coursework to keep me busy, I'd also had a weeklong trip to Barcelona and also one to Madrid, picking up another few wristbands along the way. Fenella and I had gone mad in Madrid. One afternoon when we had been allowed some free time and were set loose to investigate, we'd found this incredible little boutique in a quiet side street. It had been full of one-of-a-kind clothes and the most beautiful dresses. And the best part was they'd been an absolute steal!

We'd found the perfect dresses for us to wear to the dance at the end of the year and I couldn't wait to wear mine. Annie and Jemima had been jealous they hadn't been with us, and we'd been leaving the very next morning and so they'd had no to time to go. That was what they got for choosing to sit by a fountain and watch cute boys, rather than go with their friends to pick out clothes.

It was all about priorities…

I went home to Monaco for the Christmas holidays, and enjoyed getting to see Mummy, Daddy, Augustus and Louisa. The weather and I got better acquainted also, as winter in the south of France was vastly preferable to the winter in Kent.

The days were spent getting caught up with friends and spending quality time with my family. That quality time included searching Louisa's bedroom for *my* things the little thief had stolen.

On Christmas Day we were all spoilt rotten as we always were. There were parcels of clothes and makeup, new shoes and a stack of great CDs. The whole family went to church for the special Christmas service then later enjoyed a delicious dinner cooked by Aimee. Thankfully there were no chases with decapitated poultry heads.

The two weeks went by all too quickly and before I knew it I was at the airport again heading for Britain. Mummy hugged me tight before I boarded the plane, whispering in my ear for me to be good and that she would see me soon.

On my return to school, the pressure to do well in my A Levels really amped up. Classes were more intense, more homework was given and all my free time seemed swallowed up by revision...that I may or may not have always given my full attention to.

Most girls were up late into the night as we kept up with our schoolwork, and it ate into my valuable sleep time. But, thanks to extreme exhaustion, I'd discovered a brilliant way of sneaking in a little bit more sleep. The sound of Matron banging on girls' bedroom doors one morning had woken me up. How, I have no idea, as I'd been virtually unconscious thanks to being up so late the night before. In my drowsy state, I'd jumped out of bed and dived into my tiny cupboard. I had just pulled the door closed when Matron had knocked loudly on my room door and opened it.

"Well, at least some of them can get up in time," she had mumbled.

And once the door had closed again behind her, I'd eased out of the cupboard and jumped back into my warm bed for another half an hour's kip.

It was genius, really.

Apart from the cupboard really being too small to hold a girl of my height, it worked a treat and I had been doing it every morning since.

Athena and I walked to physics class after morning prayers in mid-February, taking our sweet time since we were in no hurry to subject ourselves to Mr Pennington and his delightful personality.

"In your own time, girls," Mr Pennington said, narrowing his shrewd little eyes as we entered the classroom.

"Sorry, Mr Pennington," we chorused. Athena and I shared a glance and rolled our eyes once his back was turned.

We took our seats at our lab table with Chloe and Rachel.

"God, I hate this class," Athena grumbled as she took out her textbook.

"Tell me about it," I agreed. "The worst part of the day. I can't wait for the year to be over. Not long now, though, I suppose."

Chloe slid her eyes over to where Mr Pennington stood in front of his chalkboard, scribbling indecipherable notes. "Play a trick on him, Freddie."

I balked at Chloe. "What! Why me?"

"Because you always get away with everything," Chloe said. She leaned in closer to me. "Go on, it will cheer us all up. *Everyone* hates this class."

Athena tapped me on the arm with her pen. "Yeah, go on, Freddie. I need something to help get me through another one of his boring classes."

A school secretary tapped on the classroom door, and Mr Pennington put down his chalk to go and talk to her.

I winked at the girls at the lab table and crept to the front of the classroom. Mr Pennington had his back to me as he talked in a low murmur to the secretary. I swiped a few pieces of chalk from his desk and placed them quietly on his chair.

There were muffled giggles as I did an exaggerated tiptoe walk back to my stool.

Just as I sat myself back down, Mr Pennington finished his conversation with the secretary and headed back to the chalkboard. He continued his scribbling and a few girls tittered.

It was an agonising five minutes before he finished. Mr Pennington instructed us to work through the experiments he had written on the chalkboard. A couple of girls groaned, and he shot them a look that quickly quietened them. Mr Pennington liked complete silence in his class, and I had earned myself more than my fair share of lines already by chatting to Athena.

At our lab table, we all held our breath as Mr Pennington lowered himself into his chair. He didn't notice the chalk and Athena choked back a laugh as he settled himself better into the chair, really working the chalk into his backside.

Mr Pennington glanced at Athena, and she quickly looked down at her jotter, biting her lip.

We waited.

And we waited.

And we waited some more.

Mr Pennington. Didn't. Get. Back. Up.

"Well, this is rubbish," Rachel whispered after fifteen minutes had passed. "His next class will end up benefitting from *our* prank."

"You should have put pins on his chair instead, Freddie," Chloe said with a wicked lift of her eyebrows.

"My gosh, Chloe!" I said with a laugh. "I'd rather not get expelled for assaulting a teacher, thank you very much."

"That reminds me—have you all heard about Meredith Sims?" Athena asked. Her eyes were as wide as saucers as she leaned in to whisper to the rest of us.

"In Upper Sixth?" I asked.

Athena nodded. "*Well*…rumour has it that she has been enjoying a little *extra attention* from Mr Stewart."

Chloe gasped and clamped a hand over her mouth.

Rachel looked as shocked as I felt. "Are you really saying that Meredith is seeing her Latin teacher?"

"Yes! Crazy, isn't it? Meredith told a few of her friends and *they* told a few more. And, I don't know how much truth there is in this, but apparently someone saw them together in his office. You know, like *together*, together."

I laughed, louder than I'd intended, but it sneaked out of me before I could stop it.

"What's going on over there?" Mr Pennington asked.

"Nothing, Sir," I said quickly, returning to my jotter and pretending to scribble something down. The last thing I needed was for Mr Pennington to get his knickers in a twist over me and my friends gossiping.

He rose from his chair and walked slowly to the back of the room where our lab table was. "It's always you I catch chatting, Frederica. Do you need the 'I shall not talk or disturb Mr Pennington's class' line one hundred times again?"

"No, sir."

The girls at the tables in front turned around and caught sight of what had to be a very white bottom, and couldn't contain their laughter.

He whirled around at the sound, allowing me and the rest of the table a perfect view of his chalky arse.

Athena released a loud, barking laugh, and Chloe and Rachel couldn't contain their giggles.

Mr Pennington spun back around to face us, and his eyes narrowed. He patted his bottom and examined his white, chalky hands. Mr Pennington stomped back to his chair and glared at the seat, before turning that angry look my way.

"Frederica Felton."

"Yes, Sir?" I asked, batting my eyelashes in innocence.

"I have had it up to here with your theatrics!" Mr Pennington's face turned an odd shade of purple as he placed his hands on his hips. He stalked closer to the table. "You have gone too far with your insolence this time and I will stand for it no longer!"

Okay, maybe it had been a bad idea to play a trick on him, but in my defence I'd had no clue that he would erupt like this. "I'm sorry, Sir, but whatever do you mean?"

Mr Pennington turned to the side and gestured to his bottom. "Are you trying to say you had nothing to do with *this*?"

I turned away sharply and shielded my eyes. "Mr Pennington!"

Athena gasped and clutched my arm. "My goodness, Frederica! Whatever would Mrs Mapherson say if she knew one of her staff was inappropriately showing himself to a poor student?"

Chloe snorted a laugh, which she tried to turn into a cough.

"What? I— Now, you listen here—" Mr Pennington spluttered.

"Mr Pennington," Rachel said quietly as she shrank back from him and into Chloe. "Please calm down. You're starting to frighten me."

Mr Pennington gestured wildly with his hand, narrowly missing our lit Bunsen burner. "*Frighten* you?" he asked in disbelief. "I cannot believe this! You silly girls are trying to upset me and *I* am frightening *you*?"

He slammed his hand down on the lab table, and Athena and I both shrieked in surprise. A flicker of brightness drew my attention to Mr Pennington's arm. More accurately, his shirt. Which was on fire.

Perhaps it wasn't as narrowly missed as I'd thought. He had caught his sleeve in it as he gestured like a crazy man.

"Mr Pennington!" I cried.

"Enough, Frederica!"

"No, Mr Pennington, sir—" I tried again.

"Quiet!" he bellowed. "I have had it up to here—"

The classroom door swung open and Miss Montgomery, who taught Chemistry in the classroom next door, rushed inside. "Mr Pennington, is everything all right? I could hear yelling."

"Everything is fine, Miss Montgomery," Mr Pennington said as he continued to glare at us all, oblivious to his smouldering arm. "Just a few insolent girls. Nothing I can't handle. Is it, Frederica?"

I widened my eyes again as I peered around him to Miss Montgomery. "Of course, Miss Montgomery. Mr Pennington was getting very upset because he accidentally sat on some chalk. So much so that he hasn't noticed his arm is on fire."

"His arm is on fire?" Miss Montgomery repeated, her eyebrows shooting up into her hairline.

I nodded, widening my eyes and swung my gaze back to Mr Pennington.

It was then he turned his eyes to his arm and he realised that yes, his arm was indeed on fire.

Somehow my luck was with me yet again and I wasn't punished for the…misunderstanding with Mr Pennington. Which was really rather fortunate as I had a lacrosse match that weekend against Wigcombe Abbey — our all-time ultimate rival.

The light faded around me as I jogged around the lacrosse field. My lungs burned from exertion but I didn't let myself stop or falter. It was the night before the big game, and just like every evening and spare moment I'd had, I was spending it running drills, practicing and making sure I was at peak fitness.

"Come on, Freddie!" Sarah, one of my teammates called from the edge of the field. She and the others had finished training fifteen minutes ago. "You'll exhaust yourself for tomorrow!"

I waved to show her I was fine. "Just a few more minutes."

She nodded then gathered up her bag and water bottle. "See you in the morning."

Twenty minutes later, I slowed my pace until I eventually came to a stop. I stretched, drank my water then moseyed back to my room.

In the morning, I made my way to the coach after a healthy breakfast of fruit, Weetabix and natural yogurt. The bus was surrounded by my teammates, our coach, Mrs Chesterfield and a few chaperones. Once our roster was checked and double-checked to confirm we were all present, we boarded the bus.

The moment we trundled down the long drive, every girl burst into cheer. I loved game days. Everyone was riled up and in high spirits. It worked wonders for getting us in the mood for a game, to become a single unit of a team than solitary players.

Someone behind me started singing a school song and a beat later the entire coach joined in. I grinned and sang at the top of my voice. We barely paused for a breath between one song and the next. We recited fight chants to get our adrenaline up and it worked so well that by the time the game started we could probably have accomplished world domination.

But Wigcombe Abbey girls had a tough lacrosse team, and they weren't easy to beat.

The first half passed in a blur of frenzied activity. My teammates moved fluidly across the field, helping each other and trying their best to feed me and the other attackers the ball. I stayed on the offensive side and tried to get around the midfielders.

The whistle blew for half-time and we were one goal down to their three.

I trudged off the field with my shoulders slumped.

"Come on, Freddie, chin up," Ms. Chesterfield, our coach, said. "All right, girls, gather round."

We all grabbed our water bottles and crouched down to listen to Ms. Chesterfield.

"It may seem grim right now, but we *will not be beaten*! We have come back from much worse than this! Those girls over there think they have already won the game — but they haven't! We're saving our best for last and we will knock their socks off." She rose to full height. "Now let's get back out there and finish them!"

With a cheer, we jumped to our feet and charged back onto the field, determined that we would, in fact, not be beaten.

We set up for a face-off with the opposition and waited for the whistle to blow.

The second half started and we were women on a mission as we won the face-off against Wigcombe Abbey.

Girls from our school who had come along on another bus to support the team cheered from the sidelines, screaming for us to slaughter the opposition.

I played harder than I ever had. I seized every ground ball, brought out all my best fake-out moves and took every chance to score that I had.

With two minutes remaining of the game, we were an even draw with Wigcombe Abbey. Some people may have been discouraged, but not me. I was a girl possessed and adamant I would not return to school a loser. I tore across the field and intercepted a pass. Seeing my chance, I reared my arm back to score a goal.

But I was ploughed into with a stick and knocked to the ground hard enough to push the wind from my lungs. As attacker, my job was a little rougher than some of the other girls and I was used to getting bashed about. What I wasn't used to was being illegally cross-checked by a girl so large she could have doubled as Miss Trunchbull.

"What was that?" I demanded as I scrambled to my feet, holding my sides as my lungs complained.

She shrugged. "It was an accident. I lost control."

My backside! I opened my mouth to say as much, but the ref blew her whistle and rushed over to us.

"Foul! Illegal cross-check! Two minute penalty!"

Two minutes…we could make this work. I exchanged a look with my teammates who all nodded their unspoken agreement.

One of the opposing midfielders tried to block me, but I spun around her in time to catch the ball from my team. I tore towards the goal and using a stutter-step dodge to confuse the defender, I threw the ball as hard as I could and…*scored*!

The ball touched the back of the net as the whistle blew for the end of the game.

All of us screamed in excitement and rushed to each other in a big, clumsy group-hug.

No power on this earth could have contained our spirits on the drive home that evening. We were victors and we wanted the world to know it.

My eyes were bleary, my head thumped and all I wanted to do was crawl into my warm, comfy bed and sleep for a week. Instead, I was sat cross-legged on my bed beside Annie, staring at the same paragraph I had read three times. It *still* hadn't sunk in.

Annie groaned and flopped back against my pillows. "Remind me why we leave revision to the last minute again?"

"Because it's a system that has worked for us so far, so why break tradition?"

It was after midnight the night before our first A-Level exams, and Annie and I were burning the midnight oil studying for it. Up until now we had coasted by with barely cracking open a textbook, but it was the final hour and we could put it off no longer.

We were armed with packets of Pro Plus, bottles of Coke and plenty of sugary sweets. Aerosmith played quietly from my new CD player, filling the room with the scratchy voice of Steven Tyler.

The rest of the House was quiet, most of the other girls all fast asleep. But I'd bet good money there were a few who resembled Annie and I and were cramming like mad.

"Can you believe it's almost the end of the year already?" Annie asked as she reached for another Freddo.

"Tell me about it," I said as I fought back a yawn. "It's gone past so quickly."

"Are you looking forward to the dance?"

"I'm looking forward to wearing my new dress!" Giving Annie a soft nudge, I asked, "What about you, Annie? Have you got your sights on any fit Stonebridge boys?"

Annie scoffed a laugh. "Yeah, right! Like I'd get a look in stood beside you, anyway."

I frowned. "What's that supposed to mean?"

My friend gave me a bland look. "You are kidding, right? Freddie...you're bloody gorgeous. We all look like a bunch of tramps when we're standing beside you."

A blush warmed my cheeks. It was sweet of Annie to say so, but I hardly felt like that myself. "I'm too tall."

"Yeah, you're tall, but you're not *too* tall. Come on, you'll probably be a world-famous fashion model by the time the rest of us finish university!" Annie let out a quiet giggle.

"I'm going to university!" I exclaimed with a laugh.

"After university then," she conceded. "You'll be on the catwalks of New York and Milan, dressed in beautiful creations by these designers you adore so much." Annie waved her hand in the direction of my corkboard, which was full to bursting with pictures I had cut out of magazines of designer clothes.

I sighed. "A girl can but dream..."

Annie laughed again. "Just don't forget about us when you're jetting all over the world."

"Like anyone could forget about you lot...you're all as mad as a box of frogs," I said, throwing my arm around Annie's shoulders. "Now, as much as I hate to say it, back to the grind!"

Annie muttered something unladylike under her breath as she sat back upright and grabbed her textbook.

We were in for a long night...

8

The school year was coming to a close. Final exams had been completed, all coursework and dissertations had been handed in. There was a buzz of excitement in the air around Mapleton Manor, from girls and teachers alike. The weather was warmer, putting everyone in good spirits, and that feeling of completion and sense of impending freedom that came with every approaching summer holiday had me walking on air.

At the end of the week I would be flying back home to Monaco for a brief stopover over before heading off to Switzerland to the summer camp that I went to every year with Augustus and Louisa. I couldn't wait for summer camp—it was always great fun and full of exciting activities.

There was only one last thing left on the Mapleton Manor School Calendar until the end of term—the dance with Stonebridge boys' school. We were encouraged to invite other people, but all my friends were already there so I didn't have anyone I particularly wanted to extend an invitation to. Some girls invited siblings and other family members, and it was brilliant to meet new people. Needless to say, every Mapleton Manor girl wanted to look her best.

Taking advantage of the good weather, I lay in a line with my friends on the great lawn behind the school. We sprawled out under the sun in our bikinis during our afternoon break from classes. We were slathered in baby oil, and my tanned skin only needed the barest of encouragement from the sun to return to its usual healthy glow. The English winters could make me pale—not as pale as my friends—but pale enough that I felt like a vampire some days.

I adored the heat of the sun and could feel its rays on my skin as I soaked up all that vitamin D.

"This is the life," Fenella murmured beside me.

"Absolutely," I agreed.

"We'll all be bronzed goddesses for the dance in a few days," said Athena. She lay on her stomach and flicked through the latest issue of *More* magazine. "Oh, look at this dress. Where is it from...?"

"I'm so excited for the dance," Harriet said beside me. "My brother and cousin are coming. I can't wait for you all to meet them."

"Brother?" Jemima asked as she sat up. "I've never heard anything about a brother before."

"I have a brother—what's the big deal?" I asked Jemima.

"Your brother is a little young for my taste, Freddie." She gave me a tight smile before turning to Harriet again. "How old is he, Harriet?"

"Pan is seventeen, like us. Mummy had us one right after the other, so we ended up in the same year at school. He's a lot of fun, I'm sure you will all like him."

"Some of us more than others," Athena muttered from my other side.

I gasped and glanced at Jemima, but she didn't appear to have heard Athena's comment.

Athena flashed me a wink when she caught my gaping look. I stuck my tongue out at her.

"Are we all getting ready together?" Cassandra asked as she pushed her large sunglasses up onto the top of her head. "It's so much fun when we do."

"Sounds great!" Fenella said with a wide smile.

"Count me in," I agreed.

"Awesome!" Cassandra beamed. "My room after dinner?"

We all nodded our assent.

I adored getting dressed up anyway, and doing my hair and makeup, but it was even better when we all did it together. We could pass on advice and encouragement and compliments on our outfits before we took the world by storm.

Every Mapleton Manor girl was a flurry of excitement as they skipped and danced down the halls. Nothing got the girls fired up like a school dance could. Half of them could barely sit still during dinner, and a couple of my friends in particular hardly ate a thing, as they were too excited.

The second we were allowed, my friends and I rushed to our rooms to get the things we needed and carted them to Cassandra's room. Using the bathroom was always a feat when there was a dance as every single girl wanted to use it. Thankfully we all arrived in the nick of time, and I actually managed to grab a shower with hot water.

Cassandra's room was full to the gunnels and bursting with noise. Makeup bags spilled their contents, dresses were hung around the room, hairdryers blasted and there were so many different perfumes that the room was more potent than the fragrance section of Harrods.

Athena, Jemima and Annie all wore floral prom-style dresses with full knee-length skirts and bright, busy patterns. Cassandra pulled out one of the fabulous pieces her dad had sent over from LA, an emerald green slinky dress with thousands of sparkling sequins. Fenella and I couldn't wait to put on our dresses that we'd bought in Madrid. Fenella's was an aquamarine number with a fitted bodice embellished with detailed stitching, Swarovski crystals and a big, tulle skirt.

And mine…well, mine was easily the best of the bunch…if I did say so myself. But then I suppose I was a little biased. I had completely fallen in love with this dress when I'd bought it, and time had not diminished my adoration of it.

It was a black halter neck with buttons down the front to the skirt, which flowed out in a nice little flare without being too outrageous. It ended a few inches above my knees, showing off my long, tanned legs. It revealed more skin than I was used to, and my back was completely bare, but it wasn't overly racy.

My dress was still fun but I felt like it was more grown-up than the other girls, with an edge of playful sophistication that theirs lacked.

I applied a smoky look to my eyes, making the irises stand out, and I kept my blonde hair straight and natural, not needing to overdo it. When I emerged from behind the screen in Cassandra's room once I had put on my beautiful dress, it was to the surprised gasps of my friends.

"*Frederica*!" Athena exclaimed. "Look at you! You look absolutely gorgeous!"

"Blimey, Freddie, you look like you should be in a nightclub," Fenella said in a breathy voice. "It looks even better on now than it did in Madrid."

"Now I'm doubly jealous I didn't get to go to that shop." Annie pouted as she gave my dress a harmless tug.

My cheeks warmed from their compliments and I waved them aside with my hand. "Stop, you'll embarrass me."

"We're the ones who should be embarrassed, sweetie," Cassandra said with a wide smile. "After all, we have to stand next to you all night with you looking like that."

"She's right," Jemima said, scanning me from head to toe. When she drew her gaze back up to my eyes, she laughed and shook her head. "No one will look twice at us."

"Stop, you are all absolutely gorgeous." I threw my arm around Jemima's shoulders. "This dress fits you perfectly, you have such an amazing figure."

Jemima popped a hip. "Yes, I suppose you're right."

We all laughed.

"Picture time!" Fenella announced. She hopped over to Cassandra's desk where a disposable camera sat. She picked it up and gestured for us all to move closer.

All of us crowded together with our cheeks touching. Fenella placed herself in front and held the camera up. "Everyone say Stonebridge!"

"Stonebridge!" we chorused through our laughter.

"Oh my gosh, I'm nervous," Fenella whispered as we walked down the corridor towards the hall where the dance was being held.

"Why?" I asked her.

She shrugged. "It's just so exciting, isn't it? I mean, we're not the young girls anymore, are we? We're the older ones. We're the ones the boys will pay more attention to. Hopefully. Oh God, what if no one pays attention to us?"

I kissed her cheek. There wasn't a chance on this earth of no one paying attention to Fenella. She looked incredible and she was such a fun person that she could win over just about anybody. The boys of Stonebridge had better watch out. "Then it will be their loss!"

Fenella giggled. "You're right, Freddie, just like always."

"Come on, you two!" Harriet called from in front of us.

We hurried to catch up with the rest of the group, Fenella sliding her hand into mine and we giggled like the schoolgirls that we were.

The hall was decked out in paper streamers and balloons. A DJ was set up in the corner, and disco lights throbbed in time with his music. There was a row of chairs against each wall and the time-honoured tradition of girls on one side and boys on the other was being strictly upheld. A refreshments table had been set up at the back of the hall where pop and snacks were being sold.

The first part of dances were always awkward until everyone got over their shyness. The younger Mapleton Manor girls crowded into one corner, forming almost a protective huddle against the scary boys. They whispered and sneaked glances, but for the most part they only showed their backs.

I followed my friends to the refreshments table so we could get a drink of squash, more for the excuse to have something to do than anything else.

Music blasted into the room, R.E.M.'s *Losing My Religion*, and a few of the braver Mapleton Manor girls danced along to it. They were watched by the Stonebridge boys, a few of them with looks of wonder on their faces as though they were observing some rare, exotic creatures.

For a while we wandered the room, chatting to friends and peeking glances at the boys. Mostly the boys were refined and appeared to be gentlemen, but there were others who were more crass, loud and boisterous.

Teachers milled around the room, a few unfamiliar ones who had to be from Stonebridge. They kept an eye on things, making sure no one was acting out of turn.

"This is agonising," Annie murmured in my ear. "Why are we always so excited for these dances? They are nothing but embarrassing when we get to them."

I shrugged my shoulders. It was the age-old question, I supposed. "Everyone is too unsure of themselves, it seems."

"Well, it's rubbish."

Glancing at my friends, all beautiful, strong, confident girls, reduced to insecure and shy individuals when faced with a room full of boys, I knew something had to be done.

"Yes, it is rubbish. So why don't we do something about it?" I asked, lifting an eyebrow. Without waiting for a reply, I marched over to the other side of the room to where a cluster of Stonebridge boy's stood. Picking the best looking of the bunch, a tall, leanly built blond with a slightly crooked nose, I grabbed his hand. "I thought this was a dance, not a stand-a-round."

His friends cheered as I dragged him in the direction of the dance floor, shouting things I couldn't make out, and I was quite glad of that fact. My friends watched with wide eyes when I stopped right in the middle of the dance floor, in full view of the entire room, and started shaking my hips and moving to the music.

I cut my eyes to his group of friends then back again to the girls, hinting for them to man up and do what I had done.

Jemima was the first. She stormed to that group of boys like she owned the place, sizing them up and choosing the next best one. After that, all the others moved over to mingle with the boys and before I knew it, there was no gaping distance between the Stonebridge boys and the Mapleton Manor girls.

"That was pretty cool of you," the boy I was dancing with said.

I smiled at him. "Thanks." Maybe this boy was worth coming to the party for...and he went to Stonebridge, so I could see him lots. Plus he was the same height as me. He wasn't taller than me, which I would have preferred, but it was definitely more agreeable than being shorter!

"I'm Miles, by the way," the boy said, flashing me a wide smile.

"I'm Frederica. Lovely to meet you."

The music changed to a slower number, and Miles wasted no time in sliding an arm around my waist and tugging me closer to him. The motion startled me and I stiffened in his arms. Miles let his hands wander south and a second later he was cupping my bottom.

An unfamiliar teacher rapped Miles on the shoulder, his face a mask of annoyance and embarrassment. "Mr Haines, might I remind you that you are a representative of Stonebridge School? This sort of behaviour just will not do."

His hands moved from my bottom to the middle of my back in a hurry. "Yes, sir, sorry, sir," Miles mumbled as he glared at the floor.

The teacher glanced at me briefly, his eyes assessing. I wanted to scream that Miles' attention was unwanted and I had done nothing to encourage his behaviour. He gave Miles another pointed look then turned away from us, no doubt trying to find another Stonebridge boy acting with bad decorum.

Once his teacher's back was turned, Miles' bashful look twisted into an angry sneer. "God, what an idiot that man is. I should have known he would be patrolling around like a prison warden."

"I think he's just making sure everyone acts appropriately," I said quietly.

"*I* think he's just out to ruin everyone's night." Miles' eyes bored into my face. "Well, he can try anyway." He moved his hands south again, and I knew I had made a catastrophic error in choosing my dance partner.

Ripping out of his hold, I stumbled back into another couple dancing behind us. "Sorry, but I think you've managed to ruin my night all on your own."

"What?" Miles asked, his eyebrows shooting up. "Are you kidding?"

"No, I am not," I huffed. "God, keep your hands to yourself next time, will you?" And with that I turned around, my hair whipping my face, and marched away from him.

I stormed over to the refreshments stand and bought myself a cup of warm Coke and a packet of Maltesers. Taking my things, I found an empty seat at one of the tables that had been set out, and sat down to watch the dance from the safety of my chair.

Fenella looked like she was enjoying herself as she danced with her guy, as did Jemima, whose body language was borderline inappropriate. I couldn't see any of the others, but the dance floor was now so crowded they could have been anywhere.

Everyone looked as though they were having a good time. Everywhere I looked, girls were smiling and dancing, either with their friends or a Stonebridge boy.

I had been sitting at the table for about fifteen minutes when I spotted Athena pushing her way through the crowd towards me. When she reached the table, she shooed me until I moved over on my chair so there was enough room for her to sit down too.

"So, you picked the wrong one!" she declared, throwing her arm around my shoulders and stealing the last of my drink.

"That I did. How did you know?" I asked her. When I'd last looked, Athena had been busy with her own Stonebridge boy, and had spared no glance for me and mine.

"I spied you marching away from him like he was the devil incarnate, and a minute ago he asked me to dance. When I said no he asked if all Mapleton Manor girls were as frigid as me and my friend." Athena's face darkened with anger and I knew it had taken all her self-control not to impale the idiot with her stiletto shoe right there on the spot.

I gasped, unable to hold in my shock. "Oh my God, what an idiot." *What I wouldn't give for Daddy's air rifle right about now...*

"Well, forget him," Athena said. "There are plenty of other cute boys here. You just had rotten luck the first time around, that's all."

A laugh bubbled in my throat. "I think that was worse than rotten luck, Athena. He was awful! And I hate to say it, but I think he's put me off Stonebridge boys for life."

"No, don't say that!" Athena cried. "You can't let one stupid boy ruin your night, or your dating prospects."

"I don't think the love of my life is going to be a silly Stonebridge boy, Athena."

She sighed like it was the saddest thing she had ever heard. "Fine, fine. But at the very least, you can't let him spoil the rest of your night. You may not be looking for a boy, but all your girls are here and we all love you."

I laughed again. "I suppose you're right."

Athena jumped to her feet and grabbed my hand, pulling me out of my chair. "Come on, I'm not letting you waste the night in the corner by yourself." She held my hand all the way to the dance floor as though she was afraid I'd bolt in the opposite direction if she let me go. A fast song came on, and Athena started jumping around like a crazy person.

Harriet and Cassandra appeared from the throng of bodies. They gave excited squeals when they reached us, and joined in with Athena's rather enthusiastic dancing.

I threw my hands in the air and lost myself to the music, letting my body take over and do what came naturally. A happy, warm feeling bloomed in my belly. Athena was right—I shouldn't let a stupid boy ruin my night. It was still early yet, and the night was young. My friends were here and that was all I needed for a good time.

Dancing with my friends felt like better exercise than a lacrosse match. My feet throbbed, my legs ached and my heart pounded. I was fairly sure I looked like a sweaty mess, but a quick trip to the bathroom reassured me the exertion had only given my cheeks a healthy flush.

"This is definitely the best dance Mapleton Manor has put on," Fenella said as she freshened up her lipstick in the mirror.

"Absolutely. Those Stonebridge boys get better looking every year," Jemima said. She caught my eye in the mirror as I carefully applied another coat of mascara. "Don't you think, Freddie?"

I shrugged. Was she intentionally trying to goad me? Or did she not know what had happened with Miles? "None of them have made me lose my head yet."

"Don't fret, I'm sure you'll meet your Prince Charming sooner or later. Perhaps later, though."

Athena groaned and gave Jemima a little nudge, making her mess up her gloss.

"Watch it, would you?" Jemima said, narrowing her eyes at Athena.

"Watch your tongue and I'll watch my elbow," Athena said with a Cheshire Cat grin. "You don't realise how half the things you say sound to the rest of us, Jem. You're lucky we know you're not a total bitch."

Jemima stuck her tongue out at Athena. But when her eyes met mine in the mirror again, there was a hint of coldness in them that hadn't been there before.

"How's your boy working out, Annie?" I asked, turning to my friend.

She smiled so wide I was surprised it didn't split her face in half. "Great! He's just brilliant. And so nice."

"Is there romance in the air?" Harriet asked, giggling.

"Maybe," Annie answered, her cheeks flushing pink.

"Will you give him a goodnight kiss?" Cassandra asked as she pulled kissy faces at Annie.

If anything, Annie's face burned darker. She shrugged her shoulders and rifled through her small handbag. "I don't know. Probably. If he wants one. He might not. How can you tell, anyway?"

Athena and I exchanged a glance, and we chorused, "You'll be able to tell."

There was a moment's pause before we all dissolved into giggles.

A familiar song started playing, the muffled sounds of it sneaking its way into the bathroom. Harriet squealed and grabbed Cassandra's hand, who grabbed Annie's, who grabbed Jemima's, who grabbed Fenella's, who grabbed mine, and I grabbed Athena's, and we all charged out of the bathroom and back into the hall where we could take the dance floor by storm.

I felt light and carefree as we shook our stuff. We fought off the boys who tried to infiltrate our tight circle. Some dances were just for friends, and no boy could ever change that.

When the song was over, most of my friends then accepted dances from the boys. I felt like a spare part, and I was so hot still, so I sneaked out of the side door and into the cool evening air.

It was barely nine o'clock but it was still practically daylight. The sun held its warmth, though it wasn't as intense as it had been earlier in the day, and the mild breeze was fresh and invigorating after being in the stifling heat of the hall.

Birdsong floated in the air, and the swallows that nested in the eaves of the older buildings on campus flew and dived. The sweet scent of the gardens created a heady perfume, topping off the perfect atmosphere of a summer's evening.

I skipped down the steps and kicked off my shoes to walk barefoot across the lawn to a large oak tree. Leaning against the cool, rough bark, I closed my eyes and let out a contented sigh.

"You look as though you're enjoying the evening air," a boy said.

The suddenness of it startled me, and I pushed off the tree and looked around for the source.

To the right of me stood a boy. "I'm sorry, did I frighten you?" he asked, his forehead wrinkling as he frowned. His voice was smooth and alluring, strong without being a bellow, refined and intelligent without being snobbish. Low enough that I knew he was on the cusp of manhood. He was tall with broad shoulders, a narrow waist and golden brown hair. His lips stretched into a friendly smile, flashing straight, white teeth. The action was so warm and open that I felt my own mouth curving in response.

Shaking my head to clear the fog he had cast over me, I let out a quiet laugh. "No, sorry. I was lost in my thoughts."

"I hope they weren't too serious." His smile widened. "Or that you can't ever find them again."

A laugh bubbled in my throat. "No, definitely nothing serious. I was just thinking how lovely the evening is. It's still warm but not too hot."

"Just right?" he asked.

"Just right," I confirmed.

"Are you having a good night?"

I felt myself nodding, but I had to question whether I really was or not. It was brilliant dancing and having a lark with my friends, but I couldn't deny that the altercation with Miles at the beginning of the night had cast a cloud over the entire thing. "I've been to better parties."

The boy's eyebrows rose in surprise. "Oh? How come?"

I shrugged. "It just hasn't turned out like I thought it would."

He seemed to consider this for a few moments. His face turned serious for a beat before he smoothed out his expression and he resumed his carefree one. "I think I know what you mean. I ducked out to take myself for a quick walk, but then realised I could get myself hopelessly lost. What do you say — feel like escorting me for a few minutes to save me the embarrassment of needing a search party?"

There was something about the boy's easy charm that was both alluring and relaxing. He wasn't threatening or imposing in the least, and I had to admit that I was curious to know more. "Sure. I'd love to." I stepped forward to walk beside him and couldn't help but notice that he was indeed tall. He wasn't the same height as me.

He was taller than me.

For the first time, I had to look up into the eyes of someone my own age. It made my stomach flutter and he became all the more appealing to me.

I didn't bother putting my shoes back on, and instead walked barefoot across the grass as we headed around the school. That was the best thing about Mapleton Manor—it was huge, colossal even, with plenty of wide, open spaces.

"I'm Peter, by the way," the boy said as we moved farther away from the building. "You know, so we're no longer strangers...just in case you started to question your decision to walk off with someone you don't know."

I giggled. "I wasn't, but perhaps I should?"

Peter's eyes widened with surprise. "Oh no, you can't do that, I'm afraid it's too late for that. After all, you agreed to escort me. You can't go back on your word."

"Ah, but what if you're dangerous to an innocent girl like me?" I asked playfully.

For a brief moment, Peter's eyes dipped as he scanned my body. I shivered under his quick perusal. "I don't think I could ever find it in me to hurt a beautiful girl like you."

My steps faltered and he caught my elbow to steady me. Warmth blossomed under his touch and for the first time in my life, I was rendered speechless.

Peter smiled like he hadn't just given me the best compliment I had ever had. "So do I get to know your name, or will this be a Prince Charming trying to find his nameless Cinderella type of situation?"

"Of course not. I like my shoes far too much to leave one of them behind," I said dryly, lifting up the shoes dangling from my fingertips.

Peter laughed, a full-bodied, throaty sound that made my skin tingle. "You have a cracking sense of humour."

"Thank you." I felt myself blooming under his attention. "And my name is Frederica, but everyone calls me Freddie."

"Frederica," he murmured. "Freddie. I like it. It suits you. You look like a Freddie."

I wrinkled my nose. "Is that your way of saying I look like a boy?"

"No, Christ, no," Peter said in a rush. "Absolutely not. Trust me, there is *nothing* boyish about you."

"That's good to know," I said. My cheeks warmed at his declaration. It was peculiar — in a lot of ways he was bolder than Miles, but he didn't have even a hint of sleaziness about him.

We walked towards the woods, and the air was a few degrees cooler once we were under the thick blanket of trees. "Won't you hurt your feet?" he asked.

"No, my feet are more at home unsheathed than they are in shoes." I smiled. "I grew up in Monaco and I was always barefoot, scrambling over the rocks at the beach or wandering around at home. And I'm an outdoorsy girl — I've always played in woods. Bare feet give better traction whilst climbing trees."

Peter laughed. "I can't imagine you climbing trees."

"I was the best in my class, I'll have you know," I said, pretending to huff. "At Bourne Park I spent as much time in the spinney as I could. If teachers couldn't find me, they checked the trees first."

"You're a total contradiction, Freddie." Peter smiled. "And definitely not what I assumed when I first saw you."

"And what was that?" I couldn't help but ask.

Peter shrugged. "You looked interesting, but not as interesting as I now know you are. More than anything, you just seemed like a beautiful girl who was into all the usual stuff girls are. Hair, makeup, that sort of thing. I can't tell you how impressed I am that you can climb a tree."

I let out a startled laugh. "Is that all it takes to impress you? Be able to climb a tree?"

"You, my dear, have never seen *me* attempt to climb one."

"Well, that does it. I have to see it now," I said, folding my arms across my chest and silently daring him to refuse me.

Peter raised his eyebrows. "And you would happily see me humiliate myself in front of the girl I'm trying to win over with my charm and good looks?"

A giggle rose in my throat. "I would be impressed with the attempt—and the fact that you were willing to embarrass yourself anyway."

He sighed and dropped his head. "Fine, have it your way. Pick me a good one." Peter gestured around him to the various trees.

"Follow me." There was a huge sycamore a short way down the path from us, and even the First Formers could climb it. It was full of handy knots and branches for holding onto and hoisting myself up. I led Peter over to it and waved in its direction. "Even a novice could climb this old girl. Just look for places to put your hands and feet and you'll be fine."

Peter peered up into the tree for a long minute as though he were facing the ultimate battle and his life depended on the outcome of this challenge. He turned back to me and pulled off his socks and shoes. He then rolled up the sleeves of his pale green shirt, and tucked his tie into the space between two buttons. "Wish me luck," he said as he took a deep breath.

"You don't need it, but good luck anyway." I smiled.

Peter stood with his hands on his hips as he perused the tree again, probably looking for the best place to start. He moved partially around the trunk and grabbed a low branch, placing one foot and then the other against the rough bark, and hoisting himself up.

His foot slipped and he yelped. In his initial panic, he scrambled closer to the trunk and tried to wrap his arm around the branch he held onto. But unfortunately it wasn't strong enough to hold his weight. It snapped with a distinctive crack and Peter skidded down the trunk and landed in a messy heap at my feet.

I bit the inside of my cheek to keep from laughing.

Peter's eyes were squeezed shut as he lay flat on his back, his arms and legs sprawled out to the sides. "Is it over? Am I dead yet?"

A laugh crept out and I pressed my fingers to my mouth. "No, not yet."

Peter cracked one eye open and peered up at me from the ground. "Are you laughing at me?"

"No, I wouldn't dream of doing such a thing."

He opened his other eye and gave me a pointed look. I could hold my laughter in no longer and it bubbled out of me. Peter sat up and got to his feet, brushing himself off. "Is that it, then? Have I completely ruined any hopes of getting to know you further? I'm sure I can find my own way back, you don't have to take pity on me and escort me to the school."

"No, don't be silly," I said once I had my laughter under control. "Are you all right? You landed quite hard."

Peter shook his head. "I'm fine. It's just my pride that's wounded. Well, that and my elbow, I think." He twisted his arm around to examine his elbow, and he had scraped a good length of skin off his arm.

I hissed in a breath through my teeth. "Ouch, that must hurt."

Peter shrugged. "It stings a little. Maybe it will scar and I can come up with a good story that isn't the horrifying, embarrassing truth of what really happened?"

"I feel terrible for insisting I see you attempt to climb a tree now," I said, frowning at my own thoughtlessness.

Peter's face softened. "Don't. You weren't to know just how much I really *couldn't* climb a tree."

Reaching my hand out, I gently touched his arm. "Just know that I am sorry you got hurt."

He opened his mouth to say something but stopped at the last moment. His eyes turned mischievous and he flashed me a wicked smile. "I know how you can make it up to me."

My eyebrows shot up into my hairline. "Oh? How?"

Peter jerked his head towards the tree. "Prove to me you're the tree climbing champion you claim to be."

I laughed. "I never claimed to be a *champion*!"

He smiled. "A pro, at the very least."

Glancing at the tree, I realised I was hardly dressed for climbing. I looked back at Peter. "You have to promise not to look up until I tell you."

He huffed. "But how will I learn where I went wrong?"

Like I would climb the tree knowing he was getting a perfect view straight up my dress! I folded my arms across my chest. "And here I thought you were a gentleman."

Peter chuckled and he reached out to stroke my arm. "I'm teasing, Freddie. Of course I won't look."

"Okay, well turn around then."

He did as he'd been told and I scampered up the tree as fast as I could.

I hadn't been exaggerating when I'd said that I spent half my time in the spinney. As a child I'd always been adventurous and the only good tree in my book was one that I could climb. I remember I'd given my mother a near heart attack when I'd climbed the tallest tree in our garden and I'd seen her through an upstairs window.

I'd been six at the time.

This particular tree, I had climbed hundreds of times during my attendance at Mapleton Manor. I knew every knot, every crevice and I was up it before a minute had passed.

"You can turn around now."

Peter trailed his eyes up the tree slowly, and I caught the disbelief in them, even from my great height. "If I hadn't been standing here this entire time, I would have said there was no possibility you could have climbed that tree that quickly."

"I am a pro, after all," I said, throwing his earlier words back at him.

"If I didn't know any better, I would have said you flew up there."

I twisted around and tried to peer down my back. "Darn—are my wings showing again?"

Peter rolled his eyes. "Ha ha. Now come down, please, before my sensitive male pride is injured any more."

I laughed. "All right, but turn around again, please."

He turned away from me. "You really are an outdoorsy kind of girl, then?"

"Absolutely," I said, taking more time to go down than I did to go up. The last thing that I wanted was to misplace a foot or a hand and land in an ungainly heap like Peter had.

When I reached the bottom, I tapped Peter on the shoulder. He turned around to face me, a sweet smile at play on his full lips.

"Well that," he murmured, "was impressive." Peter's eyes moved to my hair. Reaching out, he plucked a leaf tangled in my locks.

Though he barely touched me, it was enough to send shivers all the way down my spine.

"You're missing the dance. Would you like to head back, or…?" Peter watched me carefully.

I bit my lip and shook my head. "No. I'm not ready to go back yet."

His eyes seared into mine. "I know what you mean." Peter slipped his hand into mine, lacing our fingers together and stroking the back of my hand with his thumb.

Swallowing a sudden rise of nervousness, I took a step backwards, pulling him with me. "I know somewhere we can go."

We were quiet as we headed into the heart of the woods. It was quieter here, the whispering sway of the tree branches in the gentle breeze, the far away chirping of birds the only sounds to be heard. Mapleton Manor and the dance were but a distant dream — an age away from where we really were.

I led Peter to the clearing my friends and I had discovered, knowing it would provide perfect privacy and a place we could sit and chill out. I glanced at Peter and there was surprise all over his face.

"Not what you were expecting?" I asked him with a smile.

He gave a soft shake of his head. "No, but I suppose I shouldn't be surprised. Girls at boarding school are always more resourceful than boys. I take it this is yours and your friends' secret hang-out place?"

I shrugged. "Just somewhere private we like to come to, you know, get away from school for a bit, that sort of thing."

Peter nodded. "It's cool. I like it." He wandered around for a few moments, taking in the makeshift circle of tree logs and the campfire in the middle. "How often do you come here?"

"It depends how much time we have, really. We always come loads at the beginning of terms, but as work gets more intense it gets less and less. And in the

winter it's so cold and wet it isn't worth it. Although…"
I let my sentence trail off as I approached one of the tree
logs. This particular one had hollowed out at one end,
and it was perfect for hiding stuff in it. Reaching inside,
my fingers brushed up against a plastic carrier bag. I
tugged it out and held it up for Peter to see. "We had
our ways of protecting our entertainment."

He laughed and took the bag from me. "What on
earth is this?"

I gestured for him to open the bag. "See for yourself."

Peter rifled through the contents. "Magazines,
cigarettes…a bottle of vodka?" He lifted his eyes to
mine. "You are a sneaky lot, aren't you?"

Wasn't that the truth. My friends and I had ingenious
ways of getting our kicks. "Did you have any doubt? I
was sure all the teachers at Stonebridge had warned all
their boys about the dangerous Mapleton Manor girls.
We are terrible, you know."

Peter's smile widened. "Well, that would explain it. I
don't go to Stonebridge."

My eyebrows knitted together. "You don't? But I
thought everyone here went to Stonebridge." Oh dear
Lord…was Peter a stranger who had wandered onto
the Mapleton Manor school grounds accidentally?

Wait—if it was accidental why was he dressed as
though he was attending the dance?

Was he intentionally masquerading as a Stonebridge
boy so that he could lure some poor Mapleton Manor
girl off into the woods…much like he had done with
me…so he could murder her and chop her into tiny
little pieces?

*Christ…I'm going to be the next Polly Pearl. Girls will tell
my horror stories for decades.*

"No. I go to Upton—I was invited to come tonight." Peter sat down on one of the logs and pulled out the magazine to flick through. "This is March's issue. You haven't been here for a while, then."

I'm an absolute idiot... "Um, no, not for a while. I've been busy. Busy, busy, busy..."

Peter glanced at me. "Are you all right?"

"Me? I'm fine." *Crazy, but fine.* "So you go to Upton? How do you like it?"

He shrugged and put the magazine back in the plastic bag. He sealed it back up again and rested his elbows on his knees. "I enjoy it as much as anyone else, I suppose. Perhaps not quite as much as you enjoy your school."

"Perhaps not. It would be difficult to top. Mapleton Manor is a long way for you to come just for a school dance, isn't it?"

A soft smile touched Peter's lips. "To some maybe. But look how well it's turned out for me."

Wow. This boy was definitely a charmer. And I was sufficiently charmed. Tonight might have got off to a rocky start thanks to Miles, his repulsive wandering hands and his terrible personality, but I couldn't deny that I was more than enjoying this new turn of events. I took a seat beside Peter on the log and pulled the packet of cigarettes out of the bag. I offered him the pack. Peter took it and drew himself out a cigarette.

"Would you like a drink?" I asked Peter, gesturing to the vodka bottle.

"Sure," he agreed with a smile.

I unscrewed the lid of the bottle and took a large swig. A cough irritated my throat as I passed the bottle to Peter.

He lifted his eyebrows. "Maybe you should start off slower?"

"I have to do that to start with or it makes me feel ill sipping straight vodka. But if I take a big gulp it sort of makes it more bearable," I said, rubbing my chest and willing the burn to pass.

"I suppose that makes sense. In a convoluted sort of way." Peter chuckled. "So this is what you and your friends do for fun — sneak down here for late-night parties?"

"Hardly parties," I said with a laugh. "But we come down here and chat, tell ghost stories and have a giggle — that sort of thing. We sneak the alcohol and cigarettes out and it keeps things interesting."

"How do you even get the booze in? The housemasters at Upton are like prison wardens. We can get hardly anything past them."

I gave Peter a catlike smile. "We have our ways. I buy it in the Ville — the village just down the road — and then we hide it around our House. Sometimes we have to sneak it in in water bottles, but we're usually successful. I haven't been caught once."

Peter's dark green eyes sparkled and he leaned a fraction of an inch closer to me. "I'm beginning to get the impression that you're nothing but trouble."

"You could be right," I agreed. "But trust me, this is nothing to how I used to be."

"Oh?"

I nodded. "I was an absolute rogue when I was a child."

He grinned. "So I can imagine. Have you always boarded?"

"No, I was in day school in Monaco for the first few years, but Daddy wanted me to have an English education. I went to Bourne Park when I was eight, and then here to Mapleton Manor. What about you?"

"Day school until Upton. I can't say I like it any better or less."

"I love boarding," I said quietly, my cheeks warming under my admission. "Call me childish, but I love being around all my friends all the time. We have so much fun. Especially when we were at Bourne Park—which a few of the girls I live with now went to as well, so we've known each other for such a long time."

"I can imagine that builds amazing friendships," Peter said, softly.

"It does. I can tell them anything. And I know that one, five, even ten years could pass and I could call any one of them and they would be there for me in a heartbeat." I meant every word that I said. That was the best part about building these sorts of friendships—they truly lasted. Fenella and Annie had been with me since Bourne Park and apart from a few minor feuds—usually over someone suspecting someone else of raiding their tuck box—there had never been any conflict. I could only hope that lasted for the rest of our lives.

"Didn't you mind being sent to boarding school so young? Didn't you miss your family?" Peter asked. He passed me the vodka bottle back and I took a small sip this time.

"Of course I missed them—I still do. But I don't cry in the night, or beg Mummy to bring me home. I miss them like anyone would miss someone they loved. Just like I miss my friends during the holidays when I don't see them. If anything, boarding has made me appreciate my family a whole lot more. I didn't mind being sent away from home when I was eight. Sure, it took some getting used to, but once I settled in at Bourne Park, I had nothing but fun."

Peter grinned and took a drag on his cigarette. "I can appreciate that. Although, growing up I would have done just about anything to get away from my little sister. She drove me barmy."

I laughed, a memory flooding back to me from my time at Bourne. "You never locked yourself away in cupboard then? There was a huge one in our dormitory and we dared a girl to spend the night in it once."

His eyebrows shot up into his hairline. "In a *cupboard*?"

"A very *big* cupboard. And we were always starving, which is probably why we're all so slim. So she fit just fine."

"Did you all get caught?"

I huffed and rolled my eyes. "Of course we did — because the idiot in the cupboard didn't turn the alarm on her watch off, so it started bleating in the middle of the night and she couldn't find the button to turn it off, so it made a huge racket and woke up the housemistress. We had to stand facing the wall for hours. So long I fell asleep."

Peter threw his head back and laughed, a deep and throaty sound. "That sounds barbaric!"

"We *were* pretty naughty. There were swings at the bottom of the garden and we used to flick our shoes over the fence into the field. When we were caught we would have to go and retrieve them, but we didn't care and would always turn it into a lark. And we used to eat the wild garlic that grew in the Spinney."

"Wild garlic?" Peter's face twisted in disgust. "That must have tasted revolting!"

A laugh bubbled in my throat. "It did. But like I said, we were always starving so we didn't care. The French teacher would go mad, though, when we did it because we all stunk to high heaven."

Peter grinned. "I can imagine."

"Some of the school meals were just awful—like corned beef and fish pie. Oh, and rice pudding and semolina. And pretty much anything with custard."

"What's wrong with custard?"

"It was lumpy. We would try anything to get extra food. We would sneak into the kitchen to make marmite on toast, too. And there were tricks you could do to get sent to the sick bay where you would get extra toast, like warming up a thermometer on the radiator. But if I was given Calpol I would spit it out because it tasted disgusting."

"Poor, hungry girls," he said in a teasing voice.

I gave him a gentle nudge with my elbow. "Yes, poor us. It wasn't all like that, or we'd resemble a bunch of wretched orphans from the Victorian age. I'm not painting a very good picture of my prep school, am I? I adored it—especially because we all had tons of pets, like rabbits and hamsters. Only Peshak the cat ate one of my baby rabbits, which was quite rubbish. And there was bring your pet to school day. I'm sure you can imagine the chaos that day, especially in the science room. My windowsill in the dorm was always cluttered with jars of caterpillars that I'd keep until they transformed into butterflies. And I was forever catching tadpoles that I then kept as pet frogs. The other girls were more squeamish with the frogs, but I liked the slimy, hoppy little things."

He tipped his head back and laughed, the sound rich and full. "You're starting to make me wish I had gone to an all-girls prep school. It's not fair that I missed out on all of that," Peter said, as he flashed me a wink.

"You wouldn't be saying that if you knew how annoying apple pie beds were," I said, grinning.

"Do you have siblings? Are they in boarding school?" Peter rested his chin on his palm, seeming riveted by what I had to say.

I wasn't used to someone taking such an interest in me, let alone seeming to genuinely care about the answers. Most boys I interacted with couldn't care less. Yet again, Peter impressed me in all the right ways. "Yes, Augustus is fourteen and goes to Seaton, he's the pride of the family. And Louisa, she's eleven now, and she's at Bourne Park."

"Are you close to them? It's only in the last few years that I've started to get along with my sister. We tormented each other like crazy when we were younger."

"I'm close to Augustus because we're quite similar. We're both sporty and most holidays we disappear off together, and like going fishing or swimming, that sort of thing. Louisa, I think, just lives to wind me up. She always steals my things and constantly begs to tag along. She's a demon child a lot of the time." I shrugged and couldn't help but chuckle. "Louisa is a very *spirited* girl. But as much as she annoys me, I'm very protective of her. Like you are of your little sister, I bet."

"Of course. Never tried to sell her once. Honest." Peter smiled. "I bet you and your sister turn into good friends when she's a bit older."

"Maybe," I murmured quietly. *Here's hoping, at least.* Only time would tell. "I have two older half-brothers too, Jamie and Carr, from my father's first and second marriages. I don't get to see them very often, but I have the best memories of Jamie taking me up in his helicopter and Mummy being petrified with fright."

"He sounds like quite a character. You all do," Peter said.

"Jamie went to Upton," I said. "From what I can gather, he earned himself a bit of a reputation, too."

Peter sat up straighter. "Wait— You're not talking about Jamie Felton, are you?"

My eyebrows pinched together. "Yes. Have you heard about him?"

"*Heard* about him? Everyone at Upton knows the stories of Jamie Felton. He's legendary." Peter laughed.

I smiled. "Jamie will be pleased to hear that."

"So… You're actually Lady Freddie, then?"

"Yes," I said, giving a short nod.

There was a pause before Peter spoke again, and doubt took the opportunity to creep into my mind. Would he treat me differently now? My friends never had—but they were different. Some of them I had known since I'd been eight and barely even thought of me as someone with a title.

"I'm not sure it's entirely ladylike to climb trees," Peter said with a teasing smile.

I let out a breath I hadn't been aware I was holding, and couldn't help but laugh. "So my mother tells me. She was never impressed when I would come home with ripped dresses and skinned knees."

Peter laughed. "Do you have a big family estate then?"

"Yes, Heyworth House. Most of it is leased, but the East Wing is occupied by my family when we visit. We lived there full-time until I was about two. It's a beautiful estate, especially when you see the Rotunda as you come up the drive. And the gardens and grounds are just huge—beautifully maintained. We have a London house, too, but we live in Monaco for the most part, which I adore." I grinned. "I've never exactly warmed to the British weather."

His face warmed as he gave me a soft smile. "It sounds like you have an amazing life."

My cheeks blushed. "It may sound conceited, but I really do. I'm lucky. I know how much I am."

"Well, I feel lucky to have met you, Lady Freddie," Peter said, softly.

"I know what you mean," I whispered.

The time passed in an odd, dreamlike way. Part of me felt like I had known Peter for years, yet at the same time it felt like only a heartbeat since I had met him. His easy, good-natured personality made him likeable and the charm that seemed to come naturally to him completely won me over. Peter was the sort of person that I knew would attract people to him like he was the sun. He was easy to be around and I realised that the longer I was with him, the longer I *wanted* to be with him.

I wanted to draw the hours out until they stretched into oblivion and gave me more time with him.

Twilight settled around us, the air growing cooler as the day finally gave way to night. The dance would be ending soon, but it was as far away from my mind at that moment as the moon was from the earth.

Peter tipped his head back to gaze up at the pinpricks of stars that began to turn on in the sky. "It's getting late."

As loath as I was to admit, I nodded. "People will be leaving soon."

Peter blew out a breath and slowly got to his feet. "I got a lift here—I should head back so they don't think I've already left."

I nodded again and tried to quell the rising disappointment in my chest. What had I thought would happen? That we could stay here in the woods forever, living on berries and twigs? *Reality check, Freddie...*

He extended a hand to me, and I slid my palm into his, shivering at the contact. Peter pulled me to my feet, and to my surprise, and absolute pleasure, he didn't let go.

We walked back along the path the way we'd come, going slower than a snail's pace as we dragged it out. Peter threw a dirty look as we passed the sycamore he had fallen out of, making me giggle. He gave my hand a squeeze as he peered down at me, his eyes full of good humour.

"Will it be late when you get back to Upton?" I asked.

Peter shrugged. "It takes a few hours to drive. Maybe I'll catch a nap on the back seat."

"And not share all the driving?" I poked him in the stomach. "You're terrible."

"My friend loves to drive. He's very protective of his car and doesn't trust a fool like me behind the wheel of his precious baby." He grinned. "I read my book on the way up, but it will be too dark heading back home. I can't help it—the minute I'm in a moving car I fall asleep. Unless I'm reading."

"What is it you're reading?" I asked him.

"*The Return of the King.* Again. I'm a fan of the trilogy."

"Do you enjoy literature, then?"

"No, I *adore* literature." Peter's smile lit up his face. "Call me a geek, but I live for falling into a good book. And I reread all my favourites. It's like meeting a long-lost friend that you haven't talked to in ages. It's comforting."

"I love a good book too, but I have to admit that I'm not as ardent as you are."

"There's nothing better than the written word," Peter said, quietly. "A good writer can paint a scene for his reader, making him feel like he's right there in the middle of the story. It's why I enjoy letter writing so much, too."

We stepped out of the woods and the school campus came into view. The grass was cool under my feet as we slowly walked across the lawn towards the main building. Music pulsed from inside, and outside couples darted around corners and hid in shadows, stealing a few minutes of privacy.

"Do you write a lot of letters?" I asked Peter.

He nodded. "Whenever I can, to whoever I can. I write to my family. My mother, in particular, loves the days the postman brings her a letter from her beautiful baby boy."

I smiled. "How modest you are."

"Careful," Peter said, squeezing my hand again. "Or *you* won't get one."

My steps faltered and I looked up at his handsome face. "You would write to me?"

Peter stopped just outside the door that would take us back into the dance. "Frederica, it would be a divine honour to write to a *lady* like yourself. And why would you think that tonight would be enough for me?"

My heart thumped, a constant beat of adrenaline and excitement. I couldn't stop the wide, goofy smile that spread across my face. "I don't know. But I'm hoping it's not."

Peter grinned. "Well, I assure you that it is not. So, Lady Freddie, can I write to you?"

"I would love you to," I said with a girlish giggle.

He raised my hand to his lips and pressed a soft kiss to the back of it. My heart spluttered and for one scary second I thought it might give up all together. Peter's eyes caught mine, pinning me to the spot with his enchanting green eyes.

Peter shifted, bringing his body closer to mine. He placed his free hand on my hip and instinctively I stepped into his space.

If anything, my heart pounded harder — so hard I had no idea how it was still inside my body. I'd never had a reaction like this to a boy before. My entire being felt different — lighter somehow. And yet, at the same time, like I was full of all this burning energy, a live wire, and would surely shock anyone who touched me.

Peter dipped his head and his breath gently drifted across my face. I saw every fleck of colour in his eyes, the different tones of green, the subtle dots of gold. There was a tiny smattering of freckles across his nose that I hadn't noticed before, almost perfectly blended in with his smooth, tanned skin.

"Freddie," Peter whispered.

I tipped my face up, my lips parted as I waited for his question, which I was sure, which I hoped, I knew.

His hand skimmed up my body until he cupped my cheek.

God...this is it! I never thought I would be one of those girls who just got off with a boy at a school disco, but here I was...agonisingly waiting for him to kiss me.

He smiled before leaning even further in.

My breath hitched as I anticipated his lips meeting mine.

"Freddie! There you are!"

I wrenched away from Peter to see Fenella race down the steps towards us. "Hi, Fenella."

"Where on earth have you been? I've looked all over for you, and the other...girls...we..." Fenella's eyes started flickering between Peter and me before they widened. Fenella practically bounced on the spot. She grabbed my hand and squeezed it so tightly I thought she might crack a few bones. "Freddie, I desperately need the loo, will you come with me?"

What? Now? No! I groaned. "Oh, Fenella, do we have—"

"Yes!" Fenella exclaimed. She gave me a look that I didn't dare disagree with. "I need you to come *right now*. Okay?"

"Fine," I said with a sigh. I twisted around to see Peter. "Sorry, I'll just be a minute."

He grinned and I think he knew exactly what was going on—that my friend was a complete nosey parker and she wanted every juicy detail of where I had been and who Peter was.

"Of course. I'll wait for you inside. Look for me?" he asked.

"Of course," I repeated.

Peter smiled, and I smiled back, and Fenella hauled me inside so hard I wondered how she didn't pull my arm out of the socket. The dance was still going strong as we passed through at breakneck speed. Couples danced in tight embraces, friends formed their own circles and teachers kept watchful eyes over everything, making sure no one acted inappropriately.

I guessed they hadn't looked too closely into those dark corners — there were plenty of inappropriate activities going on.

On our way to the bathroom, Fenella grabbed Athena and Annie and hauled them along also.

"What's going on?" Athena asked once we were inside.

"Go on, tell them," Fenella said with obvious delight.

The other girls' eyes fell on me. "Tell us what?" Annie asked, lifting her eyebrows.

My cheeks flushed and I smiled shyly. "I met a boy."

The girls all screeched with excitement and huddled closer around me.

"Who?"

"Where?"

"Have you been with him all this time?"

"What's he like?"

"What does he *look* like?"

"Is he fit?"

"Did you get off with him?"

"Are you going to?"

Their questions were endless. I laughed and pulled a step away from them. "My God, you girls are endless."

"Come on, Freddie, we want the details," Athena said with a wide smile.

I released a breath and bit the corner of my lip. "Okay, I met him outside when I went for some air. We went for a walk in the woods and we've been talking ever since. He's...well, he's bloody gorgeous. Tall — taller than *me*! Golden brown hair, these intense, dreamy green eyes, really good body. And he's really nice, like

properly nice, and so polite. I didn't get off with him —
Fenella put an end to that."

Annie and Athena turned to glare at Fenella.

"What?" she asked, throwing her hands up. "*I* didn't
realise she was about to snog his face off!"

Athena rolled her eyes. "You need to get back out
there. There's only five minutes before this thing is over
and then your chance, and the moment, will be over.
You need to have the last dance with him."

Fenella and Annie squealed again — I swear I'd never
met a more excitable bunch of girls in my life — and I let
them pull me back out into the hall.

The opening bars of *Killing Me Softly* by the Fugees
drifted out of the speakers to greet us. It could only
mean one thing — the last dance had already begun.

Athena tugged on my hand, catching on to the
sudden urgency flooding through me. This was it — if I
didn't find Peter right that very minute, whatever
magical spell had woven around us in the woods
would be extinguished forever.

A shift in the crowd of dancers revealed him to me. A
wide smile stretched across my lips when I saw him
from the side. I took a step towards him and he turned,
revealing the girl in his arms.

At first I could only focus on the fact that he was
dancing with another girl. A piercing hurt stabbed my
chest, an ache I had never experienced before. That was
my guy — *my guy* — and someone else was dancing with
him! A hard lump formed in my throat that refused to
be dislodged.

The longer that I stared at them, the more I noticed.
The way his hands rested on her waist, so similarly to
how he had touched me just minutes before. The soft
smile that pulled at the corners of his mouth — the

mouth I had almost kissed. The girl's hands stroking the hair at the nape of his neck.

It was then that I let my eyes drift to her — to the girl he had abandoned me for, forgotten about me so quickly for. At first, it only distantly registered that she was familiar.

Then, the longer I looked, that she was more than familiar.

That she was a girl I had seen, spoken to, almost every day for years.

That she was a girl I lived with.

That she was a girl I had got ready with for this very dance.

That she was one of my best friends.

That she was Jemima.

It was as though the air had been punched out of me. I sucked in a breath but it didn't reach my lungs. For a brief second I imagined myself marching over to them and demanding he let her go right that very second. That Jemima back off, that he was mine and I had seen him first.

It was the smile on both of their faces that made me pause. I was unable to take that first step in approaching them and make a scene that girls, and Stonebridge boys alike, would titter over for weeks to come.

What if he was only being nice to me? What if, really, he had no romantic inclination towards me at all? What if I had created the entire flirtation in my head?

And Jemima was one of my closest friends, even if she had been acting differently this last year...the last thing I wanted was to create a divide between us. Fighting over a boy could ruin friendships, and I hadn't I only a short while ago told Peter that I would love these girls for the rest of my life?

Besides, I had never seen Jemima wear that smile before—so open and friendly. There was every chance that she already knew him, and was seriously into him.

Tears pricked my eyes as I made my decision.

"Uh...what's Jemima doing with your guy?" Fenella asked from behind me.

It felt as though I had been staring at them for hours, when in truth it would only have been a few short seconds. I whirled around and pinned Fenella with a sharp look. "My guy? Nah, he just looks a little like him. I can't see my guy, maybe he had to leave early."

Fenella frowned. "But—"

"Jemima looks happy, doesn't she?" I asked, turning back around to look at them.

There was a pause before Fenella answered. "Yeah, Freddie," she said quietly. "She does."

I knew then that she got it, and that this would be the last time we ever spoke about the boy I had met at the school dance.

The song came to an end, and the lights were turned back up to their usual harsh, artificial brightness. Peter dropped his hold on Jemima and started to look around the room.

My cheeks flushed and I whipped around to face my friends. "I'm exhausted now, I'm going to go to bed."

"*Bed*?" Annie exclaimed. "But we never go straight to bed after a dance! We always sneak out and keep the party going, or dissect every detail in someone's room."

"I know," I said. "But I think I ate some bad Fruit Salads, I feel quite sick. And all this crap music has made my head pound."

Athena studied me with her sharp eyes and I knew she more than likely smelled a rat. "As long as you're sure. Come on, I'll walk you up."

"That's okay, I'll take her." Fenella looped her arm through mine, keeping her lock iron tight so there was no chance for escape.

So much for the unspoken promise that we would never talk about Peter or Jemima, or Peter *and* Jemima, again. Perhaps Fenella needed to brush up on her silent conversational skills.

We pushed our way through the crowd of students and headed out into the cool night air. It was full dark now, the stars illuminating the heavens and the moon a swollen, glowing orb suspended in the sky.

Fenella didn't push for information like I'd thought she would as we walked back to Masters. Gravel crunched under our feet, and was soon the only sound that could be heard.

Housemistress was sitting on a couch just inside the entry hall in Crosby House, waiting for all the girls to return. She placed the book she had been reading beside her as we came inside. "You two are back early. Everything okay?"

I nodded. "Just not feeling well."

"Too many sweets," Fenella supplied. "You know our Freddie."

"Yes, I do," Housemistress murmured. "Are you all right, Freddie, dear?"

"I'll be fine," I said, forcing a smile. "Nothing a good night's sleep won't sort out."

Like Athena, Housemistress's eyes seemed to see right through my cover, and know there was something deeper going on with me. "You know where I am if you need me, don't you, Freddie?"

"Of course. I really am fine, just a bit of a bad tummy."

"As long as you're sure, dear." Housemistress's eyebrows pulled together in a frown, as though she wasn't happy with herself letting me slip away.

I nodded and tugged Fenella upstairs.

"So are we really not going to talk about the fact that you just totally let Jemima steal your guy?"

A sigh pushed past my lips. "He was never *my* guy, Fenella. I lost my chance with him, and Jemima didn't. She's my friend, I'm hardly going to pick a fight with her over a random boy. End of story."

Fenella fidgeted with her fingers as we slowed to a stop outside my bedroom door. "Well, maybe this makes me an awful friend, but I have to say it—you do realise that if the situation were reversed, she would never have just done what you did? Jemima is a lot of things, but capable of bowing out gracefully, and letting her friend's happiness come before her own, is not one of them. Sorry, two of them."

The lump lodged in my throat again. I tried to swallow past it. "I know. But I believe in putting other people first. I just want people to be happy, Fenella."

She nodded, and her chin quivered. Fenella threw her arms around me and hugged me so, so fiercely. "I love you, Freddie."

I squeezed my eyes shut to stop the tears from escaping. "I know. I love you, too, Fenella."

When she let me go, I slipped inside my bedroom and closed the door tightly. I scrubbed at my eyes until the tears no longer threatened to fall.

The dress that I had adored now chaffed. I pulled it off in a hurry, not caring if I snagged the fabric. I paced my small bedroom like a caged tiger and suddenly all I wanted was wide, open spaces.

I threw on a pair of pyjamas then eased my window open so I could creep out into the night. Somewhere in the distance was the sound of voices, the grumble of bus engines as they started to take all the boys back to their own school.

Taking care as I shimmied along the ledge to our usual spot, I then sat down and lit a cigarette. The tip glowed amber in the dark, almost matching the rear lights of the buses that trundled down the drive.

I wondered if Peter had left yet. What sort of car he would be in.

Stop it, Freddie…

This was ridiculous! I had only met him tonight. Yes, we had talked for hours but what did that mean? Absolutely nothing. He clearly preferred dancing with Jemima to talking with me.

She was the better girl in this situation, and I had lost.

There would be other boys. Other dances.

I stayed outside until I heard the sounds of the girls returning home — I didn't want anyone to spot me up on the roof. Athena would keep everyone away from my room tonight, so I didn't have to worry about being disturbed.

I crept back inside my room and climbed into bed. As I went to stretch my legs out, they met resistance.

Huffing my annoyance, I threw back the duvet and set about unmaking my apple pie bed.

I curled up in a tight ball once my bed was corrected, and tucked the covers up under my chin. My nose tickled and I wiggled it.

You will not cry, you will not cry, you will not cry!

I marvelled at how other people could make you feel. Could change you. Because Peter had changed me. Before him, I hadn't taken much interest in boys. But he was different—interesting and funny and utterly charming.

Maybe I should look on this experience as a good one. Peter had opened my eyes where it came to boys. I should start giving more of them a chance. After all, he couldn't be the only tall boy on the planet who made my heart flutter like a hummingbird.

It was late when I awoke the next morning. Sunlight streamed through the curtains, hinting at another beautiful day. For a moment, I considered pleading with Matron to let me stay in bed, to let me skip church in the Ville. But I decided against it, knowing I had to show my face sooner or later and it might as well be sooner. After all, someone only hid away if they had something to hide.

I approached the group of girls gathered in the entry hall, waiting to go to the church. I found my friends by the corner, all chatting over the top of one another.

"Freddie!" Cassandra exclaimed, her face lighting up when she saw me. "What on earth happened to you last night? You totally disappeared!"

"Sorry," I said, smiling. "I ducked out early, I wasn't feeling well. So, what's the gossip? I must have missed tons!"

It turned out to be the perfect diversion. Soon, all my friends were speaking in a rush about who had danced with who, who'd got off with who, and who had seen whose parts that should have remained unseen.

"It's a shame you disappeared, Freddie," Jemima said. "You didn't get the chance to see the fitty I pulled."

I forced a smile and prayed it looked genuine. "Good on you, Jemima. Are you seeing him again?"

She gave a nonchalant shrug. "Maybe. I haven't decided if I'm done with him or not yet."

It took everything in me to not give Jemima a cold, hard look. For a brief second, fury tore through my body. How dare she be so cavalier when it came to Peter? Didn't she realise just how special he was?

But on the other hand, if he was so quick to discard a girl in favour of a different one, maybe he wasn't as special as I'd thought.

"Knowing you, Jemima, there will be one more broken heart out there with your name on it," I said, throwing my arm around her shoulder as we headed outside.

Jemima frowned for a moment before she smoothed out her features.

"They ought to start a club for the poor boys, Jemima!" Athena called from behind us.

Jemima twisted around to stick her tongue out at Athena.

"Ladies, ladies, do I *have* to remind you all on the importance of decorum? Again?" Housemistress asked.

"No, Housemistress," we chorused.

As soon as Housemistress moved away from us, Harriet clutched my other arm and started telling me all about the Stonebridge boy she had met the night before. They had sneaked away from the dance to be alone for hours. She was a welcome distraction, and I encouraged her to tell me every minute detail.

The halls were a flutter of activity as all the girls started to get their things packed. Usually I was one of the ones who left everything to the last minute and ended up forgetting something, but this time around I was organised and ready to go. Perhaps I was more than ready for the summer holidays, and the welcome break it would bring.

The school year ended and another year at Mapleton Manor was done. It was bittersweet as always, saying goodbye to my friends, but this year was especially so.

Fenella wouldn't be returning to Mapleton Manor for Upper Sixth Form, and instead was going to day school. She would be closer to London, so we were already planning many visits and sneaking into the odd party!

"I'm going to miss you all so much!" Fenella said, tears streaming down her face.

"Not as much as we will miss you," I said, hugging her fiercely.

"Promise you will all call and write? And come and see me?" she asked, sniffling.

"We promise," Annie and Athena said in unison.

"Oh, God, this is hard," Fenella said. "Freddie, will you post me sweets when you get your hoard in?"

"Of course. I'll get some extra Push Pops just for you, okay?"

Fenella nodded and sniffed again.

"Fenella, come along, darling, we must be on our way," Fenella's mother called from their car.

"Coming, Mummy!"

She gave us all one last hug and kiss on the cheek, then Fenella was gone. It wouldn't be the same without her and I knew everyone would miss her terribly.

One by one, each of us departed with our trunks and tuck boxes.

Before I got into the car that would take me to the airport, I turned to look back at the school. Next year I would be returning for my last year at Mapleton Manor. Upper Sixth would be a true test of not only my academics, but also my character. It was the last year I had as a schoolgirl, before I stepped out into the big world.

Yes, next year would be a challenge, and I would see a lot of changes. But first there was summer, and all the fun it brought.

With a jaunty salute to my beloved school, I jumped into the car and sped off towards months of fun and mischief.

10

Crans-Montana, Switzerland, had been the setting for my summers for years. It was set on a sunny plateau above the vineyards of the Rhone Valley and was surrounded by sprawling pine forests and soaring mountains capped with pristine snow.

Every summer I spent two months in the Swiss mountains, enjoying a jam-packed schedule of horse riding, sports, swimming and discos twice a week. And this year was extra special, for the simple reason that it would be my last. Some of my best childhood memories had come from Camp Monte Leone and they would stay with me for a lifetime.

Like the year I'd won special awards for the best grass stains in camp and also for being a keen chocoholic. I still had those awards, and I probably always would. Not everyone can brag about having the best grass stains.

Augustus, Louisa and I stepped off the bus that had collected us, along with a dozen or so others who were attending the camp for the summer, from the airport. Camp Monte Leone was an international summer camp, with children coming from fifty different countries. Most of them were American, with lots of French and Brits, and a handful of other Europeans and some Australians.

Camp Monte Leone was nothing if not diverse.

A young counsellor stood waiting for us to disembark. She was pretty — in her early twenties with golden tanned skin, a wide smile that flashed straight, white teeth and glossy blonde hair pulled into a sleek ponytail. She wore a pair of tan shorts and a blue T-shirt with the Camp's logo stitched onto the chest.

"Good afternoon, everyone!" she said in a cheery voice once we had all got off the bus and stood in a row in front of it. "I'm Hannah, one of the counsellors here at Camp Monte Leone, and I wish to give you all a super warm welcome."

These counsellors got cheerier every year, I was sure of it.

Hannah waved her clipboard in the air. "I'm going to get you all taken to your accommodation for your stay with us and get you all settled in. So, first of all, can I have the Seniors, please?"

The camp was split into four different levels — Juniors, for the eight to nine year olds, Pioneers for the ten to eleven year olds, Champions for the twelve to thirteen year olds, and Seniors, for the fourteen to seventeen year olds. My last year would also be the first that Augustus and I would be in the same group.

Camp Monte Leone was co-educational, so while boys and girls shared accommodation, it was on different floors, and a lot of the activities were together also.

Augustus and I stepped forward, along with three others — two boys and a girl. Hannah introduced us to Derek, this gorgeous young guy with dark hair and muscles on his muscles. Derek ticked our names off his list and instructed us to follow him to the Seniors Chalet. We waved goodbye to Louisa, who barely even noticed we had gone as she was too busy chattering like an excited little bird to a girl she had met on the bus.

The younger groups all housed together in a large chalet, but the Seniors got their own. It made for a lot of late-night parties, room hopping and general mischief, at which I excelled. There were shared rooms of small groups, and on the first floor there were large communal areas. The lounge had huge couches and armchairs I loved to sprawl out on after an energetic day.

Downstairs there were also a TV room, games room with pool table, a ping-pong table along with a selection of board games also kept us occupied — and out of trouble — in the evenings.

Most people hung out in the main lodge chalet, but it was nice to chill in your own chalet sometimes, especially at night, and with the people you were rooming with. Camp had a similar feel to boarding at school, and bonds were formed with the people you spent loads of time with.

The girls' floor was first, so I got dropped off at my room — number seventy-six — before Augustus. I gave him a smile and a wave as I skipped inside the room I would share with three other girls.

My room was empty and two of the beds had items on them, so I guessed I was the third resident to arrive. Choosing the free top bunk beside the window, I dumped my suitcase on the floor and moved to the window to peer out.

The main chalet in all its tall and traditional Swiss beauty took up most of the view. The camp teemed with life and activity, and people were everywhere — carrying sports equipment, running around a football pitch, and I even spotted some horseback riders heading for the trail into the forest. If I was at a different side of the chalet, I would be able to see the almost Olympic-sized pool and the enormous Lake Moubra where sailing boats floated on its crystalline waters.

Camp Monte Leone was as close to idyllic perfection as any place could be, and I would miss spending my summers here. Many of the campers returned to become counsellors…maybe I could do that, and return during the summer holidays while I was at university.

God…university.

It felt like years off, a distant dream that I would never really reach because it was so far away. But it was actually little over a year from happening.

The door to the bedroom swung open and two laughing girls stepped inside. They paused when they saw me, but soon recovered themselves.

"Hello, I'm Paulina, and this is Zuzu," a short brunette girl said. She had a French accent and these huge, beautiful, feline brown eyes. "Have you just arrived?"

I nodded. "I'm Freddie, lovely to meet you."

"You, too," Zuzu said. Zuzu was only a fraction taller than Paulina, and far less exotic looking. Her nondescript black hair was pulled into a messy ponytail, and her cheeks were flushed from exertion. "We've just been playing tennis. I'm so out of shape!"

The best thing about being so active at Mapleton Manor was that I never really found myself getting out of shape.

"Do you like tennis, Freddie?" Paulina asked. She crossed the room to a bed and dropped her sweatshirt onto it.

"Yes, I do. Horseback riding is more my thing, though," I said. I moved to the vacant bottom bunk below my own bed and sat down, folding my legs beneath me. "When did you two arrive? Last week?"

Zuzu shook her head. "Just a few days. Have you been here before?"

I gave her a wry smile. "It's my fourth summer."

Zuzu's and Paulina's eyes widened. "Wow! This is our first year. Zuzu and I go to school together in Paris, and we begged our parents to send us here," Paulina said. She turned to give Zuzu a wink. "Freddie here can show us the ropes."

A laugh bubbled in my throat. "How old are you two anyway?"

"Fourteen," they choroused.

Fourteen seemed young to be showing them the hidden secrets of Camp Monte Leone...but then again I had been fourteen when I had sneaked my first drink here.

It was this weird Swiss Absinthe that I'd had two sips of then had thrown up in the bushes.

I hadn't touched any other alcohol for the rest of the summer.

"I suppose I could show you a few things. But really, it's pretty cool here anyway. The counsellors here are all in their early twenties so they're a lot of fun. The discos twice a week run for the Seniors, and they aren't, like, totally strict while we're there."

Zuzu grinned. "Sounds brilliant! We went to the disco a few nights ago, but there was hardly anyone there."

"It will get busier. How long are you two here for?" I asked.

"For the whole summer," Zuzu said.

"Me, too," I said. "By the end of July things will really get going because that's when the camp is at its busiest."

"What's the best thing to do here? What do you look forward to doing every year?" Paulina asked. She had an inquisitive nature, but I found it charming. Better that she was friendly and inquisitive than aloof and hostile.

"The camping, for sure. We build fires, toast marshmallows and tell ghost stories. It's super fun. And the boys go, too. You go in groups and there's always a big camping trip at the end of camp."

"The *boys*?" Paulina asked, her big eyes widening even more. "Zuzu, the *boys* go, as well!"

Zuzu rolled her eyes, but cracked a smile at her friend. "Yes, so I heard, Paulina." Zuzu walked across the room to a cupboard and pulled out a wash bag. "I'm going to go grab a shower before dinner."

Once Zuzu had left the room, Paulina sprawled out on her stomach on her bed and flicked through a French teen magazine. I took the opportunity to unpack my things, hang up my clothes and arrange my cosmetics.

Dorm life was usually on the cramped side, with each girl arguing over every available surface, drawer or hanging space. I noticed that Zuzu and Paulina had already claimed most of the shelves under the mirror. If they wanted this to be a peaceful communal space, they would have to realise there were more people than just the two of them now.

It took no time at all to get myself settled. Zuzu returned from her shower, and she and Paulina set about giving me their life history.

Which was actually quite extraordinary.

They both originated from Zaire, in Africa. Their families had fled because of the war, leaving all their possessions behind. They'd escaped to Belgium, where they had family, before moving on to France.

They were very sweet girls, so lively and full of good spirits, but so very young too. I left them to their girlish antics as they struggled to decide what to wear to the disco, and headed across the camp to the main chalet where the dining room was.

The dining room was gorgeous, with huge, panoramic views of the camp and the picturesque landscape beyond. I joined the end of the already lengthening line, and felt my stomach rumble at the sight of all the delicious food.

When it was my turn, I was served by a smiling gentleman in a white chef's coat with the camp's emblem on the chest, checked trousers and a white cap. I went mad helping myself to the home baking. The pastries, breads and cakes were second only to Aimee's. I carried my tray to one of the empty round tables. There were no seating arrangements in the dining hall and we were free to sit where we liked. Most people usually sat with their groups anyway.

Augustus came in a short while later, laughing with a group of boys. He gave me a short, distracted wave and I had to smile—he was far too cool to be seen with his older sister now, it seemed.

Louisa didn't even see me.

The dining room began to fill up, and I spotted Paulina and Zuzu arrive with a handful of chattering girls.

"Hey, is this seat taken?" A tray landed on the table with a loud clatter, making me jump a mile out of my skin. A girl of about my age with dark blonde hair, a lean build and an American accent dropped down into the chair beside me. Clearly not waiting for an actual reply, she started tucking into her lush green salad.

"Uh, no, not it's not," I said, lifting my eyebrows at her brashness.

"Thank God. Otherwise I'd totally be stuck over there with the prepubescent crowd." She rolled her eyes. "So who are you?"

"I'm Freddie. Who are you?" Done with my meal, I dropped my napkin onto my plate and sat back in my chair. This girl, however candid and frank she may be, was a curiosity.

"Amber. I'm from Wisconsin."

"I'm from all over. Born in England, but my family now live in Monaco."

"Sweet, I bet it's great for shopping there."

My lips twitched with a smile. "Yes, it is quite. How are you enjoying the camp?"

Amber shrugged and made a not very impressed face. "It's okay, I guess. I sort of thought there would be more going on than there is."

I laughed, short and loud. "What else could you possibly want? Haven't you found *any* sort of activities that you enjoy?"

"I just figured there would be more of an underground scene than there is." Amber slid her eyes over me, her gaze cool and assessing—she seemed to see right through me to my bones. "You look like a girl that knows what the score is. You can hook me up, right?"

I could indeed hook her up. The truth of it was, it was spectacularly easy to get away with things here. The counsellors who were in charge of us wanted to find their own fun as much as we did. Which made for easy stealthy parties.

"I can," I said. "Are you planning on going to the disco tonight?"

Amber nodded. "I'll be there, for all its Whitney Houston glory."

"Good," I said with a grin. "When there's ten minutes to go before the end, meet me outside and I'll walk back to the Senior chalet with you. We'll find something."

Amber's eyebrows pulled together in a frown. "Why ten minutes before the end?"

"If you leave too early it's suspicious. If you leave right at the end, you have more of a risk of getting caught sneaking in places you shouldn't."

"And just where is it we shouldn't be sneaking in?"

I smiled. "You'll have to wait and see." Picking up my tray, I stood and flashed Amber a wink. "See you tonight."

Paulina and Zuzu were typical fourteen-year-old girls as they got ready for that night's disco. They chattered and giggled and plastered on far too much makeup and insisted on wearing platform shoes they could barely walk in. I watched them with amusement, smiling at their innocent naïvety.

"Are you coming, Freddie?" Zuzu asked as she and Paulina picked up their tiny handbags, ready to leave the room.

"I'll be there shortly," I said as I applied a coat of mascara. "Save me a dance!"

Paulina giggled. "Will do."

The pair left the room, but I could still hear their shrieking laughter as it bounced off the walls of the corridor. Other girls my age might have been annoyed at their immaturity, but I found them charming.

I finished getting ready but I hung around in the room for another half an hour. It was practically social suicide to be seen at a disco during its first hour. When it was time, I headed outside to the main lodge.

Music thumped as I approached, Peter Andre telling the world about this *Mysterious Girl* he wanted to get close to. As I entered, the room was full of people, a mixture of girls and boys and older teenagers. The discos were only for the Seniors, and ran until ten o'clock, eleven on a Saturday night.

I wandered over to the refreshment stand and got myself lemonade, which was almost knocked out of my hand as a body collided with mine.

"Freddie, Freddie, Freddie!"

Immediately recognising the voice to be that of Gabrielle, my Australian friend, I flung my arms around her shoulders. Gabrielle was gorgeous — almost as tall as me, with shapely legs and fantastic body shape, long, glossy brown hair and beautiful hazel eyes.

"Oh my gosh! How are you?" I asked, unable to keep the enormous smile off my face. Gabrielle and I had been coming to Camp Monte Leone together for years, but she had been unsure whether or not she'd be able to attend this year. I was ecstatic to see my friend. She was just as mad and excitable as I was, and always made the summers memorable.

"Hi, Gabrielle," Paulina said as she and Zuzu approached us. "Freddie, have you met Gabrielle before?"

Gabrielle and I exchanged a glance. "Just once or twice," I said in a teasing voice.

Paulina's eyes lit up. "Oh good, so you're already friends! Gabrielle is our new roommate. She only just got here and Zuzu and I met her when we had to run back to our room." Paulina leaned closer and lowered her voice. "I forgot my lip gloss! *Sacrè bleu!*"

I whirled back around to face Gabrielle. "Wait a minute—you're the new roommate?"

Her eyes widened. "I guess I am!"

We both let out an excited squeal and threw our arms around each other. We probably looked as silly and immature as Zuzu and Paulina had earlier, but in that moment I couldn't have cared less. Gabrielle and I had waited *years* to be roommates, and in our final year it had finally happened!

Jazzy Jeff and the Fresh Prince boomed across the speaker system and I snatched Gabrielle's hand to pull her onto the dance floor for a celebratory boogie. We shook our hips and tossed our hair like the best of them, laughing and giggling as though no time had passed at all since we had last seen each other.

After an hour or so, Amber found us. Gabrielle and I had sat down at one of the tables to grab a drink since we had danced ourselves silly. I stood up when I saw Amber approaching, and gave her a quick hug and peck on the cheek.

"I've looked for you all night, I thought maybe you weren't coming," I said.

Amber smiled. "And miss this awesome party? Not a chance in hell, sweetie. Who is this?" she asked, glancing at Gabrielle.

"I'm Gabrielle, nice to meet you," Gabrielle said as she also stood.

"Likewise," Amber said. "Are you one of these girls who knows what's what?"

Gabrielle arched a solitary eyebrow. "I'm one of the girls who *started* the what's what."

For a second Amber did nothing—barely even reacted to Gabrielle's bold claim. But then a slow smile spread across her mouth and she gave her a nod of recognition. "Glad to hear I met the right girls, then."

After that, Gabrielle and Amber chatted like they were lifelong friends, swapping stories. Amber ate the ones up about camp, loving all the tales of mischief we got up to. Even though I had only met her that evening, I knew I was going to like Amber, and hopefully would stay in touch with her for a long time afterwards. She was bold and confident and I couldn't help but admire those qualities.

The three of us danced the night away—part of the night, anyway—with more people joining our little group. Some Gabrielle and I already knew, others we didn't, like two gorgeous American boys.

By nine-thirty, the numbers at the disco slowly started to dwindle. Not enough to be noticeable and slowly enough that there wasn't a mass departure.

At nine-forty-five Amber, Gabrielle and I bade our counsellors goodnight and ambled outside like we had all the time in the world. When we were clear of the main chalet, we glanced around to make sure no one was looking, then darted off towards the forest that almost surrounded the camp. There were some trails that were used for hiking or horse treks, but there was an overgrown one that not many knew existed.

But Gabrielle and I did.

A few hundred yards into the forest was a disused cabin. No one knew how long it had been there, but we concluded that the camp had used it for a time as there was dusty sporting equipment—old enough that my father probably hadn't even used it—littered around the place.

The cabin's history mattered little to us—we only cared that it was the perfect place for us to hang out away from the camp and enjoy a drink or two. I pushed open the creaky door to the cabin and stepped inside. There were maybe twenty other people already inside, a couple of whom raised their hands in a wave or flashed us smiles.

Someone had set up a portable CD player and the worst trance music known to mankind belted through the speakers. There was a thick cloud of cigarette smoke in the air. A bottle of vodka was being offered around, and both Amber and Gabrielle swallowed a large gulp when they got their hands on it. I did the same then quickly passed it on, my eyes watering from the taste.

We pushed our way through the throng of people to a cluster of beanbags in the corner and each grabbed one.

"Now *this* is what I had in mind," Amber said with a grin.

"I'm glad to hear it," I said, having to shout over the music.

"Okay, I have to ask, do either of you know those guys?" Amber pointed to the two hot American boys I had noticed back at the disco.

"No, but I wouldn't mind getting to know one of them. Or both," Gabrielle said with a giggle.

The boys, either hearing our girlish laughter, or realising they were being discussed, turned their heads to look at us. One elbowed the other and jerked his head in our direction. His friend nodded and led the way over to us.

"Hey there," one said. He was nice to look at — dark brown hair, lovely white teeth, tanned skin and great complexion. "I'm Zach. This is Rick."

Rick smiled, revealing a smile just as nice as his friend's. He was an inch or two taller than Zach, with bleach-blond hair that flopped into his eyes. He looked like a typical surfer, and even wore flip-flops and board shorts.

"Hi, I'm Freddie," I said as I smiled at the good-looking boys. "This is Gabrielle and Amber."

They both murmured their hellos. Rick took the empty beanbag beside me, lounging in it as though he was perfectly comfortable and at home. I always felt like the stupid things were trying to eat me — and God help me when it came to getting back out of them. *Turtles stuck on their back are more graceful.*

"Hi," Rick said. He leaned on his elbow, angling his body towards mine.

My cheeks warmed at his attention and before I could even think, Peter's face flashed in my mind.

Why on earth are you thinking about him, Freddie? Come on, get a grip, girl...

I studied Rick's handsome face — the smooth angles and contours that all came together to make one beautiful boy. As far as I could tell, there was absolutely nothing wrong with him. But that first flutter of butterflies I get when I first meet someone I'm really into...those butterflies weren't there.

But did that mean they never would be? I didn't know him, not yet, at least. What if over the course of the summer I did, and he turned out to be amazing and I had cast him aside because of absentee butterflies? What an idiot I would be!

Besides, I very much doubted Peter was thinking about me. He was probably too busy thinking about Jemima.

Jemima lives in London when she isn't at school. Upton is in London...is that where he lives?

I wonder if Jemima has seen him.

"Are you all right?" Rick asked, his forehead pinching in concern.

Shaking away my reverie, I forced a smile and told myself to relax. "Yes, I'm sorry, I was... My mind took a holiday, I think. Hi, hello."

Rick laughed, a rich baritone sound. "Hi. And don't worry about it, I tend to have that effect on people."

A startled laugh burst out of me. "Modesty isn't your thing, I take it?"

He shrugged and smiled wider. "Why bother with modesty when honesty is so much better?"

"Can't argue with that logic, I guess."

Rick grinned. "Can I get you a drink? I've got some beers hidden."

"Sure, thank you."

He disappeared for a moment then returned with a beer for each of us. Gabrielle and Amber seemed to be vying for Zach's attention — the perils of a situation when girls outnumber boys. It could get ugly. Fast.

"Uh oh," Rick said, leaning over to whisper in my ear.

"Yeah, tell me about it," I said. Gabrielle and Amber had only just met and their friendship could be doomed before it even got properly started.

Rick groaned. "Hang on a sec." He jumped out of his beanbag again, and this time when he returned he had another boy with him. This one I recognised from around camp as a nice guy from Germany, with blue eyes and gorgeous dark blond hair. "Girls, look who I found — this is Jakob. No need to rip poor Zach to shreds with your nails."

Amber and Gabrielle exchanged a look before both releasing a giggle. "Come sit, Jakob," Amber said as she patted the beanbag beside her.

I turned back to Rick and gave him an impressed nod. "Crisis averted — well done."

Rick smiled and leaned back in his beanbag. "Nothing worse than angry girls. My dad taught me at an early age to just keep them happy."

"He sounds like a wise man."

"He is."

Smiling, I lifted my beer bottle. "Here's to keeping us girls happy."

"To keeping you happy," Rick said, tapping his beer bottle against mine.

I took a large drink of my beer. "What part of America are you from?"

"California. Zach too."

"Did you come here together?"

Rick nodded. "It sounded fun and our parents thought it would be a good idea — keep us busy and out of trouble."

"Are you awfully naughty?" I asked, smiling over the top of my bottle.

"Oh yeah, I'm the ultimate bad boy," Rick said with a laugh. "To be honest, between school and surfing, we barely have time for anything, let alone trouble."

I grinned. "I knew it. I had Zach pegged as a surfer, but you too?"

Rick nodded. "I love it—being out on the water, riding the waves. It was the water sports programme here that made us come." He leaned a fraction closer to me. "Though, if I'd known there would be such a cool underground scene going on, I'd have asked to come sooner."

"Stick with me, I'll keep you right."

"Are you leading that poor boy astray, Freddie?" Gabrielle asked. She had settled into the crook of Zach's arm and I had to smile at how fast my friend moved.

"Me?" I asked incredulous. "Would I do such a thing?"

"Hey, leave the girl alone," Rick said, jumping to my defence. "I am more than willing to be led astray."

Amber and Gabrielle let out peals of laughter.

Zach held his hand up. "Hang on, that's not fair. If he's being led astray than I want to be, too."

Gabrielle planted a quick kiss to Zach's cheek. "Don't worry, I won't forget about you."

We finished our drinks and the boys left to get us fresh ones.

"I am having the best time," Amber said. "Jakob is *so* cute."

"So is Zach. He is totally going to be my summer romance." Gabrielle swung her gaze to me. "What about you, Freddie? Is love on the cards for you this year?"

I shrugged and trailed my eyes over to Rick as he made his way back to our little group. "He seems nice. I guess I'll have to wait and see."

It was super late when we all walked back to the chalet. Rick and I led the group, with Zach and Gabrielle stopping every few moments to kiss or disappear into the shadows. Jakob and Amber walked a ways behind, their heads pressed close as they murmured to each other.

We reached the door to the chalet and, after checking the coast was clear, crept in like a bunch of misfit ninjas. Gabrielle laughed and grabbed my hand as we raced up the stairs as quickly — and quietly — as we could.

Amber's room was first, so we dropped her off and bade her goodnight.

Gabrielle took her time snogging the face off Zach outside our room, leaving me and Rick to smile awkwardly at each other.

"Jeez, man, you could have done that outside and saved us all this embarrassment," Rick said, smacking his friend on the shoulder.

Zach and Gabrielle separated, grinning like idiots at each other.

"Goodnight, then," Gabrielle said in a dreamy voice. She waggled her fingers in a wave then darted inside our room.

Zach punched Rick good-naturedly on the shoulder as he walked past him, heading for the stairs.

"Thanks for sitting with me tonight, it was nice getting to know you," I said. My stomach fizzed and I couldn't tell if it was because I was nervous about what Rick expected of me, or because I was starting to like him.

"You, too." Rick stepped forward. He placed his hand on my waist and dipped his head to kiss my cheek. As he pulled back, he winked and turned to follow his friend to the stairs.

I pressed my fingertips to my cheek, a smile spreading across my face.

The door to the bedroom swung open and Gabrielle popped her head out. She grabbed my arm and hauled me inside. "Get in here! We have to talk about tonight."

We flopped down on my bed and pulled the sheets up over our heads. "You like Zach, then?" I asked her.

She shrugged. "He's a good kisser, and *so* good-looking. What about you? Are you into Rick?"

I released a long breath as I thought about her question. "I think he's nice. Gorgeous, obviously. But I don't think I'm really feeling it."

"Poor Rick," Gabrielle said, pouting. "Oh well, at least you have something nice to look at all summer."

I blinked at her before we both dissolved into giggles. One of the other girls made a noise in her sleep, so we clamped our hands over our mouths to smother our laughter.

This summer was set to be spectacular.

The days and weeks dissolved into each other. Every day my schedule was jam-packed with sports and activities, or sunbathing in the spare moments I had with Gabrielle and Amber. Most nights we hung around with the boys. Amber's and Gabrielle's romances were going at breakneck speed, with both of them often disappearing to be alone with their respective boyfriends.

I had told Rick the morning after the first disco that I wasn't really looking for romance. He seemed to take it well enough, and hadn't disappeared in search for a girl who was interested like I'd thought he would. Instead he'd proved to be a really nice guy, and he always kept me company when our friends were off…being busy.

July bled away to August and before I knew it, my time at Camp Monte Leone was half over. I wrote postcards to Mummy and Daddy to let them know I was having such a good time. I was looking forward to the final two weeks of summer, when I'd return to Monaco to be with my family.

Three weeks before the end of my time at Camp Monte Leone, I joined a horse trek through the mountains with Gabrielle, Amber, Paulina and a handful of other girls. Zuzu didn't want to go because she was deathly afraid of horses.

It was a tough trail with narrow paths and often steep inclines. My horse, Shetân, was beautiful, as black as night. He was enormous, the biggest the camp owned, and young, too. He didn't feel completely trained to me, at least not to the standards he probably should have been. But because I was the tallest and most experienced when it came to horses, I was always given him to ride.

Over the last few weeks, I had got to know him better, but I didn't fully trust him. I trusted him enough to ride, but there was just a slight nagging in the back of my mind that I couldn't quiet.

We paused in a grassy clearing for a break after riding for a while. Vicky, the counsellor leading us, handed around bottles of water. It was boiling hot and I was sweating beneath my hat.

"I'm going to miss this," Gabrielle said, tipping her head back to bask in the sunshine.

"Because they don't have sunshine in Australia?" Amber asked.

Gabrielle pulled a face at her and flicked her with some water. "Shut up, you know what I mean. There's nowhere else on earth like Crans-Montana."

Amber nodded in understanding. "I can't believe this is my first year coming here, and I don't ever get to come back."

"You know, I sort of toyed with the idea of coming back as a counsellor during my summers from university," I said.

Gabrielle twisted her mouth in displeasure. "I don't think I'd enjoy this place half as much if I had to look after a bunch of brats."

A laugh bubbled in my throat. "You were one of the brats, once."

She smiled and tossed her ponytail. "I was a delightful brat, thank you very much."

"Of course you were," I said. "That's why all the counsellors groaned when they saw you coming. They used to call you Grumbling Gabrielle because you complained about everything that first summer!"

Gabrielle huffed. "The bed was lumpy, the salad was almost always soggy and there were never any rowboats free when I wanted to go out on the lake. Who wouldn't complain at that?"

Amber stared at Gabrielle in disbelief. "I take it back. I'm so glad this is my last year."

Gabrielle stuck her tongue out at Amber.

"Well, I for one am glad I have a few more years left to come here," Paulina said, joining into the conversation. "And soon I'll be one of the crazy older girls who show the younger ones where the secret parties are."

Amber lifted her eyebrows and gave Paulina a condescending look. "What makes you think we're going to tell you before we leave?"

The smile fell from Paulina's face. "What?"

"Well, if we don't tell you about them, you'll never know where they are or what they are like...so you can never pass on the knowledge yourself," Amber said. She gave Paulina a cruel smile. "I don't think you're quite up to knowing such privileged information."

Paulina stared at Amber for a few seconds. Her chin wobbled and I wanted to thump Amber for being such a nasty bitch. Paulina pulled on the reins to turn her horse, Apache, away.

Amber's eyes widened with horror. "Oh, Paulina, I was kidding! Please don't be upset!" She dug her heels into her horse's side to start after Paulina. "Paulina!"

"No!" Paulina shouted. "I don't care if you were kidding, that was a horrible thing to say, Amber!"

Amber rolled her eyes. "Oh, for God's sake, stop being such a Frenchie drama queen."

Paulina twisted around and threw her bottle of water at Amber.

It smacked against her hat, and bounced off to hit the back of her horse's neck. Amber gasped in shocked and glared at Paulina. "Are you kidding me? What are you, five?"

It was clear to anyone who was watching the episode that Paulina was hurt, and her pride was smarting. But Amber had clearly lost her temper after Paulina hadn't laughed it off when she'd told her it was a joke. "Amber—" I started.

"It's okay, Freddie," Paulina said, cutting me off. "You don't have to defend your fille soumise friend."

I gasped at the description she'd just given Amber, and also the venom in her tone.

"What did you just call me?" Amber demanded. She swung around to pin me with an angry look. "What the hell did she just call me?"

No way in heck was I taking that bullet...and Amber sure as anything was the sort to shoot the messenger. "Er...I don't think it translates."

Amber sneered and swivelled back around to face Paulina.

"Girls, girls, what's going on?" Vicky asked as she approached the situation. She wore a broad smile and clearly had no idea what was really going on, otherwise she would have entered wearing protective gear.

Paulina yanked on Apache's reins again, too hard, and I saw the animal shake his head.

I glanced between Paulina and her horse. Paulina was so rigid with adrenaline it had to have been feeding through to Apache. Horses are so sensitive, especially to their rider, and right now Paulina and Apache made for a dangerous combination. "Paulina, I think you should —"

Paulina groaned. "Stay out of this, Freddie!" She gave another hard yank on the reins to turn her horse, making him more and more agitated. He huffed and swung his head and I could almost see what was about to happen.

The rest of the girls with us on the ride were completely oblivious to the mess we had found ourselves in, and laughed at something one of the other girls had said. One of the girls laughed so hard she dropped her whip. It hit the ground with a sharp crack that provided the final straw in spooking Paulina's horse.

Apache reared up with a frightened whinny, dismounting Paulina. She rolled away as soon as she hit the ground, immediately finding shelter beneath a tree.

But Apache's spooking created a domino effect with all the other horses. They whinnied and moved around in an agitated state. Well, all except Shetân, of course.

Shetân reared up but I held on for dear life, hoping that after one outburst he would be fine. Except he wasn't fine, and his flight instinct kicked in with me still on his back, and we charged through the dense forest.

There was nothing I could do except hold on as tightly as I could and hope that he would stop soon. A spooked horse could bolt for miles before it even realised it was far from the danger it had fled from in the first place.

Shrieks and yelps pierced the air behind me, and I guessed that Shetân bolting had spooked the others into doing the same.

I had no idea how long Shetân had been galloping for. It could have been seconds but it felt like hours. My heart was hammering in my chest and my vision had blurred. I could barely make out any of the scenery, it passed by too quickly.

In the distance, a sort of thundering could be heard.

It was another few seconds that I realised what it was.

A river ran through these mountains, but not a slow flowing river, a roaring river with rapids and an impossibly strong current. We'd all been warned to never attempt to swim in it. So many visitors to the area over the years had thought they could handle it. They were wrong, and as a result there had been more than one death.

I peered over Shetân's head and focused my eyes — confirming that yes, we were fast approaching the rapids. My breath caught in my throat at the sight of the white, churning water and I wondered idly if my parents would be cross to receive the news that I'd died whilst enjoying my summer away at camp.

I was running out of time.

Shetân showed no sign of stopping.

There was no other choice — I had to jump.

Squeezing my eyes shut, I whispered, "Please stop, Shetân, please, please, stop. Don't drown." And I threw myself to the side.

I landed with a thump that knocked the wind out of me. Pain lanced through my foot, but it was secondary to the burning in my lungs as I tried to suck in a breath.

The ground was hard and lumpy beneath me, littered with rocks and solid clumps of earth. But I lay there until my breath came back and my heart rate slowed.

I forced myself into a sitting position and took stock of my surroundings. There was no indication of how far away I was from the rest of the group. I didn't know where Shetân was.

And I was fairly sure my ankle was broken.

"Freddie! Freddie, can you hear me?" Gabrielle's voice pierced the air, somehow audible over the gush of the fast-flowing river behind me.

"Here! I'm here!" I called.

A moment later Gabrielle and Vicky came into view as they emerged from the forest. Gabrielle jumped from her horse and crouched in front of me.

"My God, are you all right?"

I nodded, but winced when I tried to move my ankle. "I think my ankle is broken, but other than that, I'm fine."

Gabrielle's breath left her in a rush. "Gosh, Freddie, you're lucky to be alive! Did you jump from him?"

"Yes, I didn't know if he would stop for the river."

"You did the right thing, Freddie," Vicky said. "And right in the nick of time, I'd say." She pointed to something behind me.

I turned around to see what she meant, and saw I was less than a yard from a fierce barbed-wire fence. "I didn't even see it," I whispered. Glancing at the other two, I said, "Is there any sign of Shetân?"

Gabrielle nodded. "We passed him, it's how we knew to look this way."

"When you threw yourself off of him, it must have been enough to get through to him. I bet he turned at the right time and headed back the way he came. He's slowed down, not as spooked. He'll be fine, Freddie," Vicky said. My worry must have been all over my face.

"Thank God," I breathed. I wouldn't be able to stand it if something bad had happened to him. "What about everyone else? Is Paulina okay?"

Vicky's face hardened. "Everyone is fine, but as for Paulina, she's on kitchen duty for a week after that stunt. And banned from horses for the rest of the summer."

I winced. "Poor Paulina. You know, she was just reacting to what Amber said."

"That's exactly what Amber said, which is why she will be joining Paulina in the kitchen."

Glancing at Gabrielle, I bit my lip to keep from laughing. What a calamity... I wish I had been around to see the look on Amber's face when she'd been told that little nugget. Though if anyone ever told Amber that Paulina had called her a prostitute, then I doubted the messenger would survive.

Vicky hooked a hand under my armpit and heaved me to me feet—well, foot—and Gabrielle took my other side. "Come on, we'd best get you back so you can get checked over."

They helped me onto Vicky's horse, and she held the reins as she walked beside it back to the others.

It was like walking through a battlefield.

Girls were scattered everywhere in all sorts of positions, hats at awkward angles and clothes ripped from tree branches. Half the horses were missing and the other half were tied to trees.

We made our way slowly back to camp and it took us twice as long as it had on the way up the mountain. I was rushed to the first-aid centre, then to the small hospital in town where, after an x-ray, they confirmed that I had a hairline fracture on my ankle.

I was fitted for a cast, given a set of crutches and I was on my way back to camp. Gabrielle had gone with me to the hospital, and helped me into our chalet. The minute I arrived we were all sent to the office where we could make our calls home.

"Your mother is on the phone, Freddie," Charlotte said. "She's been frantic and calling every fifteen minutes."

I wasn't surprised Mummy was worried. We had tried calling the house in Monaco while I'd been waiting to be taken to the hospital, but she hadn't been home. I'd left a message with Aimee.

Hobbling into the office, I smiled my thanks and took the receiver from Charlotte. "Hi, Mummy."

"Frederica!" Mummy said in a shrill voice. "I've been worried sick! Are you all right, darling?"

A laugh bubbled in my throat. "I'm fine, Mummy, I promise."

Mummy let out a long breath. "Good. Are you well enough to travel? I can have a flight arranged for you in the morning."

"Mummy, no! I have three weeks left here, I don't want to go home yet. I'm fine, honest."

There was a pause before my mother spoke again. "I don't think so, Frederica. You'll be more comfortable at home."

I rolled my eyes. "My ankle will feel the same no matter where I am. Besides, it's just a hairline fracture. It's not even a real break. And also, how much more damage could I possibly do now that I'm practically immobile?"

Mummy stifled a laugh. "It's rather skewed logic, but I understand the thought behind it. Fine, darling, you can stay as long as you promise not to break anything else?"

A grin spread across my face. "I promise."

"Good." Mummy sighed. "Now, you had best tell me all about this latest adventure of yours."

I giggled and told Mummy all about the afternoon — added drama and suspense so it made the story better...but not too much. I didn't want her to change her mind, after all. And I left out the bit about Paulina calling Amber a prostitute.

"What a tale!" Mummy cried. "Well, I had best be off, darling. Telephone me if you need anything at all."

"Okay, bye, Mummy."

"Goodbye, darling."

Gabrielle's eyes were as wide as saucers when I hung up the phone. "Well? Are you being shipped home?"

"Nope, I'm staying!" I smiled. "Not that I can do very much of anything now, but I shall enjoy the sunbathing."

Gabrielle grinned and took my arm again as I struggled out of the office. "And I daresay I could be persuaded to join you!" She helped me up to our room and once there, she set about swapping our bunks so I didn't have to attempt the climb to the top one. She piled pillows at the bottom of my bed for me to rest my foot on, giving my ankle much-needed rest and elevation.

"How are you feeling? Do you want anything?" Gabrielle asked.

I shook my head. "I'm fine. It's dinner time, you should go. I'll want to grab a nap anyway."

"Okay, are you sure?"

"Of course, I'll be fine."

Gabrielle kissed my cheek before leaving the room.

My eyes fluttered shut a second after she'd left, and what felt like a second later, they were flying open again. Only the darkness outside the windows indicated that any time had passed at all.

A knock sounded on the door and I wondered if that was what had awoken me.

Without thinking, I lifted my leg to stand. My ankle ached and I winced as I replaced it on the pillows again. Answering the door in person was out. "Come in!" I called.

The door opened and Rick poked his head inside. "Hi, can I come in?"

I smiled. "Yes, quickly, before you get caught."

Rick slipped inside and crossed the room to sit on the edge of my bed. "Gabrielle just told me what happened. How are you feeling?"

"A little sore, nothing terrible," I said with a shrug.

Rick cleared his throat. "I was worried when I heard."

"That's sweet, but I really am fine."

He nodded. "Can I keep you company for a while? Unless you're tired, then I'll clear out."

I shook my head. "No, company would be good. But don't you want to go to the disco?"

A small smile touched Rick's lips. "I'd rather hang out and eat junk food with you."

"Okay then," I said.

"Great." Rick rose from my bed. "I'll go get some supplies and I'll be right back."

I smiled as I watched him leave. I was glad I had given him a chance, because he had turned out to be a really lovely guy. It was just a shame those damned butterflies still weren't there.

Gabrielle insisted that even though I was practically a cripple, I couldn't miss the gala night in the clubroom. It was only a few days after the accident and I hadn't got the rhythm of my crutches yet, so I looked a bit of a hop-a-long. But hey ho. Gala night was a time-honoured tradition at Camp Monte Leone, and I looked forward to it every year. I couldn't let a silly thing like a broken ankle stop me from going.

The evening of the gala, Gabrielle, Amber and I got ready together in my room. We wore designer gowns and created beautiful hairstyles. There was a tap on my door, and Amber rushed across the room to open it.

Rick, Zach and Jakob were dressed to kill in their suits.

"Not bad, huh?" Zach asked with a grin as he entered the room. He pulled Gabrielle into a kiss that made her swoon when he let her go.

"You all look so good," Paulina said. "I wish *I* had a handsome boy taking me."

I smiled at her as I picked up my little bag. "Just wait—it will happen for you, too."

"Come on then, hoppy," Gabrielle said with a laugh. "We don't want to be late."

I stuck my tongue out at her and hobbled out of the room. Rick walked beside me as the other two couples took the lead, engrossed in their little romances.

"You doing okay?" he asked me.

"Better than yesterday. And tomorrow I'll be even better than today," I said. "These crutches take some getting used to though."

Rick chuckled. "I'll bet."

We walked into the clubroom, which had been transformed for the gala night.

Casino games were set up all around the room with people crowding around them. The noise in the place was astronomical, with many crying out in excitement at a win.

Everyone was dressed up, like me and my friends. It was a sea of satins and sequins, tuxedos and cravats. The dresses created a gorgeous rainbow of colour, and we surely resembled a flock of dazzling peacocks.

Amber grabbed Jakob's hand and dragged him to the roulette table, and Gabrielle and Zach headed to blackjack.

"Are you feeling lucky?" Rick asked as he motioned to the craps table.

I grinned. "I grew up in Monaco. I *always* feel lucky."

"Freddie, hand me another tissue please."

I grabbed the box beside my bed and hopped over to the dressing table where Gabrielle sat attempting to do her makeup. She dabbed under her eyes, trying to remedy another mascara-tear disaster.

"Maybe you shouldn't wear mascara if you're just going to keep crying," I suggested.

Gabrielle shook her head. "No way. I want to look my best for Zach."

"And panda eyes is the way to do that?"

She held my eye in the mirror for a long moment before releasing a breath and reaching for a makeup remover wipe. She swiped it across her eyes, and caught the last of the smudged mascara. "You're right."

"Anyway, Zach won't care. He's getting you all alone for most of the night. He isn't going to be looking at you and wondering why you aren't wearing mascara."

Gabrielle giggled. "No, I don't suppose he will." She sighed, her melancholy returning. "I just can't believe it's time for them to leave already. It isn't fair."

It was the pitfalls of a summer romance — the dreaded departure.

A week had passed after I'd broken my ankle and it was now time for Zach and Rick to leave.

"Come on, you've been crying all day," I said as there was a knock on the door. "That will be the boys. Are you okay?"

Gabrielle nodded and dabbed her eyes with a tissue once again.

I crossed the room to open the door. Rick stood a little behind Zach and rolled his eyes at him before giving me a wide grin. Zach, to give him his due, looked just as forlorn as Gabrielle.

Gabrielle let out a squeak and threw herself into his arms. He pressed his face into her hair and murmured something I couldn't make out.

"Okay, you two, you'd best disappear before you end up getting caught," I said.

The pair broke apart, and Gabrielle gathered her things.

I scooped up the bag filled with *my* entertainment for the evening — namely some films and lots and lots of junk food. We left the room, and downstairs Rick and I distracted Vicky for a few moments so Gabrielle and Zach could slip away unnoticed.

They were spending their last night together in the woods camping, and Rick and I were covering for them, should anyone come asking about their whereabouts.

We were watching a cheesy horror film in the lounge of the senior chalet, surrounded by sweets, fizzy pop and huge bags of crisps.

"Are you excited to be heading home?" I asked Rick as I reached for another fizzy lace.

Rick shrugged. "Sort of. I miss my friends back home, but I'm having a pretty amazing time here."

"I know what you mean. Leaving school, leaving home, leaving camp, it feels bittersweet no matter where I'm leaving." And wasn't that the truth. I was a resident of the world and I loved to move around and be in different places. My worst nightmare was the thought of being stuck in the same place for the rest of my life.

But the leaving never got any easier. Only more tolerable.

The film ended and Rick turned the TV off.

"It's getting late, I should head up to bed. I doubt anyone will come looking for Gabrielle and Zach now," I said.

Rick nodded and rose from the couch. He extended his hand to me to help me up. I slid my palm into his and he gently pulled me to my feet. Rick didn't let go of my hand like I'd thought he would, and instead gave it a light squeeze. "Freddie, I have something I need to say."

My stomach dipped, and not entirely in a pleasant way. "Okay. What's wrong?"

"Nothing is wrong." Rick let out a nervous laugh. "I'm crazy about you, Freddie. I've been giving you space because you told me you weren't looking for anything more than a friend right now. But I have to admit that all summer long, I've hoped you would change your mind."

"But, Rick, you're leaving in the morning," I said quietly. "And we live on opposite sides of the world."

"I know...I know. But I would be a total moron if I left without telling you how I feel. And I'm not asking you to promise anything, or even reciprocate my feelings. I just want you to know that I've had the best summer with you." Rick's eyes seared into mine, the passion in them fierce.

I reached out with my free hand to touch his cheek. He had been an amazing friend to me this summer, and I was sad to see him leave. But what on earth could I promise him, even if he wasn't expecting anything? "Thank you, Rick. You've been an incredible friend. I'm glad to have met you."

He squeezed my hand again. "I want to ask if I can kiss you, but I don't want you to feel pressured or anything."

My heart picked up speed.

A kiss? He was a good friend, sure...but could he be anything else? I wouldn't find out by doing nothing, and maybe a kiss was the perfect way to find out if there really was anything more between us than friendship.

"You can kiss me, Rick."

He smiled, wide and happy. Rick cupped my cheek and leaned in to press his lips to mine. His kiss was dry and bordered on chaste, which I was grateful for. At least he wasn't one of those boys who shoved their slimy tongue into your mouth with no warning.

The kiss only lasted a few seconds and while it was nice…that was all it was.

Rick pulled back and scanned my face. "I'd love to call you when you get home. I don't want to lose contact with you."

For a fleeting second, all I could think of was that I wished he had said he would write me a letter.

"Freddie? There's a call for you in the office."

I jumped at the sound of Vicky's voice. Turning my head to see her leaning into the doorway, I nodded my thanks. "Okay, thanks, Vicky."

Vicky glanced between Rick and me. "It's your mother. She sounds a little off, you shouldn't keep her waiting."

"Okay." Turning back to Rick, I gave him a small smile. "I should go. Mummy is probably going to try and talk me into coming home. Again. I'll see you in the morning? Before you leave?"

Rick grinned. "Count on it."

"Night, Rick." A small part of me was thankful at Mummy's timing. Rick's kiss hadn't been in the least bit horrible, but I knew I didn't want any others. That kiss had told me everything I needed to know, and confirmed what I'd already suspected. There truly was nothing but friendship between Rick and me.

I hobbled into the office and picked up the receiver that rested on the desk. "Hi, Mummy."

"Frederica."

My stomach dropped at the sound of my mother's voice. I had never heard her sound like that, not ever, and I dreaded what had caused it. "Mummy?" I whispered. "What is it?"

"I'm sorry, darling," Mummy said. Her voice broke. "It's Daddy. He—he died, my love."

My ears rang, a high-pitched whine that only got louder. Distantly, I heard the phone clatter as I dropped it.

"Frederica? Freddie, darling, are you there?" Mummy's tinny voice came from the speaker.

No...no, I didn't think I was.

It was my last conscious thought before darkness swamped me.

12

The morning after my mother made the call to me at camp, Augustus, Louisa and I flew home to Monaco.

I'd had to tell them.

I'd had to tell my little brother and sister that our father was dead.

Our father was dead.

I wasn't not sure if had sunk in, even now.

Augustus was reacting much the same as me, in his quiet, reserved way. Louisa chewed on her fingernails and tapped her feet constantly, her little mind whirring. We barely spoke a word on the flight home, could barely respond when Samantha picked us up at the airport in her battered little blue VW Golf.

Our house was the same, but it was so, so different. There was no booming voice from the office as Daddy made his phone calls, there was no vibrancy, and the whole place, though it was filled with people, was devoid of life.

People arrived and left with regularity as they came to pay their respects and check on how we were all doing. We children would be trotted out like exhibits so the well-wishers could give their condolences. All wanting to know what had happened.

I heard without really hearing that my father had been enjoying a rare walk home one night after the evening's festivities at the Beach Club. It was almost ritual for Daddy to be driven everywhere, to show the world who he was and what he had. But every now and then, he liked to walk and enjoy the night air. As a child I used to join him on the infrequent occasions I'd been allowed up that late.

The car had hit him while travelling at illegal speeds.

He'd lived long enough to make it to the hospital and to say goodbye to my mother. He hadn't survived the surgery that had been an attempt to save his life.

The driver, who had been high on cocaine, had been found and was awaiting trial.

Friends and family had flown in from all over the world to be at my father's funeral later that week. Part of me wanted to scream for them all to go away, because if they weren't here then all of this wasn't really happening.

When I woke up the morning of the funeral, for a brief second I was fine. My mind hadn't reminded me what I would be doing later, hadn't seen the freshly pressed black dress hanging on the back of my wardrobe door in a plastic garment bag.

But then I remembered, and a heavy wave of pain crashed through my body. I lay in my bed, curled in a protective ball. The breeze that carried with it the scent of the garden and the ocean beyond was usually a comfort but today it did little to soothe me.

I hugged my arms around my chest and squeezed my eyes shut, feeling the familiar burn of tears behind them. My bedroom door gave a low squeak as it was pushed slowly open.

"Freddie?" Louisa whispered, her little voice broken with anguish.

Raising up onto my elbow, I brushed my knotted hair from my face. "Are you all right, Lou?" My little sister had hung from my mother's skirts this past week. For all her boisterousness and large personality, Louisa had shrunk before our very eyes. She was a child again, the smallest.

Louisa shook her head and bit her lip.

My heart ached for her. None of this made sense to me, so how on earth could it make sense to Louisa? I patted the bed beside me and she rushed across the room.

Louisa dived into bed with me and I pulled the sheets up over our heads, shielding and protecting us from the world. She cuddled up to me and popped her thumb in her mouth — something she hadn't done for years.

Whatever helps her.

"Did you sleep at all last night?" I asked her.

"Some," she whispered. "Did you?"

I shrugged. "Some."

We were quiet for a few minutes and I knew there was something she wanted to say, but for whatever reason couldn't find the nerve right away. There was no rushing Louisa — in anything. She did what she wanted exactly when she wanted to do it, and no force could make her any different. So I would give her all the time she needed.

"I'm scared for today," Louisa finally admitted.

"Which part?"

"All the parts." Louisa sniffed and her eyes filled with tears. "Will it be very scary? Seeing the coffin?"

"I don't know, Lou. I don't know how it will make you feel. What you have to remember, is that it is Daddy. Was there anything scary about Daddy?"

She shook her head. After a moment, a slow smile pulled at her lips. "Remember when he caught us using his chair to go up the stairs?"

A laugh bubbled in my throat. After Daddy had had his hip replacement, the house had been fitted with a stair lift—much to our delight. "Yes. I thought he was going to tell us off, instead he told us to give him a shot as we were hogging it."

"What about when Harry ate all his new flowers?"

"Ah yes, Harry the horrid tortoise. What a menace he was." I tapped Louisa on the nose. "My favourite photograph of you is still that one of you bending over peering at little Harry in your gorgeous frilly dress. You must have only been two or three."

The smile that had been so full and happy on Louisa's face slipped. "I'm so sad, Freddie."

I hugged her tighter. "I know, darling. We all are. It's okay to be sad."

"But Daddy hated it when we were sad, he said it made *him* sad too, and I don't want Daddy to be sad in Heaven."

The first tear slid down my cheek at Louisa's innocent worry. "Daddy won't be sad in Heaven. He's up there with his family who have passed away. And he's with Harry."

"Will Harry look after him?" Louisa asked, hiccupping.

"He had better, or William and Charles will tell him off." I wiped away Louisa's fresh tears that streamed down her young face. "I tell you what," I whispered, "every time we start to feel too sad today, why don't we tell a story about Daddy that makes us laugh or smile?"

Louisa nodded and scrubbed at her face. "I like that idea."

My bedroom door squeaked again and Louisa and I threw off the sheet to see Augustus standing in the doorway.

"What are you two doing?" Augustus asked, glancing between us.

"I think right now we're hiding." I looked at Louisa. "Is that what we're doing, Louisa?"

She nodded her head vigorously. "Do you want to hide with us, Augustus?"

Augustus lifted his eyebrows but crossed the room without having to be asked twice. "Too right I do. I poked my head into the kitchen and all I could see was people I don't know." Augustus climbed into bed beside me, taking care of my ankle, and sandwiched me between my two siblings. "I wish it wasn't here yet," he said quietly.

"Me, too," Louisa agreed.

I grabbed both their hands and squeezed. "We'll get through today, I promise. We'll get through it together."

I don't know how much time passed with us hidden away, but the world outside my bedroom door grew louder as more and more people arrived at the house.

It wasn't a shock when my door opened for the third time, and I knew it was someone looking for the three of us.

Mummy stepped inside, her face softening as she took stock of us all in bed together. "I should have known I would find you all together."

"We're hiding, Mummy," Louisa said.

"Can I hide with you for a moment?" Mummy asked as she stepped forward.

We all nodded and scooched over, making room for Mummy to climb in and join us. At first no one said anything. We lay there in my cramped and full bed like it was the safest place in the world.

"Wouldn't it be marvellous if we could stay here all day?" Mummy asked quietly.

"Could we, Mummy?" Louisa asked. "We could get Aimee to bring our lunch in here, and I bet Samantha would read us a story if we asked her nicely."

Mummy chuckled under her breath and reached across to pat Louisa's hand. "I wish we could, my little darling. But we have to say goodbye to Daddy."

Louisa nodded and tucked her chin into her chest.

A few minutes later there was a gentle tap on the door. It was pushed open and Samantha stepped inside. She gave us a small, sad smile.

"I'm sorry to disturb you all," Samantha said, looking at Mummy. "But people are asking after you all."

Mummy nodded and pushed back the sheet. She rose from the bed and Samantha touched her arm as she paused in front of her. "See that the children get dressed, please," Mummy said.

"Of course."

Mummy left and Samantha faced us with a look we were all familiar with. "Come on then, gang."

"We want to hide, Samantha," Louisa said with a pout.

Samantha stepped towards the bed. "Hiding won't stop today from happening, poppet. Besides, you heard your mother. We don't want to give her anything else to fret about today, do we? We all have to be on our best behaviour, and be kind to one another."

After a moment, Louisa gave a nod in agreement and climbed out of my bed, somewhat reluctantly. Samantha held her hand out and Louisa slipped hers into it.

They headed for the door, and Samantha looked back at Augustus and myself. "And you two. I'll send Aimee in here with a few chicken heads, if that will get you both moving."

I chuckled. "All right, Samantha, we're getting up."

"Glad to hear it," she said with a smile.

Augustus and I both got out of bed and I noticed how weary and aged my brother looked — far older than his fifteen years.

"How are you, Augustus?"

He paused at the door, his back facing me. "I'll get there, Freddie. I'll get there."

"Let's all disappear tonight, what do you say? You, me and Louisa. We'll take her crabbing and buy some ice creams. She's always nagging us to take her."

Augustus threw me a smile over his shoulder that didn't quite meet his eyes. "Sounds perfect."

My brother left my room, and it was just me and a little black dress I didn't want to wear.

Hundreds of people crammed into the church in Champ Doree to pay their final respects to my father. He was loved and respected by many, and it showed in the turn out for his funeral.

I held Louisa's hand as we listened to my father's vibrant life and how much he'd adored his children. When it was time, we followed the coffin into the churchyard and stood at the front beside Mummy and my two half-brothers.

Daddy's motto was inscribed on his tombstone. Reading the words made a hard lump form in my throat and tears stream down my face. I scrubbed them away, hoping they didn't make my makeup run. I wanted to look perfect for Daddy. I didn't want to give Mummy another reason to fret.

After the funeral, our house was jam-packed with people again. So many strangers wanted to talk to me, to ask how I was feeling with my ankle, to ask how I was coping. I wanted to scream. My father was dead, how did they think I was coping? What a stupid question!

By early evening, I could see that Louisa had had enough. She sat in a chair in the corner of the lounge with a lost and forlorn look on her face. I found Augustus and grabbed his arm, pulling him in the direction of Mummy.

She touched my cheek and gave Augustus a slight smile. "How are you both?"

I shook my head. "Can we take Louisa out for a bit? She's reached her limit, I think."

Mummy looked over at Louisa in her chair. "Of course. Slip out quietly. Do you need some money?"

"No, I'm sure we'll find some," I said, smiling and trying to lighten the tone.

She giggled. "Yes, I daresay you will."

We bade our mother goodbye and crossed the room again to get Louisa.

"Come on, Lou, we're getting out of here," Augustus said.

Her eyes lit up and she jumped out of her chair. "Are we really? Where are we going?"

"Crabbing, now hurry up or we'll leave you behind." Though his words were mean, the smile took any harm out of it.

We quickly changed into some old clothes and hurried out of the house. The second I was on the beach I felt better. The air in the house had been stifling and I'd felt as though I was slowly being suffocated by a fog of expensive perfumes.

The headache that had throbbed behind my eyes all day finally began to dissipate as I shrugged off the heavy oppression of the day.

Louisa shrieked and ran down to the shoreline. She kicked in the surf and ran away from Augustus as he chased her, threatening to throw her into the ocean.

When we were out on the water, Augustus and I let Louisa win at crabbing, discreetly throwing our catches overboard when she wasn't looking. Louisa loved to win, but she hated someone letting her win. She was feisty and strong-willed and I adored that about my little sister.

It was also the reason she made me want to throttle her at times.

In the end, Louisa threw all her crabs back anyway. She said they belonged in their watery home and we didn't have any right in taking them out of it.

I treated them both to a ginormous ice cream cone back on the beach and we sat licking them and watching the sun go down. It reflected off the water, sending brilliant ripples of orange and pink across the ocean.

Augustus gave Louisa a piggyback ride home as she was beginning to fall asleep on the beach. I hobbled home on my trusty crutches – I couldn't wait to see the back of them. Mummy took Louisa to bed when we arrived home, and Augustus disappeared off to his room. It had been such a long day and we were all clearly feeling the effects.

The house had emptied of surplus bodies, but a few still remained. My step-brother Jamie and his mother were still around somewhere, as were a few of Daddy's friends.

I wanted solitude, but I couldn't stand the idea of locking myself away in my room like I had done most of the week. I wanted to be near Daddy, to smell him, to be immersed in him.

Pushing open the door to his office, I found it was the same as it had always been, yet it was also vastly different. Tears stung my eyes as I stared at his desk, my mind conjuring up the image of him laughing into the telephone.

The doors to the garden were flung open, and the sound of Daddy's friends talking drifted in. They were telling stories about him, laughing and sounding animated. I curled up in one of the blue and gold chairs to listen to them and even found myself smiling.

I sat up in my chair to see Jamie leaning against the patio doorframe, wearing his usual candid smile. His tailored suit looked good on him, as his suits always did. Jamie dressed in old-world aristocratic wealth, just like Daddy.

Jamie was a good ten years older than I was, and thus we had never had much in common. But I still adored my elder half-brother. He was mad and eccentric and so much fun.

Jamie took the chair beside me and lowered his tall frame into it. "I didn't see you much today." He tapped his fingers on my cast. "How's the ankle?"

I shrugged. "Fine, I guess. Hopefully I can get the cast off in a few weeks since it's just a hairline fracture. Besides," I said, giving him a smile, "you were too busy to pay me any attention. Everyone wanted to talk to the new Marquess."

Jamie nodded. "That they did. I imagine you had your ear chewed off a great deal also."

"Pretty much," I admitted. "Everyone wanted to know my plan after next year."

"This is your final year at school? What are your plans? Crazy gap year jetting off all over the world?" Jamie asked.

I snorted a laugh. "I wish! I'll be at St Finbars for university."

"You don't sound overly thrilled at the prospect."

"It's always been the plan," I murmured.

"According to who? Your mother and father?"

I nodded. "Daddy always said he wanted me to go to a top uni like St Finbars."

"Daddy always wanted you to be happy first." Jamie reached across to take my hand. "It's your life, Frederica, and you're the one who has to live it. Don't waste it by doing what you think other people expect of you."

Jamie's words sent a thrill down my spine. Not going to university had never even occurred to me before. I couldn't deny that the prospect of doing a gap year first was exciting and so, so tempting.

But could I really do it?

Mummy would be furious…

I shook my head. "It's a silly dream."

"You're only young once," Jamie said as he got up. "Don't blow your chances, and for God's sake, don't make choices you'll regret."

"I won't," I said quietly. My mind churned and I knew I would be thinking all night about this conversation. "How long are you staying with us, Jamie? It's been ages since we've seen you properly."

Jamie glanced at the door. He turned back to me with a small smile. "I'll be off in the morning. I expect it will be quite some time before I see you again."

I opened my mouth to question his meaning, but changed my mind at the last moment. "Never say never."

Jamie's smile widened. "Exactly. Goodnight, Frederica."

"Goodnight, Jamie."

When Jamie left, I stayed curled up in the chair in Daddy's office for a long time. His words swam in my head over and over again. Was I really living my life the way other people expected it? How many choices did I make that were actually my own?

Even at school, while I was rebellious and I sneaked out a lot, I was hardly like some of the girls who disappeared off to London, or to their boyfriend's schools. I was a saint in comparison.

Maybe it was time I started enjoying life like Jamie had said.

Maybe it was time I started living for myself.

13

I felt irrevocably different. My entire centre of balance had shifted. I was no longer a young, carefree girl. I was changed and altered by grief. My shoulders felt heavier these days, my soul a little darker.

Death affected everyone differently. Augustus became insolent and stroppy, Louisa became clingy. She followed us everywhere for the rest of the summer, and for once I didn't mind.

I felt older, more mature.

Shortly after the funeral, Mummy took us on a trip to Venice, to where she and Daddy had spent their honeymoon. She wanted to show us a place that meant a lot to her and Daddy, and it would always be a place that reminded me of him, even though I'd never visited it with him.

We stayed at the Cipriani and drank Bellinis at Harry's Bar. Mummy always said 'start at the top!'

Thankfully I didn't have to return to school with a cast on my foot—pretty as it was. Louisa had spent many an hour scribbling intricate patterns on it until it resembled a piece of fine art. I had it removed a few days before the end of summer, and no longer needed the crutches. It was a relief to leave home and fly to England. Mapleton Manor was a welcome refuge after such a terrible summer.

Everything was different now. Everything felt more intense.

Daddy wouldn't answer the phone when I called home. Fenella was gone. I was a prefect, because it would look brilliant on my university application — which I also needed all As for. The pressure was on for my final year at Mapleton Manor.

I no longer knew if I wanted to attend university, at least right away.

My Masters house was bustling with activity when I arrived. Athena could be heard signing along to her radio, Cassandra, Alicia and Harriet chatted in the common room and Annie was yelling something about someone raiding her tuck box already.

It felt great to be back — like a huge weight had been lifted from my shoulders. I dumped my things in my room and headed into the common room to see the girls.

"Freddie!" Cassandra exclaimed when she saw me. She vaulted off the couch and wrapped her arms around me in a fierce hug. Before long, most of the girls had appeared and did the same.

"How are you, sweetie?" Annie asked as she hugged me.

I shrugged. "I'm getting there. A party tonight will certainly help! Who's in for going to the woods after lights out?"

"I'm in," Athena said without missing a beat.

"And me!"

It was a unanimous decision.

Jemima arrived shortly after I did and I felt the same stab of betrayal that had plagued me at the end of term. But if this summer had taught me anything, it was that life was too short, especially to hold a grudge. So I hugged Jemima in welcome and accepted her sincere condolences.

I disappeared into my room to unpack, itching to raid my tuck box and pin posters to the walls. I had been hard at work for maybe half an hour when Housemistress tapped on the open door.

"Hi, Freddie," she said as she stepped into the room. "How are you, sweetheart? I was so sorry to hear about your father."

I gave her a tight-lipped smile and nodded. "Thank you, Housemistress. It was quite a shock."

"So I imagine," she said. She stepped forward and held an envelope out to me. "This arrived for you just after term ended. I've kept it safe for you."

I accepted it. "Thank you."

Housemistress nodded and left the room.

Turning the envelope over, I didn't recognise the looping scrawled handwriting. I carefully opened the envelope and pulled out the single sheet of paper inside.

I sat on my bed and unfolded the paper.

Dear Freddie,

Well, I promised a letter, did I not? I hope it finds you before you leave school for the summer, as I expect it will be an agonising wait for your reply as it is. If you even want *to reply, that is.*

I looked for you at the dance after you disappeared with your friend, but to no avail. I can only hope you didn't have second thoughts about me. That night as I drove back to Upton with my friend, I couldn't have slept or read my book even if I wanted to – you were all I could think about.

My mind whirled with the beautiful tree-climbing girl I met, so funny and down to earth. I want to get to know this girl better.

I want to see her again.

I've left the number you can reach me at school on at the bottom of the page – please call me if you wish to keep up our contact.

Yours,

Peter

My heart thumped as I read his words.

It was as surprising as it was unexpected. I had thought I'd never hear from him again...only to discover he wanted me to call him? A smile spread across my face before it froze.

But if he was so enamoured with me, why had he danced with Jemima? He couldn't have looked too hard for me if he had found her to dance with so quickly. And Jemima had all but said they'd done far more than dance together.

With a heavy heart I refolded the letter and slid it back inside its envelope. I carried it over to the waste-paper basket, meaning to drop it inside. But I found I couldn't. For whatever reason, I tucked it between the pages of a novel and placed it in a desk drawer, out of sight from nosey Mapleton Manor girls.

Being a Mapleton Manor prefect meant a few things. I had more responsibilities, there were younger girls to look after and I had to be a model student — and I had a new uniform. Instead of the navy blue jumper and house tie I was accustomed to, I wore a pink and white striped blouse, a grey jumper and my prefect's badge.

The night before, we'd spent a touch too long in the woods. We'd drunk leftover alcohol from the year before and had smoked loads of cigarettes. Dawn had only been an hour or so away when we'd sneaked back inside, tiptoeing and trying not to giggle.

I spent my first day as a prefect completely hungover.

By the end of the day all I wanted to do was crawl into bed, shut out the world and sleep away the headache that didn't want to leave.

My friend Athena, it seemed, had other ideas. She barged into my room just as I had climbed into bed. "What are you doing? You're not seriously going to bed already are you?"

I groaned and flopped back against my pillows. "Athena, I am absolutely exhausted...and I feel like death. The question should be why are you *not* going to bed?"

Athena grinned and sat down cross-legged on my bed. She waved a white envelope in her hand. "Guess who I just got a letter from?"

"Who?" I asked past a yawn.

"Our darling friend Fenella. Seems she's missing us already and wants us to go down next weekend to see her in London. I'm thinking some fake IDs and a London nightclub?" Athena lifted her eyebrows and waggled the envelope again like the proverbial carrot on a stick.

I sat up straight in bed. "Really? Gosh, that sounds fun."

"Fun?" Athena exclaimed. "Freddie, that sounds *amazing!*"

"Who else is going?"

"Why don't we keep it just us? It will be so suspicious if we all disappear. Plus the three of us have always been the closest." Athena's face softened. "I think you could use a night of fun."

I nodded. It sounded perfect—a night away with my two best friends. Especially a night away in London. Freedom, the chance to let my hair down and let loose...I couldn't wait.

Athena told me to stay put, and that she would be back in a moment. A few minutes ticked by, and when she did return, it was dressed in her pyjamas with her arms laden down with treats from her tuck box, and with the other six girls.

A laugh bubbled in my throat at the sight of them carrying their own weight in junk food.

"What are you all doing?"

Annie threw herself across the bottom of my bed. "We never got our first night midnight feast. And we're all knackered, so we're having it now instead of the middle of the night."

Athena nudged me until I scooted over in my bed. She climbed in and rested her head on my shoulder as she chewed her way down a Curly Wurly. "You guys, how is it even possible that this time next year we won't be doing this?" she asked.

Cassandra sighed. "I know, weird, right?"

Jemima rolled her eyes. "Yes, how absolutely tragic. I'm sure we'll find other people to eat rubbish with."

"Jemima, it's not the same," Annie huffed. "God, you're miserable sometimes."

"Here, here," Harriet said with a laugh. "I don't think she's worthy of being a part of early-night feasts."

"Harriet's right…" Alicia murmured. "Seize the ingrate!"

We launched ourselves at Jemima who gave a squeal of fright and held her snacks to her chest as though they were her first born. We ended up a laughing, rolling mass of hair and limbs as we tried to prise Jemima's things out of her grip. But she must have really liked those Wagon Wheels because she wasn't for parting with them.

My bedroom door flew open and Housemistress stepped inside. She stared down at us, a perplexed look on her face. "I'm not even going to ask. Keep it down, girls, or I will have to send you to your rooms."

The moment my bedroom door was closed again, we burst into uncontrollable laughter. I clutched my belly and laughed so hard I went silent.

This was what I needed. My girls, my family. They made me feel like me again.

Upper Sixth was like being thrown in at the deep end when I couldn't swim. There was no easing into the new term, no slow departure from the station. Just a head dive into the busiest year I had ever faced.

The trips for this year's classes were fabulous, including one to China after Christmas. Rome and Russia were two I looked forward to also.

On the first day of classes after the summer holidays, each teacher took it upon themselves to give us a ten-minute lecture on the importance of the year. How this was the year to make all our past Mapleton Manor years count, and to have something to stand up and show for our dedication to learning.

If we wanted to get into a top university, then we had to work hard and buckle down to get the As needed to beat out the competition.

It left me with a sour feeling in my mouth and uneasiness in my belly. A heavy pressure settled over my shoulders again, made worse by the telephone call with Mummy the first Sunday of term. She reminded me again to work hard...and to make Daddy proud.

The trip to see Fenella couldn't have come any sooner. The days leading up to it saw me and Athena hopping about like crickets who couldn't contain our excitement.

We didn't tell the other girls where we were going. Partly because they would have only wanted to come with us and therefore make getting caught likely, and partly because...it was sort of exciting to sneak away twice, in effects. Once from school, once from our friends.

On Saturday morning, we started to lay the groundwork to get away. After breakfast I complained loudly of a stomach ache, and Athena pulled back on her usual big personality. By lunch I had gone to my room to lie down, and hopefully people had begun to think there was something wrong with Athena, too.

Housemistress came to check on us, and I told her I felt quite sick and tired. She mentioned Athena felt much the same, and she quickly advised me to stay in bed like Athena was. Bugs and viruses ripped through dormitories like wildfire, and it was best to keep it as contained as possible.

When everyone left for dinner, we made our escape.

Athena and I stuffed our beds to make it look like we were sleeping soundly in them. We pulled the curtains closed tight and Athena even placed a bucket by the side of her bed for effect.

Dressed in our party clothes with jeans and flannel shirts on top, we climbed out of my window and shimmied down a drainpipe to the bottom. From there we darted into the woods so we were out of sight, and made our way through the thickets to the road into town.

We had to walk to Dambrook Station in the Ville, as stashing our bicycles would have been too conspicuous, but we didn't care. It didn't take us long to make it to the Ville, though it would have been quicker if we hadn't dived into the hedges every time we heard a car trundle down the road, convinced it was someone from school come to fetch us.

At the station, we shed our outer layers, leaving us in our party clothes. We stuffed the others in a plastic bag and hid them in the hedge surrounding the train station for us to collect in the early hours of the morning when we returned.

The two hour journey into London took forever and a day. We just wanted to get there and see Fenella and enjoy the night. It was just before nine p.m. when the train finally rolled into the station. We stood at the doors, hopping on the balls of our feet as we waited for them to open.

They finally did, and we jumped out of the train and rushed to the exit. We spotted her next to a news stand, searching the crowds.

"Fenella!" I shouted.

She turned in our direction, her face morphing into undisguised excitement when she spotted us. Fenella ran towards us at full speed and almost knocked us to the ground as she wrapped her arms around the two of us.

We laughed and squealed, jumping up and down in our little huddle.

"I am so pleased to see you both!" Fenella gushed as she released us. "Tell me, how is it without me? Is it just awful? Is everyone just ever so sad?"

"*Ever* so sad, Fenella," Athena said in a teasing voice. "Seriously, though, it's good to see you."

Her smile widened before it turned softer as she directed it my way. "I'm so sorry about your dad, Freddie. How are you doing?"

I shrugged. "Better now I'm here," I said with a forced smile. The truth was, while I appreciated everyone's sympathy, I didn't want it anymore. I wanted to get back to normal. But first I had to accept that this was my new normal — accept that I had to live a life without my father.

Fenella nodded and didn't say another word about the matter, and I knew she got it. Situating herself in the middle, Fenella linked her arms through Athena's and mine and guided us out of the station. "I hope you two are prepared, because we're going to this amazing club tonight that will blow your minds."

Athena whooped, and I cheered.

Bring. It. On.

Fenella took us to her friend's studio apartment where we could do our makeup and freshen up a little before we hit the town. It turned out to belong to the sister of a girl Fenella went to Sixth Form College with, who was away for the weekend. She didn't mind us using the flat, so long as we promised not to destroy it.

We drank cheap, horrific tasting wine that made me screw up my face as I drank it, and danced to the music on the radio. At eleven, the three of us, half drunk on that foul wine, hopped on a night bus to Leicester Square.

Liquid, the name of the nightclub, was emblazoned on the front of the building in a luminescent light, a two-tone theatre mask above it. There was already an enormous queue to get in and we grudgingly joined the end of it.

Thankfully it was a warm night and not intolerable to wait. But the longer we did wait, the more I vowed to one day make it to be the sort of person who never had to queue to get in places. Ever.

It's all about ambition…

"These IDs had better work, Freddie," Fenella whispered as we neared the front of the line.

"They will," I assured her. "But they won't unless you get that frightened look off your face. Confidence, Fenella, it's all about confidence."

When it was our turn, I went first, strolling up to the bouncers and not stopping when they didn't ask me for ID. Just inside the door, I turned to watch my friends.

Athena, who had confidence in spades, did the same as me, and marched straight for the door as though she owned the place. But Fenella, who hung behind Athena like a shadow, was stopped as the bouncer placed his hand on her arm.

She tilted her head and smiled, looking gorgeous. I bit my lip to stifle the giggle that bubbled in my throat. Fenella's plan was obvious — if she couldn't blag her way in with confidence, she'd knock their socks off with her charm.

Fenella pulled the fake ID I had made for her earlier in the week out of her purse. She handed it to one of the bouncers and laughed at something he said. Fenella accepted the ID back from him, and gave him a sultry smile as she sauntered past him to join us.

Once she was clear, Fenella mouthed, "Oh my God" and grabbed my arm. "That was bloody terrifying!" she exclaimed as we made our way farther inside so we could pay our admission.

"But you did it. The first time is the hardest, you know." Athena paid for the three of us and we headed inside. "It's all downhill after this!"

I pulled open one of the heavy double doors that led into the main entrance of the nightclub. Rave music blasted, hitting us as we moved inside. The chrome and mirror style of the interior made the place look and feel edgy with people reflecting off of every surface.

Bodies were crammed into the sunken dance floor, writhing and moving to music that blasted my eardrums. I pointed to the bar, and the girls nodded. Leading the girls, I pushed my way through the throng of people.

We were served our vodkas and lemonades with no trouble, the bartender not even blinking at our order. Athena gulped hers down and slammed the empty glass on the bar.

"Who's dancing?" she yelled over the music.

Fenella held her hand up and quickly finished her drink, and I followed suit. Athena led the way to the dance floor and we found a great spot near the DJ booth where we could shake and shimmy the night away.

We danced for hours, the best exercise ever. Guys bought us drinks, wanted to dance with us and paid us so much attention it threatened to give me a fat head and an inflated ego… I doubted my friends felt differently.

I felt free.

I felt capable of anything, the world was my oyster and all that. Most of all…I felt happy.

It could be explained by the vodka, but at the point I really didn't care. I was with my two best friends, guys were paying me attention and I had made a decision because I wanted to — not because of anyone else. Once upon a time, I probably wouldn't have even gone. I'd have been afraid of disappointing Mummy if I got caught.

Sneaking out into the woods was a far cry from sneaking out to *London*.

But something told me that I wouldn't be missing my dear friend Fenella too much…because I would be visiting her often.

In the early hours of the morning, the three of us stumbled out of Liquid and headed back to the apartment. Athena sprawled across an armchair, and Fenella and I took the couch.

We hadn't intended on falling asleep because our train was stupidly early, but exhaustion combined with quite a lot of vodka made this an impossible task.

I woke to Athena shaking me, a look of panic on her face. "What's the matter?" I asked, grimacing at the awful, furry texture to my mouth. "And what's that smell?"

"You. That smell is you. Now get up or we're going to miss the train!" Athena groaned like the last thing in the world she wanted to do was rush around and catch a train. Which I completely empathised with, because it was also the last thing in the world that *I* wanted to do.

I shoved Fenella's foot away, which had been embedded in my ribs and staggered to my feet. In the bathroom, I smeared some toothpaste onto my finger and attempted to use it as a makeshift brush. Fenella had risen when I came out, and had poured us all massive glasses of water.

We downed them then rushed out of the apartment to the train station.

Bleary-eyed and feeling quite drunk still, I was pulled into a huddle with my friends. We hugged each other tightly and promised to see each other soon. An announcement was made over the loudspeaker that our train would be departing in one minute.

With a last goodbye, Athena and I raced across the platform and threw ourselves onto the train a moment before the doors slid closed.

We found an empty table and sat beside each other so we could put our feet up on the seats across from us. Less than a minute into the journey, I was asleep.

Somehow we woke in time to get off the train again as it rolled into the Ville. Athena and I picked up our things and stumbled towards the door. They opened and I almost fell out of the train.

I rubbed my eyes that stung from the bright morning sun.

Athena yawned and stretched her arms above her head. We fetched our clothes from the hedge and pulled them over our party dresses.

I almost fell into the hedge trying to get my Levis on.

Snails could have beaten us on the walk back to Mapleton Manor. We went so slowly we practically went backwards. It was the most demanding physical test of our lives. My head thumped and I felt so sick I had to pause every few minutes in case I actually was.

But it was nothing compared to the task of sneaking back *into* Mapleton Manor. Shimming down a drainpipe is easy. Shimmying *up* one, is slightly harder.

"We didn't think this one through properly, did we?" Athena asked as we stared up at my window, which seemed like a million miles away.

"Oh, sod this," I mumbled. "Come on, we'll go in the front. People should be at breakfast by now, or still asleep, and if we get caught we say we went for a walk to get some air but now we feel rubbish again so are going back to bed."

Athena blew out a breath. "Sod it," she agreed.

Luck was on our side and we didn't see a single soul on our way up to our floor.

At my door, Athena gave me a limp hug. "That was brilliant. And I'm sure I will think more fondly about it once this hangover clears off."

I laughed and immediately clamped a hand over my mouth. "Urgh. Right, I'm going to bed."

"And me. See you later."

My bed felt blissful as I slid between the cool sheets. I snuggled down as gingerly as I could, taking care not to make any sudden movements to risk upsetting my tender tummy, or to make the pounding in my head any worse.

I had just got into a seriously comfortable position, and had probably dozed off for around thirty seconds, when my bedroom opened.

"Morning, Freddie, love," Housemistress said. She marched across the room and flung open my curtains, making me groan and wriggle further down in my bed.

"It's not morning, please, please let it be bedtime," I grumbled.

"Nope. Up you get, the fresh air will do you the world of good."

"Fresh air?"

"Yes, on your walk into the village for Sunday service."

Oh, God…Sunday service! "Oh, Housemistress, I'm still not feeling one hundred per cent…"

"Just as I thought, which is why the fresh air is the best thing for you. Now up you get, or you'll never get a hot shower and then you will be late."

She left my room and I had no choice but to get out of the bed I had only just got into.

I felt mildly more human after a shower, certainly a slightly more alert one.

Athena leaned against the stone façade of the Sixth Form Centre, looking as crap as I felt. She cracked open one eye as I leaned beside her. "Why did we think Saturday night was a good idea, again?"

"I don't know. But next time we either go on a Friday, or come up with better cover stories as to why we can't go to Sunday service. A broken leg should do it, right?"

Athena snorted a laugh. "It should. Are you volunteering?"

I gave my ankle a shake. "Nah, this one is only just mended. I'd best not give my mother another fright."

The walk back into the Ville was just as awful as the one Athena and I had only just finished. Whoever wanted more cigarettes could bloody well go themselves next time—I didn't want to make this journey again for a while.

It was hot and stuffy inside the church. The reverend had a soothing, hypnotic quality to his voice that made my eyes droop and body relax. I scooted down lower in my seat, as low as I could in a pew, anyway, and folded my arms across my chest.

The next thing I knew, I was blinking away drowsiness and wondered why everyone was staring at me. Glancing at Harriet beside me, I whispered, "What's everyone looking at?"

"You," she whispered with a giggle. "You were snoring, Freddie. Quite loudly, too."

I cringed and gazed over to Mrs Macpherson, who did not look impressed. There went my plans for sleeping the rest of the day away until it was time to return to school. I'd bet my Doc Martens that I would be scrubbing the red staircase in Hemston with a toothbrush.

Oh, bugger…

14

It took until the following weekend to forget how terrible the hangover was, how horrid the punishment had been, and how bone-tired the night out had made me. So when Fenella wrote another letter saying she and her friends were having a party and asked if I wanted to go, I couldn't think of a reason not to.

Sneaking out had been exhilarating and I had developed a taste for it. Why should I do what was expected of me all the time? I was young! This was the time in my life where I should be breaking the rules and getting into mischief.

Athena couldn't go to the party, so I sneaked out myself. She promised to cover for me if anyone came looking and I knew I could count on her.

This time, instead of getting the train to London, Fenella had arranged for me to meet her at a little village on the outskirts of the city. She was waiting for me at the station when my train arrived, sitting on a bench with large-framed sunglasses covering half of her face.

Fenella smiled wildly when I stepped off the train, and draped one arm over my shoulders. "How are you, sweetie?"

I slung my arm over hers as we started walking towards the exit. "Good. All the better for seeing you."

She laughed. "That's what I like to hear. What about Louisa and Augustus? How are they managing now they're back at school?"

"I haven't spoken to them. Louisa is going to be visiting Grandma a few times for exeats." I shrugged. "I might join them so I can keep an eye on her."

"Poor Lou," Fenella murmured. "It must be so hard for her, she's so young."

"She barely left my side after Daddy's funeral. And you should have seen her at the airport saying goodbye to Mummy. I thought she was going to break the glass windows with her screeching."

"Poor Lou," Fenella repeated.

I gave a heavy sigh, my heart aching. "Let's not talk about this. What's the plan for tonight? What are we doing out in the sticks anyway?"

"Okay, keep an open mind about what I'm going to tell you."

"This sounds worrying," I said dryly.

"Perhaps." Fenella giggled. "The party...it's sort of in a sheep field."

"*A sheep field*?" I exclaimed. "Are you mad?"

"No, not in the least." Fenella led the way towards a parked car. "They have these parties all the time. We're going straight there, it's sort of an 'as long as you last' sort of thing. Last weekend, some people were there until Monday morning."

I glanced down at my fitted T-shirt and Levis. "And here I thought I would be under dressed."

Fenella giggled and unlocked the car. "You look gorgeous as always."

"Is this yours?" I asked her as I climbed into the passenger seat.

"It is indeed. Mummy and Daddy said if I passed my test on the first try then they would get me a little run around. I've been practicing on the estate all summer and passed my test this week. Nice, huh?"

"Very," I said, impressed. I had no time to learn to drive. I barely had time for school these days.

Fenella drove the country lanes like a rally driver, speeding around the corners and narrowly missing driving us head first into a tractor. She parked in a wide layby and locked the car once we had climbed out.

"Are you sure this is it?" I asked, peering around. Though she had said the party was in a field, I had expected it to be a touch livelier than the empty green pasture that I was staring at.

"Of course it's not," Fenella said with a laugh. "We have to cross a couple of empty fields to get to the right one."

"You never said I had to trek through a bunch of *other* fields to get to the right one!" I huffed.

Fenella patted my shoulder and motioned for me to follow her. "Come on. I promise it will be over before you know it. And it will be well worth it when we make it."

"It had better," I muttered as I followed after her. We climbed over the gate that led into the empty field, and started making our way across it to the other end.

"You're going to love all these new people, Freddie," Fenella said. "I've made so many new friends it's unbelievable. They're always doing mad stuff like this, and I get the *best* party invites."

It sounded as though she was having an amazing time at her new school. I ignored the sharp stab of jealousy to hear her talk about her new friends. Mostly I hated that other people got to see her more than I did.

But if she wasn't at a new school, then we wouldn't be about to attend a party in a sheep field. I would decide afterwards if this was a good thing or not.

We climbed over a gate into the next field. There was a cow in the middle, staring right at us.

"Are you sure we're allowed over here, Fenella?"

Fenella snorted a laugh. "Of course we're not allowed in here. Why do you think the party is in such a faraway field? It's so we don't get caught."

"Well what about that cow over there? Is it safe to be in here with it?" I looked at the cow again, and saw it meander over to us.

"Yeah, it should be fine. Though, it is weird that it's on its own, right? I feel like that means something, but I can't remember what."

The animal padded closer and unease grew in my belly. "Isn't it bulls you should be wary of if they're in a field by themselves?"

"Yeah, that was it!" Fenella exclaimed. "Why?"

"Because I think that is a bull," I whispered.

Fenella looked over at it, and swore under her breath. "Okay, don't panic. Let's just walk nice and slowly to the other gate. We're almost there, it's not far."

"Yep, we'll walk nice and slowly..." I agreed in a quiet voice.

The bull snorted and we screamed and started running for the gate. We practically flew over it and kept running until we were half way across another field and realised that the bull hadn't scaled the hedge and chased after us.

"Oh my God," Fenella said on a breath. "I think I had a heart attack."

"*Think*? I know!" I sucked in a deep breath, trying to slow my racing heart. "Fenella...do you think perhaps we're lost?"

"I think...perhaps you're right."

We walked for so long I thought my feet would fall off, climbed so many fences I became a pro and managed to avoid being chased by any more bulls. But we eventually found the right field. Half a dozen large tents were erected in the middle, and the chatter and laughter of people drifted across to greet us. A guy spotted us and stood up out of his camping chair.

"Fenella! You made it! Where on earth have you been?"

"We got chased by a bull! I think we may have gotten a little lost. But never mind, we're here now. What's happening? Where's the booze?" she asked.

I couldn't help but grin at my flustered friend. Something told me that this story would be one she told to all her new friends. There was nothing for me to be jealous about. Fenella might have a separate life from me now, but I was still very much a part of it.

I stretched out in my bed, wrapping the warm duvet tightly around me and snuggling deeper into the mattress. Letting out a contented sigh, I smiled at the memory of my dream about Keanu Reeves.

With a yawn, I cracked my eyes open.

Annie and Athena's faces were about an inch from mine.

I yelped and scrambled so far back in my bed I fell out the other side with a thump.

My friends, helpful as they were, cackled with laughter. Athena helped untangle my legs from the duvet and gave me a hand up.

"What on earth are you two doing?" I asked as I rubbed the sleep from my eyes.

Athena and Annie exchanged an excited look. Athena nodded, and Annie reached for something hidden on the other side of my bed. She held up a bulging pillowcase.

"Happy birthday, Freddie," Annie said.

Athena threw her arms around me. "Happy birthday, gorgeous."

I laughed. "I can't believe you did this."

"We all did." Athena opened my bedroom door and Jemima, Harriet, Alicia and Cassandra all poured inside. They piled onto my bed and pulled me down with them.

"Come on, come on," urged Harriet. "I can't wait to see if you like my gift."

A lump of emotion rose in my throat. I had the most thoughtful friends.

Annie's face softened. "You didn't think we wouldn't do something special for your eighteenth, did you?"

I smiled at her. "I'm so glad you did. How did you remember about the pillowcases?"

Annie rolled her eyes. "We all loved pillowcases on our birthdays, but no one more than you."

Receiving a pillowcase full of gifts was one of my favourite memories of Bourne Park. The night before your birthday, two girls from your dormitory would go around all the other girls with a pillowcase. Anyone who liked you popped a little gift into the pillowcase and in the morning the two girls would present it to you. Not to sound conceited, but my pillowcase was always the fullest. I put it down to the fact that I got along with everybody and was genuinely a nice person.

That, and I was the sweetie queen of Bourne Park.

I swiped away a stray tear and dived into the pillowcase. The girls helped me to open my gifts, some fun and quirky, others lovely and meaningful. Soon my bed was covered in piles of CDs, makeup and books, jewellery and accessories.

As well as presents from my individual friends, they had all gone in together to create a memory book. There were pictures and anecdotes from my years at Bourne Park and Mapleton Manor.

We laughed for hours that morning as we poured over the book, reminiscing and being nostalgic.

It was the best birthday ever.

Louisa had morphed into the clichéd rebel child, acting stroppy and being disrespectful. It was obvious to us all that it was because she was hurting so much still, but it made being around her difficult sometimes.

The presence of Daddy was still so strong in the house, too. A few times Mummy and I swore we got a gentle waft of his scent, like he was still there, still keeping an eye on us. It made my grief return. At Mapleton Manor, I had felt as though I had almost returned to normal, but back home the waves of anguish came swift and often and all I wanted was for someone to make it better.

Augustus was now every bit the sullen teenager, and spoke in grunts and shrugs. So it fell to me to be the good one...the one not to do anything to upset Mummy.

By the time I left for school again after half term, that awful pressure and suffocation was back.

One night after returning for the new term at school, I was elbow deep in my History of Art textbook when Athena and Annie slipped into my room. I glanced at my digital clock on the bedside table and saw it was almost eleven.

I gave them both a disapproving look. "Now, girls, aren't you aware it's past curfew?"

Athena rolled her eyes and flopped down on my bed. "Sorry, Miss."

"What are you two up to anyway?" I asked with a grin.

"We were bored and saw the light on under your door," Annie replied. "What are you studying?"

"I have my history of art test next week." I shoved the textbook away and got to my feet. "But the dates are making my head spin. Fancy a cig?"

Athena and Annie didn't have to be asked twice. We grabbed my packet and eased out onto the ledge to shimmy across to the lower part of the roof. Athena and I sneaked out so often that it was like second nature to us now. We knew where to stand, where to hold on and most of all...where to avoid. Annie, it seemed, had forgotten about the row of loose shingles and inadvertently grabbed hold of one as she climbed onto the roof.

It slipped free of its holding, and free of Annie's hand as it fell to the ground, quite a few storeys down. It broke with a sharp crack that seemed to echo across the grounds.

I held my breath and looked at my friends with wide eyes. Annie and Athena also appeared to have stopped breathing. When after a minute or two, no one came to investigate, I began to relax.

"They'll just think it slipped loose," Athena said with a shrug.

"Do you really think so?" Annie asked. Her eyes were big and round and her body was stiff—she was noticeably shaken.

Athena nodded and handed out the cigarettes. "So what's next on the party girl's agenda?"

"Fenella said there's this really cool party happening at King's Cross the week before the Christmas holidays. It should be pretty good. And I bet that guy you meet the other week will be there," I said with a smile at Athena. She had come with me to the last party in a sheep field. Like me, she hadn't been overly impressed with the trek to get to the right field, but luckily for her, we'd gone the right way and hadn't been chased by any cattle. Athena had hit it off with Simon, one of Fenella's new school friends, and I knew she was itching to see him again.

Athena's eyes lit up. "Sounds brilliant! I'm there!"

"Oooh, can I come too?" Annie asked as she shuffled across the roof to sit closer to us. "I haven't sneaked out in ages."

Athena and I exchanged a look and pretended to consider the request. I giggled. "Of course you can come, Annie, don't be daft."

She squealed and leaned over to kiss my cheek. "I can't wait. Do you think there will be any good-looking boys for me?"

"I think we should tell Fenella off if there aren't," Athena said.

Annie laughed. "What about you, Freddie? Are any boys on your radar?"

For a brief second, Peter's face flashed in my mind. *God, why am I still thinking about him?* I forced a smile and shook my head.

"You know, you never did tell us what happened with that boy from the end of term dance last year," Athena said, giving me a keen look.

My cheeks flushed. "I did, I told you that I couldn't see him when we went back out to the dance. These things happen, I guess."

"Hmm," Athena said, clearly not believing a word I'd said.

"Uh, guys…" Annie said slowly. "What's that?"

I followed her pointed finger and saw two cars speeding up the drive towards the school. With flashing lights on the roof.

There was a split second when it didn't properly sink in what I was looking at. Then someone swore very loudly and we all jumped to our feet and scrambled back down into my room.

We had just closed the window when the handle of my door turned. "Quick! Hide!" I whispered as loud as I dared. I dived into my bed and pulled the covers up to my chin to disguise the fact I had just been outside and was clearly not in my pyjamas.

Annie hid on the floor between my bed and the wall, and Athena stood behind the door, squeezing herself into the small space.

Housemistress poked her head into the room. "Frederica, are you all right?"

"Yes, I am. Why?" I asked, trying to make my voice seem groggy as though she had woken me up.

"I don't want to alarm you, but there is an intruder in the House. The police are here now, so don't worry. They will take care of everything."

"An *intruder*?" I exclaimed. "Whatever makes you think that?"

"We heard them on the roof. They loosened some shingles and one broke, alerting me to their presence. I heard them creeping around up there so I called the police right away. But do not worry yourself, Frederica. I have every faith the police will catch the criminals."

Housemistress gave me a smile and closed my door again.

I rolled over to peer down at Annie who lay curled up on my bedroom floor. "Well, I found the intruder first."

"Bugger," Annie swore.

It was a few weeks later that the three of us sneaked out to get the train to London and join Fenella for the party at King's Cross. We knew nothing about it except it was an all-night sort of thing and hundreds of people were going.

Annie bounced around in excitement in her seat on the train, much to Athena's annoyance — she was so cool she could chill the sun. Fenella met us at the station again, and took us to another friend's flat to get ready. Like always, we were wearing our party clothes, and so only needed to put the finishing touches to our makeup.

Before we left, Fenella passed us each a rolled-up sleeping bag.

"What are these for, Fenella?" Annie asked her as she accepted her sleeping bag.

"Yeah, what sort of party are we going to that we need sleeping bags?" Athena asked with a bemused look on her face.

Fenella laughed. "You'll see. Trust me."

Our trust in Fenella slowly dwindled the closer we got to the party. No one gave us strange looks, though strange we did indeed look, four girls dressed up in party dresses and carrying a sleeping bag each, but then again, it was London after all.

Fenella led us down a narrow side street to a large abandoned warehouse that looked as though it had seen better days. It was dark — I could barely even see the end of my nose. Athena's hand was in mine as we huddled together and I tried not to wonder if my friend had lost her mind.

She pulled open a heavy metal door and ushered us quickly inside.

"This is how every horror film starts, you know," Annie whispered from behind us. "Just wait — some chainsaw-wielding maniac will jump out and hack us all to pieces."

"Shut up, Annie!" Athena hissed through her teeth.

"But it's true!"

"*I* will hack you to pieces if you don't give it a rest!"

We followed Fenella down a corridor and across a metal walkway. Our footsteps echoed around the empty building, eerie and haunting. The deeper into the building we ventured, the louder I could hear a thump of music.

Fenella threw open another door, and this time, the rush of music almost knocked me to my knees. In the sunken pit below was a writhing mass of bodies, crammed together like fish in a net as they danced to the music.

She found a place to stash our sleeping bags, then gestured to follow her down the wrought-iron twisting staircase to the party below.

Everywhere I looked it was crowded. Some hot or sweaty person or other pushed against me as we navigated the scores of bodies. Annie, Athena and I exchanged looks, but no one said anything for fear of upsetting Fenella.

We stayed glued to each other, none of us even daring to try and find a toilet as God only knew how disgusting it would have been. So we danced and tried to have a good time, but I knew the other two, like me, were counting down the hours until we could leave.

Drugs were being passed around and we declined them every time. Loads of people were completely off their face and it just made me want to leave all the more.

We didn't even have a drop of alcohol.

When we were able to convince Fenella to call it a night, she led the way into another room where there was just a sea of bodies laid out on the floor, with tons and tons of sleeping bags all crammed together.

It was the worst night's — or few hours' — sleep I had ever had.

I think we were all relieved when we could leave for the train station the next morning. It was the first time we'd journeyed back to Mapleton Manor without a horrific hangover, so the change was quite refreshing. Even if I did feel like I had been coated in filth.

"I can't wait for a shower," Athena grumbled as the train doors closed and we left the station.

"And me."

"And me," Annie agreed. "I might have two."

"And me."

"And me." I picked at the corner of my nail, flicking a piece of nail polish away.

"Are you okay, Freddie?" Athena asked. "You're quieter than normal this morning."

The truth of it was, the King's Cross party had been somewhat of an eye opener. Was sneaking out of Mapleton Manor to go to a party like that even worth it? I'd had an awful time. I was pretty sure someone had lifted the twenty pound note out of my pocket and it was the grottiest and grossest place I had ever been.

"I was just thinking that maybe I should pull back on the partying for a bit," I said quietly. "That place was disgusting."

"Tell me about it," Athena agreed. "It wouldn't be a bad idea to just chill out for a while. Fenella will understand. She can't expect you to go running down there every time she asks you to. Besides, isn't she thinking about going to St Finbars too? You'll be together for another four years before you know it."

Athena's words, while well meant, gave me an uncomfortable squirm in my stomach. *Another four years...*

I shook my head to clear my thoughts and forced a smile. "You're right. And she will understand, I'm sure."

"I just can't wait for Christmas," Annie said as she stretched out on her seat. "Two whole weeks in Aviemore."

Athena nodded. "It was so nice of Harriet to invite us, though it's a shame Jemima and Alicia have to miss it. I wonder what her family is like. Have either of you met any of them?"

Annie and I shook our heads. "Her brother was supposed to be at the dance last year, but I don't think he turned up," Annie said.

"Typical boy," I said with a teasing smile. "I just can't wait to get out on the mountain. I've missed skiing."

"Hmm. I've missed sitting by log-burner fires and sipping hot chocolate," Athena said.

Annie and I groaned and rolled our eyes at her. Athena made a very unladylike gesture and slid down in her seats, closing her eyes for a nap. Annie soon did the same, and it was just me left alone with my thoughts.

Aviemore would be the perfect escape for me to try and clear my head. To try to figure out just what I wanted to do with my life. I was eighteen now — I wasn't a little kid anymore. But it was clear that no matter what I decided, someone would be unhappy.

Did I want that someone to be me?

15

It was a chilly morning. The moon was still out and the last dark remnants of the night hadn't dispersed yet. I hopped from foot to foot as I hugged my arms around myself. Athena was around the side of the building, sneaking a sly cigarette. Annie and Cassandra huddled close together to ward off the cold air and Harriet was a bundle of uncontained excitement.

"I can't wait until you all see the chalet," Harriet said with a wide smile. "It's huge! And so pretty. We're going to have a fantastic holiday, I can just feel it."

"I love Aviemore," Athena said as she rounded the building. "The night skiing there is amazing."

"Tell me about, I can't wait," I agreed. I had always loved skiing — we had enjoyed many a family holiday to ski resorts and Mummy had always fretted dreadfully because Augustus and I would disappear all day.

Mummy had sent all my equipment over the week before so I didn't have to bother with renting anything.

"How long until your parents get here, Harriet?" Annie asked as her teeth chattered.

Harriet checked her watch. "Any minute now, I think."

"That's what you said an hour ago," Cassandra grumbled.

Harriet, in all her excited glory, had pestered us relentlessly until we'd finally crawled out of bed. It was an early start to the day anyway, but Harriet had insisted we get up even earlier just in case her parents were here pronto.

They weren't.

And now we were on the verge of revolt.

"Oh, look!" Harriet cried. "They're coming!"

We all turned to see a vehicle creep up the drive.

Thank God! "Guys, I'm going to run to the loo quickly before we get going."

Athena nodded in acknowledgement and started to pick up her gear.

I hurried inside to the bathroom. The drive to Aviemore could take around ten hours…not including breaks. In the past when I'd visited, we had driven overnight so it hadn't felt as long, or we'd flown straight in from Monaco. Today would be a special kind of torture.

My backpack was stock full of snacks, drinks and a couple of books. The reading for my English Literature class this year was incredible, and I was looking forward to reading most of them. I was in the middle of *Birdsong* by Sebastian Faulks and I was completely in love with it. Also tucked away in my bag was *The Great Gatsby* by F. Scott Fitzgerald and *In Cold Blood* by Truman Capote.

When I returned outside, the girls were busy loading their gear into a comfortable looking people carrier. I touched Harriet's shoulder so she knew I had returned as I grabbed my backpack up off the ground.

"Good, you're here," she said with a smile. She gestured to the two people who were busy filling up the rear of the car. It was starting to look as though we had packed for a six-month excursion. "This is my father, Glen, and my mother, Julia."

"Hello," Glen said.

"Lovely to meet you," Julia said.

"You too. Can I help?" I asked them.

Julia shook her head. "We've got it, don't worry. You had best go find a seat, I think the others have already started squabbling."

Why didn't that surprise me?

"Where's Pan?" Harriet asked.

"Trying to get the radio to work," Glen said. "All we got was static on the drive over here."

Harriet grabbed my hand and tugged me to the front of the people carrier. "You have to meet my brother. All the girls love him, though I can't for the life of me understand why."

I laughed. "All sisters feel that way, I imagine. I'll probably be the same about Augustus."

Harriet opened the passenger door at the front seat to reveal a boy crouched over and tinkering with a mass of exposed wires under the dashboard. "What on earth are you doing?" she asked curiously.

"Ensuring I don't have to listen to girlish chatter for the next ten hours," he said. "The radio is broken and I'm trying to fix it."

A shiver crept up my spine. There was something familiar about that voice. I couldn't quite place it, but a billion butterflies took flight in my stomach when I heard it.

"Ha ha," Harriet groaned. "I wanted to introduce you to my friend."

"I met them all."

"Not this one. She was in the loo when you got here."

"Good. Thinking ahead and being considerate of others — I like her already."

Harriet swatted his shoulder. "Will you just get up, please?"

The boy huffed and sat back upright. He looked at Harriet with an exasperated look on his face. The boy slid his green eyes over to mine and I watched them, in a disjointed sort of way, widen in recognition. "Freddie."

Harriet glanced between Peter and I. "Do you two know each other?"

"No," I said quickly. My heart pounded in my chest at his sudden appearance in my life. Blood roared behind my ears and I wanted to be far, far away from the situation. "We met very briefly at the dance last term."

"You never said you had met my brother," Harriet said.

"I didn't know he was," I said, unable to help but give Peter an accusing glance.

"And I didn't know she was your friend."

"Did you know that Jemima was?" The question was out of my mouth before I'd even known I was going to ask it. *Stupid mouth.*

"What?" Peter asked with a frown.

I shook my head and plastered on a fake smile. "I'm going to find a seat," I told Harriet.

She nodded and followed me as I turned and fled like the hounds of hell were snapping at my ankles.

I jumped inside the people carrier, ducking my head at the last minute so I didn't whack my head off the roof. I'd topped out at five feet eleven and I thought I was finally done with growing. Most of the seats were taken. My friends occupied the first two rows of seats and in the third there was a lone grey backpack—the only backpack that I had never seen before—on the double seat.

Ten hours sitting next to Peter...hearing him potentially talk about Jemima... *No thanks.*

Harriet was about to take her seat next to Athena. I grabbed her arm and tried to wipe the terrified look off my face. "Would you mind if I stole your seat? The only other one is in the back and I might get car sick."

Harriet frowned. "Seriously? But you travel everywhere."

I nodded. "True, but I usually have tablets that help but I forgot them."

"We're still here, you can run up and grab them."

"Er, I meant that I have run out of them. Please, Harriet?"

She glanced past me and I could sense another argument was coming. I felt awful—she obviously didn't want to be stuck sitting next to her brother all day. But however much she didn't want that, I wanted it considerably less for myself.

"You don't want to be in a car that reeks of vomit, do you, Harriet?" Athena asked from her seat.

Harriet cringed. "Uh, no. Definitely not. Fine, Freddie, you can have my seat."

Athena scooted over from her window seat and patted it. "Sit here, Freddie."

I heaved a sigh of relief and scrambled over her to the seat. I hugged my backpack to my chest and felt like I had just dodged a bullet. My gaze was pulled to the front seat, where Peter was twisted around to look at me. A confused, almost hurt look radiated in his eyes. I knew he understood what had just happened—that I had just thrown a fit to get out of sitting beside him.

But what did he expect?

Stupid boy.

A few minutes later, the car was fully loaded, Harriet and Peter had taken their seats and someone slammed the doors closed.

"What's going on?" Athena whispered once we'd started going.

"Nothing, why?" I asked, twisting my fingers.

"You're on edge. Do you want to talk about it?"

"No," I whispered. I leaned my head against the cool glass of the window and closed my eyes. My body was taut with adrenaline and tension. How on earth was I going to get through two weeks of living in the same house as Peter?

It wasn't fair…I felt cheated and blindsided.

Most of all, I was so, so glad that Jemima had gone on a holiday abroad with her family.

I hadn't intended on falling asleep, I had just wanted to put an end to the questions. But the soft murmur of my friends' voices as they chatted in the dark car must have lulled me to sleep.

The next thing I knew, a hand gently shook my shoulder, coaxing me awake. I prised open my eyelids, and had a near heart attack when I saw Peter's face was mere inches from mine.

I swore and reared backwards, smacking my head on the window. "Ouch," I mumbled.

"Are you all right?" Peter asked, his eyebrows pulled together in concern.

"Fine, fine," I said in a hurry. Glancing around, I saw that the car was empty save the two of us. A quick look out of the window confirmed we were at a service station. It was full light now, and a soft sprinkle of rain fell from the grey skies. "Where is everyone?"

"Inside," Peter said, jerking his thumb over his shoulder. "I only woke you in case you wanted to get something to eat, or use the loo or something."

"Right, yes, of course." I stood up and damn near body-checked him out of my way. "Thank you." I practically vaulted out of the car and hurried up the steps into the service station.

"Wait, hang on a second," Peter called. He jogged to catch up with me, rushing ahead to hold the door open. Peter motioned for me to go in. "I don't want to push you, but I can't help but think I've done something wrong. Is everything okay?"

I smiled so wide it hurt my cheeks. "Of course, what could be wrong?"

He shrugged and jammed his hands into his jeans pockets.

I had to admit, he had looked scrummy all dressed up the night of the dance, but he looked down right delectable now in jeans, a navy blue fleece and trainers. His hair was natural with no product in it, and the golden brown locks bordered on scruffy. I'd bet his parents would nag him to get a haircut, or to do something with the unruly looking hair, but I thought it looked good on him. Loose, carefree and casual. And hot. So, so hot.

"I know I was caught off guard when I saw you this morning, so you had to have felt like that too."

"A little," I admitted. "But I'm fine. Promise."

Peter nodded. He opened his mouth to say something else, but I jumped in before he got the chance.

"I have to pee. Like, really bad. Excuse me," I said as I darted around him and rushed away.

"The toilets are the other way, Freddie," Peter drawled.

Of course they are... This was going to be a long two weeks.

Somehow I survived the journey to Aviemore. I stayed awake the rest of the way, so I could stick to my friends like glue when we stopped for breaks. I didn't want to risk being alone with Peter again.

I was a pretty frank and open person, and usually gave honest answers when questioned. The last thing I wanted was for him to keep pushing me, and I ended up telling him just how hurt I was — *had been* — over his choosing my friend rather than me.

So my plan of action was avoidance. I could manage that, surely. The days would be spent out on the slopes, and I'm sure he would go out at night to the local scene.

Maybe.

I hope.

I just had to make sure we weren't alone together. Ever.

The scenery as we ventured farther in Scotland was gorgeous. Snow-capped mountains dominated the views and sparkling white snow covered every surface as we drove into Aviemore. I loved seeing all the chalets, like rows of small wooden palaces with warm, glowing light pouring from their huge windows.

Harriet's family chalet was huge. It was absolutely gorgeous, made of gleaming thick tree trunks. The chalet was surrounded by tall, snow-laden pine trees that bowed under the weight.

We clambered out of the car. I was eager to stretch my legs and to investigate my home for the next two weeks.

Athena grinned and draped her arm over my shoulder. "Not bad, huh?"

I snorted a laugh. "Yes, Athena. Not bad."

She was about to say something else when a snowball smacked Athena right in the face. I darted away from her in case there was another one coming with my name one it—which I would bet good money there was—and spluttered a laugh at the sight of Athena wiping snow from her face.

"This means war!" she bellowed. Her voice reverberated around us, bouncing off the mountains. She bent to scoop up a handful of snow. Athena played rounders, and had an excellent, very accurate, throwing arm. She flung the snowballs at anyone in range, and she hit her targets every time.

I shrieked as an icy ball of snow hit the back of my head and dripped down my collar to my neck. Annie laughed and ran away when I turned to glare at her. I made my own snowball and crept around the side of the car to get her back.

Spotting movement, I waited a few seconds until she was in prime range, drew my arm back and let it fly...straight in Glen's face. I had just inadvertently pelted my gracious host with a ball of snow.

I gasped, my eyes widening in horror. "Oh, God, I'm so sorry!" I said in a rush.

The other girls came running, and seeing my stricken face, burst out laughing.

"I think we should unload the car before any more snowballs are thrown my way," Glen said in a dry voice.

"I'm very sorry again," I said quietly.

"You should be." Glen gave me a stony look. "I have fantastic aim. I will get you back...when you least expect it."

Athena coughed back a laugh and elbowed me in the side. "Come on, let's get our stuff."

We helped Glen and Julia unload the car, and hauled all our stuff inside.

If anything, the interior of the chalet was even more beautiful than the outside. The great room had spectacular views of the snow-covered woods and mountains, and I would bet it filled with light as the sun rose in the morning. A large wood-burning stove was the central point in the room, with comfy, over-stuffed couches and armchairs surrounding it. Most had thick, warm blankets thrown over the back and plump pillows resting on the cushions.

Intricate wooden carvings decorated the space, and most of the furniture seemed to be handmade pieces from wood, including an enormous dining table with matching chairs.

A huge, perfectly decorated Christmas tree dominated one corner, stretching almost as high as the ceiling. Underneath were piles of exquisitely wrapped gifts.

Harriet gave us a quick tour of the downstairs, which consisted of a beautiful, state-of-the-art kitchen. All the countertops were solid marble and the appliances were gleaming steel. The bathroom was just as large and elegant. On that level were three bedrooms—two of them were for guests and the other belonged to Peter.

Of course we were on the same level.

The guest bedrooms were stunning with wide windows giving beautiful views, and large bunk beds with thick, luxurious looking mattresses.

Upstairs was another bathroom, Harriet's bedroom, her parents' bedroom and a gorgeous loft space with a comfy armchair, bookcase and floor lamp. It allowed for the most amazing views out of the front sloping windows that reached all the way up to the roof, and of the great room below.

I could quite happily spend the rest of my life living in this chalet.

"You girls must be starving," Julia said when we returned from our tour. "I had a cook come in and prepare some things for us, I just have to heat it up. Cottage pie okay with everyone?"

We all nodded and offered our thanks. By the time we had unpacked our things and got situated, it was ready.

The lot of us gathered around the table to sit down to eat. Peter took the chair opposite me. I felt his eyes on me, but I focused instead on my food.

"Everyone looking forward to hitting the slopes tomorrow?" Glen asked as we all tucked into our dinner.

"I can't wait," Harriet answered. "But it's Freddie who is most excited, I think. She's so good."

"Is that right?" Glen asked.

I nodded. "I go most years with my family on a skiing holiday. My brother and I really enjoy it."

Glen smiled. "Then I imagine it will be you and Peter on the black slopes, then. He's the best out of all of us."

When I risked a glance at Peter, his gaze was glued to my face.

"Sounds like we'll be spending lots of time together," he said.

I forced a smile and nodded. *Awesome.*

Aviemore was exceptionally beautiful. An idyllic winter paradise, it had everything a snow sport enthusiast could ever want. The slopes at Cairn Gorm Mountain were some of the best in Europe, and provided not only excellent skiing, but plenty of routes for different levels. Making it easier to hide from people you didn't necessarily want to see.

For the first three days of the holidays, I joined the other girls on the easier slopes. It was simple and boring, especially for me who had been skiing since I was tiny. I itched to carry on up the mountain to the more difficult slopes, instead of following my friends everywhere. But needs must.

We traipsed into the lodge at lunchtime to grab some food. The other girls were tired after their exertion, but I felt my muscles lagging, demanding to be put to good use instead of wasted on unchallenging slopes.

"Thomas is absolutely gorgeous," Cassandra said after we had ordered. "How lucky are we that there's a group of boys all handsome and single and *we* met them?"

That morning on the slopes a large pack of boys had migrated our way. They were on a big family holiday full of grandparents, parents, aunts, uncles, brothers, sisters and cousins. And my friends had almost fainted with their own good fortune that, as Cassandra had mentioned, it made for a pack of good-looking boys close to our age.

"No way, Steve is nicer," Annie argued.

"As if!" Harriet cried. "The best looking has to be Simon. What do you think, Freddie? Who do you think is the handsomest?"

"Oh," I said quietly. "Um, all of them, I suppose."

"*All* of them?" Annie asked with a laugh. "Are you feeling greedy, Freddie?"

The truth was I had absolutely no interest in any of the boys we had met. My head was far too full with one boy in particular to take notice of any new ones. I forced a smile and shook my head. "They were all handsome. But none tall enough for my liking, I'm afraid."

Cassandra sighed. "Typical Freddie logic."

I sat back in my chair and let the rest of the conversation drift over me. Our meal came and I ate mostly in silence. The others were too busy discussing their boys' merits and looks to pay me any attention, which suited me just fine.

"Aren't you bored, Freddie?" Annie asked, suddenly.

She snapped me out of the ramblings I had just reminded myself to try to get out of, and I sat up straighter in my chair. "Me? Bored? Not at all, why?"

"Because you're miles better than all of us at skiing and you've been on the beginner slopes for the last few days," Annie replied.

"Who's on the beginner slopes?"

My heart began to gallop when I heard Peter's voice behind me. He pulled out the only free chair — the one beside me — and placed his plate on the table.

"Freddie," Harriet answered. "She's so good, Pan. She's wasted on the easy slopes with us."

I felt his eyes on my face and my cheeks warmed in response. But I couldn't look at him.

"Are you nervous about being alone, Freddie?" Cassandra asked. "I know it's not like you, but I'm sure Peter would take you—"

"No!" I exclaimed, far louder than I had intended. My cheeks burned hotter and I gave Cassandra a wide smile. "Sorry, I meant, no, thanks. It's...er...my ankle! Remember I broke it over the summer? It's been giving me a spot of bother and I don't want to risk re-injuring it by pushing myself."

Annie giggled. "You could have just told us that. We've been wondering what on earth was wrong with you for the last few days."

I gave her another ridiculously wide and cheesy smile. "Well, now you know!" My friends were going to think I had gone mad...

Athena swiftly changed the subject onto the boys they had met again, taking the attention off of me. That girl really knew how to look out for me.

Once lunch was finished, we trudged back outside. I wasn't particularly looking forward to another stint on the baby slopes, but it was better than being stuck indoors as I faked some ailment or other.

I finished putting all my gear on first, then I wandered away from the group. My eyes found the top of the mountain, and the skiers on the black routes. Colourful, tiny bodies zoomed down the mountainside as though they'd been born with skis on their feet. I longed to be up there.

Peter appeared beside me, though he didn't look at me as he finished shrugging on his ski jacket. There was a pause before he spoke, as though he was choosing his words carefully. "I could take you on one of the more difficult routes if you didn't want to jump straight on the black ones. Your ankle should be fine, but I understand it might be scary for you."

The easy confidence that had made him so appealing the night of the dance was absent from his voice. He sounded tentative and unsure as he spoke, like he had no idea how I would react to his offer.

My heart pinched because I knew he was just trying to be nice, but the memory of him with my friend refused to leave and my pride was too damaged to even think about brushing it aside.

I forced a smile and shook my head. "I'm fine with my friends, but thanks."

"No problem. The offer stands if you change your mind," Peter said, his face sombre. There was no hint of his playfulness or teasing nature. And I couldn't help but feel guilty that I had caused him some amount of hurt feelings.

"Come on, back to it, Freddie," Annie called as she walked past us. "You need the practice!"

I smiled at my friend, and with one last quick glance at Peter, I hurried after her.

If I had to spend one more day on the easy slopes, I was going to lose my mind. I'd spent the day after Peter had made his offer with the girls again, and come that evening I had more or less decided to fake that ailment and stay at the chalet. I was morose and forlorn, and a little bit angry at Peter for ruining my holiday.

I had given up Christmas with my family to come with my friends to Aviemore, and I felt even guiltier since I wasn't even having a good time. I was pretty much sabotaging the trip for myself because I couldn't act like a grown up and get over my wounded pride to go with Peter on the harder slopes.

Stupid boy. Why did he have to be Harriet's brother anyway?

After dinner, the girls wanted to go in the hot tub that was out on the back deck, but I cried off. In truth, I wanted a little bit of time alone. I wanted to disappear into my book for a few hours so I could forget about real life for a while and melt into a fantasy one.

I curled up in a big squishy armchair and covered my legs with a soft blanket. Soft snowfall fluttered past the windows, and Christmas carols that Harriet's parents were listening to downstairs drifted up to complete my little escape in the reading loft.

In fact, the only thing that could top it off would be —

"Hot chocolate?" Peter asked.

I jumped about a foot in the air and dropped my book on the floor. My heart pounded in my chest and I glanced up at him to see the cringing look on his face.

"Sorry, I didn't mean to frighten you," he said. "I should know better, I'm always so far into a book it takes a bomb going off to pull me out of it."

"Hmm," I mumbled, reaching down to pick up my book.

"*Birdsong*," Peter said as he glimpsed at the cover. "How are you enjoying it?"

"Uh…a lot?" *Shoot me, shoot me now.*

Peter cracked a smile. He placed the two mugs of steaming hot chocolate onto the small table between the two armchairs. *Good Lord, he's even added whipped cream and chocolate Snickers…*

"Thanks," I said, offering a small smile.

"No problem." Peter then lowered himself into the empty chair.

God. He's staying.

My mind started racing though all the plausible excuses I could use to leave. What a wimp I was.

"I hope you don't mind the intrusion, but I was hoping that we could talk," Peter said, his voice low and sombre.

"What about?" I asked, my voice anything but low. In fact, it was high and shrill and so, so unflattering.

"That night at the dance." Peter blew out a breath and scrubbed a hand over his face. "I had thought that we'd— I had fun with you, Freddie. I thought we'd really hit it off. And I know you got my letter. So, at first I thought you were just making it clear that you weren't interested without hurting my feelings. But now…you're acting like *I* hurt *you*. And I have no idea how."

My throat tightened. Could he really be so obtuse to not think that I would be hurt over him ditching me for another girl?

"Freddie, please tell me what I did, because I genuinely don't have a clue and it's driving me crazy. But most all I want to know so that I can apologise and we can hopefully move past this."

What on earth could I say? *Well, I had sort of got my hopes up that you could have been my boyfriend, but I saw you and my friend pressed up against each other like superglue was involved, so I sort of got a bit upset by that? But never mind, don't worry about it. I'm soooo over it…not.*

I looked over at Peter. His eyebrows were drawn together and his eyes did seem full of remorse. A part of me wanted to reassure him just to take that look out of his eyes. I hated people in pain.

But no way did I want him thinking I was this hung up on him still. So I slapped on a smile and prayed it looked genuine. "I'm sorry. You were right, I...wasn't interested in you like that. I couldn't think of a way to tell you, so I tried to act indifferent and just avoid you so things wouldn't be awkward." *Liar, liar pants on fire.*

Peter's eyebrows rose. "Right. I see. So I didn't do anything to upset you?"

"Nope. Nothing. Not. A. Thing." *My nose had better not grow like Pinocchio's.*

For a moment, Peter didn't speak. He processed what I'd said, then relaxed into his chair and sipped his hot chocolate. Not exactly the reaction I had expected. "Fair enough. Now that that's cleared up, are you going to stop avoiding me? You must be bored useless on those baby slopes. I take it the ankle excuse was just that — an excuse?"

Well bugger, I'd walked right into that one. I had hoped that if I told Peter I wasn't interested then his sensitive male pride would take control of his sense and he would go in a strop like a child, and therefore he would want to avoid me as much as I wanted to avoid him. But now he wanted to spend more time together? I was starting to question this boy's sanity.

Peter grinned and took another sip of his drink. "I'll take your silence as a yes. We've cleared the air, there's nothing to feel awkward about anymore. And I do like you, Freddie. You're a cool girl. I'd like us to be friends."

My smile faltered. "Sure. Friends." *The last thing in the world I want is to be friends with you...*

16

The following morning, Peter waited for me at the ski lift so we could head farther up the mountain. My heart raced and I thought I would puke, but somehow I kept it together. Peter chatted like we were old friends, as though I hadn't acted like an ice queen for the last few days.

Part of me appreciated it, was glad that he was acting like the boy I remembered from the night of the dance. But a small voice whispered in my mind that the more he acted like the guy I had really liked, the more I would forget who he *really* was.

There was a moment as I stood at the top of trail, looking out at the world before me, where I felt…better. My heart wasn't so heavy and weary, my nerves weren't so rattled. The scent of crisp, white snow teased my nostrils, the pale winter sun warm on my face. It reminded me of every skiing holiday I had gone on as a child. I would brag to Daddy about how well I had done that day and he would cheer me on and make me feel like I was his entire world.

Daddy had always said I was his greatest gift. And I was—literally. I was born on his birthday and it made me feel all the closer to him.

I tipped my face towards the sky and closed my eyes. *God, I miss you, Daddy.* Grief didn't wash through me, sorrow wasn't making my eyes tear. For the first time, thinking about Daddy wasn't painful.

With a deep breath, I opened my eyes and threw my body forward. Wind howled in my ears as I hurtled down the trail. The world raced past me and I laughed. The greatest feeling about skiing for me was when I felt like I was flying.

A body came forward and matched pace with me. I glanced over to see Peter on his snowboard, cutting through the snow like an expert. He grinned at me, and I couldn't help but return it.

I felt free...like I was capable of anything. Including my own happiness.

"You're amazing," Peter said as he caught his breath. We had reached the bottom of the trail and were waiting for the next ski lift to take us back up. "How did you last four days with your friends?"

I shrugged, a little embarrassed to be reminded of my behaviour. I think Peter knew without my having to say a word that I'd had more fun with him those first few hours than I had in four whole days with my friends. It felt great to let my muscles loose and really go for it.

"It's nice to finally have someone to go down the mountain with," Peter said. "Harriet never bothered to push herself enough to progress, and our parents are more interested in socialising."

"I always had my brother to ski with. Augustus is like me and really sporty, so we did a lot together growing up."

"You're lucky to be so close to him. Harriet and I, while really close in age, are so different in the things we like and are interested in," Peter said.

We climbed onto the ski lift, our legs pressed together. Even through all the layers I wore, a shiver managed to snake down my body.

"I love Harriet," I said, trying to shake away the unsettled feeling of being so close to him. "She's a great friend."

"She always speaks highly of all you girls. I never realised you were one of them the night of the dance." Peter opened his mouth like he had something more to say, but changed his mind at the last minute.

We jumped off the ski lift and got ready for another trip down the mountain. As I put my mask into place, Peter touched my arm. "Loser buys the hot chocolates?"

I got ready to take off. "Hmm...sure!" And I pushed off, leaving him at the top.

"Hey! Wait up, you cheat!" he bellowed after me.

He caught up to me in seconds. We were neck and neck for a few hundred yards but then Peter crept in front of me, creating a fragile gap.

Not going to happen...

Twisting my hips and narrowing my gaze in determination, I closed the gap and grasped a tiny advantage that put me in front of him. *Yes! I'm going to...*

Peter passed me again with a grin.

I stumbled, caught unaware.

He peered back at me over his shoulder, and I gritted my teeth. I would not be beaten.

Using every amount of force in my body, I pushed myself forward with renewed vigour.

The distance closed.

A foot.

Half a foot.

An inch.

Then...

I sailed past him at the very last second, stealing the win right out from under him. Skidding to a stop, I gave Peter a triumphant grin. He returned the smile...and it warmed me to my cold toes.

Peter treated me to a hot chocolate in the lodge. And whether it was from the peace I'd found at the top of the mountain, or the exercise, I felt relaxed around him. We found seats on a large couch in front of the fireplace, and we sipped our hot drinks, chatting and getting to know each other again.

The longer I sat with him, the harder it was to remember what a bad idea it would be to let myself enjoy his company too much. After our hot chocolates we browsed the gift shop and I found a new wristband with the Cairngorm National Park emblem and I also bought a postcard to send to Mummy.

Peter and I had a quick lunch before getting back to our sports and spending the rest of the afternoon competing with each other. It wasn't until we headed back to our rendezvous point to be picked up by Glen and Julia that I got a chance to see my friends.

The girls gushed about the boys they'd seen again. They'd ended up spending the afternoon together in the lodge and forgetting all about their skiing. But that was my friends — who wants to bother with skis when boys are involved?

When we got back to the chalet, I grabbed a quick shower to wash away the day's exercise. I was bone-tired and weary as I trudged back to my room. Pulling on leggings, a T-shirt, a thick woolly jumper and cosy socks, I lay down on my bed…just for a second.

I was startled awake by Athena jerking the door open, letting a flood of light from the hall into the room.

"Are you sleeping?" she asked as she stood over the bed.

"I *was*," I grumbled. A yawn almost split my face in half.

Athena laughed quietly. "Well get up, dinner's ready." She whipped off the blanket that had covered me.

I swore and curled up in a tight ball.

"Hurry up, Freddie."

"Coming, coming," I mumbled. I sat up in bed and stretched my arms out. One last yawn and I stood up to leave the room.

As I closed the bedroom door behind me, another door opened. Peter stepped into the hall from the bathroom with just a towel around his waist.

Water droplets ran down his bare chest. His bare, beautifully sculpted, tanned chest. The planes and curves held me riveted as I dragged my eyes down his body to the thin trail of hair that began under his belly button and disappeared beneath his towel.

Snapping my eyes back up, I took in his damp hair, which was a darker shade than normal. His brilliant green eyes were bright and heated as he watched me watch him.

"Freddie, do I need to come back in there?" Athena called from the great room.

My cheeks burned. "No!" I yelped, quickly turning away from Peter. "I'm coming!" I darted down the hall and the sound of Peter's amused chuckle followed me.

I had no idea how long I'd lain staring up at the wooden slats of the bunk above me. Athena breathed softly in her sleep, a hypnotic, rhythmic sound that did nothing to aid my own sleep.

At dinner I had hardly been able to concentrate on the meal in front of me, even though I'd been starving from burning so many calories on the slopes that day. I hadn't been able to stop seeing Peter virtually naked with water droplets clinging to his skin.

It made one thing perfectly clear—I was still completely, undeniably attracted to him. My pulse had raced all night and I hadn't dared raise my eyes from my plate for fear of inadvertently locking eyes with him.

I had disappeared off to bed early in the dim hope that I would be so exhausted I would slip into a dreamless sleep and not have to think any more about Peter and his naked body. Instead, I lay awake, my mind and my body a thrum of nervous energy. Athena had crept into the room around eleven, and settled into her bunk. And at almost two a.m., I was still waiting for sleep.

After another few minutes, Athena's rhythmic breathing turned into a guttural snore. There was no possible chance for me to fall asleep now. I climbed out of bed and tiptoed down the dark hall to the kitchen.

Pale moonlight filtered into the room, the thick covering of snow illuminating the night. I made a cup of tea and raided the cupboards, looking for some biscuits or anything else I could snack on.

"For a burglar, you're not very quiet."

I yelped in fright at the sound of Peter's voice, and I spun around to face him, clutching my chest as my heart pounded. "What on earth are you doing, creeping up on people in the middle of the night?" Even in my fright, I couldn't help but notice how good Peter looked in his pyjama bottoms and worn grey T-shirt.

His clothes did nothing to help me forget about how good he looked beneath them.

I tugged at the hem of my shorts, wishing I had worn more. I felt all sorts of exposed, especially given the pyjamas were just a little on the small side now and hugged my curves and showed off quite a lot of leg.

He shrugged, seeming unperturbed at having just scared me senseless. "I heard someone raiding the kitchen. I thought it was either an intruder or some pest had broken in to eat all our food." His lips twitched. "I can see the latter is right."

I stuck my tongue out at him when he turned around to open the fridge. He took out the milk and made himself a cup of tea from the freshly boiled kettle. Once it was made, Peter opened the cupboard next to the oven and pulled out a packet of chocolate Hobnobs.

"You must be starving since you barely touched dinner," Peter said as he left the kitchen, jerking his head to signal for me to follow him. He placed his drink and the biscuits on a coffee table in the great room, and sat down on one of the big comfy couches.

The red lights of the eight-foot tall Christmas tree gave a beautiful ambiance to the room and I couldn't believe Christmas was only a few days away.

He had noticed I had only picked at my food? My belly dipped at the thought of him watching me...noticing me. "I'm sorry if I woke you," I said as I sat at the opposite end of the couch.

Peter shook his head. "I was awake anyway. Then I heard you tiptoeing around and decided I could use a drink. So what's keeping you up?"

You... "I'm not sure. Thinking about home, probably." While this was an excuse, it was also completely true. Mummy had told me to go off and have fun with my friends for the holidays and they were going to Barbados anyway, but I couldn't stop thinking that they were already one family member down this Christmas, and now I was missing too. Louisa would either love all the extra attention or would act like the 'spirited' girl we had all come to...mildly put up with.

"Have you ever been away from your family at Christmas before?" Peter asked.

"Once or twice," I answered. "But I feel guilty this time because it's the first Christmas since my father died."

Peter blew out a breath. "I'm sorry, Freddie. Were you close?"

I nodded. "Very."

He reached out and stroked the back of my hand. "Then this must be really hard for you. No wonder you've been quiet."

That, and I had been completely thrown off guard by the reappearance of Peter in my life.

"Or have you just been completely distracted by all the trees around here and you're busy trying to restrain yourself from climbing them?"

I barked out a laugh. "No, of course not!" My lips twitched into a smile as I slid my eyes over him. "But at least I could climb them if I wanted to."

Peter laughed—I had forgotten how rich and inviting the sound was. "You know, it took weeks for my arm to heal. What are Mapleton Manor trees made out of, anyway?" He shook his head and chuckled quietly. "None of my friends believed me about the cool, tree-climbing chick I met that night. They think you're a figment of my imagination."

I couldn't help the smile that spread wider across my face. "Maybe you hit your head on the way down and I really am all in your head."

Peter's hand that had been drawing lazy circles on the back of mine stilled. He threaded his fingers between mine and squeezed my hand gently. "You feel pretty real to me."

My pulse skyrocketed. What was he doing? What was I doing? God...this couldn't be good for my health.

"Is this okay?" Peter asked, nodding to our clasped hands.

I nodded, unable to speak.

"Tell me another mad story from when you were young." Peter's eyes were soft and encouraging and he gave me a warm smile at my startled expression.

Whatever I had thought he would say next...that hadn't been it. But I was grateful for the reprieve nonetheless.

"Once, after a hurricane at my prep school, the cricket pitch completely flooded. One of the work staff put a shark fin in the middle of it so we would all think a real shark was swimming around," I blurted out.

Peter laughed. "Brilliant. What else?"

"Um...I once I rescued a chameleon from a souk in Marrakesh. I smuggled him back home in my coat pocket."

He grinned. "Big animal lover then?"

I nodded. "The biggest. We were allowed loads of pets at prep school, and I took my hamster, Butterscotch, to church with me in my pocket once. But he bit through the lining and ended up scurrying around in my hem. We don't really have many pets at school now. Though there is a house rat called Templeton, but if anyone wants to take him out they have to use a lead because he's so fast."

Peter stroked my hand again and shuffled closer to me on the couch. It was then, when I didn't panic at his invasion of my personal space, that I realised what he had been doing. In encouraging me to talk he had put me at ease and I'd started to relax.

"You lead a very interesting life, Freddie."

"It's never dull, that's for sure," I said quietly.

"Is it weird how much I like to hear your stories? I never know what to expect—you're the exact opposite of predictable." He dropped his gaze for a moment before lifting his eyes to mine again. "I'm glad we got things sorted out. You're making this holiday one of the best ever for me."

"I am?" I asked quietly.

Peter nodded. He brought his free hand up to cup my cheek, his thumb stroking in featherlight sweeps across my cheekbone. "I never stopped thinking about you."

His words made my head swim. I wanted to drown in them.

"I know what you said the other day, but I can't help but feel that there is something more here. Don't you feel it, too?" he asked in a low, throaty voice.

"I—"

Peter leaned in a fraction closer. His breath warmed my cheek, his scent flooding my senses. My eyelids fluttered closed as I waited...for what?

The moment I imagined his lips landing on mine, I was assaulted by the image of Jemima in his arms—pressed against him, smiling at him, him smiling at her...the kiss they had to have shared when I'd looked away.

I jumped to my feet, my momentum knocking Peter back against the couch. "Sorry," I squeaked. "This isn't— I don't..." I sighed. "I'm going back to bed." So I left Peter, and the untouched tea and biscuits, and hurried back to my room.

If finding sleep had been hard before, it was flat-out impossible now.

Come morning, I was tired, cranky, and not at all my usually upbeat and colourful self. Over breakfast, I kept my head down so I didn't risk catching Peter's eyes, and on the drive to the resort, I made sure to sit as far away from him as I could.

I tried to appear cool and collected, but under the surface was simmering anger. How could someone be so at odds with the person they appeared to be? For all intents and purposes, Peter was my absolute dream boy. He was funny, smart, adventurous and absolutely gorgeous. Not to mention his number one quality — he was taller than I was.

And the worst part was that he seemed really into me. If I hadn't seen him with Jemima at the dance, I probably would never have realised he was a serial charmer, only interested in whatever girl was in front of him at the time.

Sometime before dawn I had decided to ski with my friends again. But when we arrived at the resort and I looked up at the mountain, I steeled my resolve and vowed not to let a silly boy ruin my holiday. I loved skiing and I was bloody good at it. There was more than enough mountain to go around and if I was careful I needn't see him all day.

Unlike the day before, where I had felt free and at peace whilst hurtling down the side of the mountain, today my thoughts kept me from truly feeling at ease. My mind was a whirling dervish that I couldn't seem to calm.

It hurt my concentration, and it came as no great surprise when I wiped out and ended up with a face full of snow. Huffing my annoyance at myself, Peter and the world in general, I unclipped my skis and shoved my mask up on top of my head.

A spray of snow was kicked up as someone skidded to a stop beside me.

"Are you okay? You came down pretty hard," Peter said, out of breath.

Peter...of course it's bloody Peter. "I'm fine," I said, rising to my feet.

"Are you sure? It looked—"

"I said I was fine, didn't I?" I snapped. I cringed at the poison in my words. It was hardly ever that I bit someone's head off, and I hated doing it. Even if they totally deserved it.

Peter's eyes narrowed, his eyebrows drawing together. "Right, am I missing something here again? What have I done now?"

"Nothing, just leave me alone," I mumbled, staring at the snow as though it held the answers that I needed.

"No," Peter said. He sat down and unclipped his snowboard. "You don't get to treat me like crap and avoid me without telling me what on earth is going through your head."

Guilt pinched in my chest. But why should I feel guilty? "Please, just leave me alone. And stay out of my way for the rest of the trip."

Peter huffed a laugh. "You're kidding, right? What happened to clearing the air and being friends?"

That was it—the final straw. "Because I don't want to be friends with you!" Turning away from him, I stomped towards the treeline, hauling my skis along with me. It wasn't easy to make a dramatic exit in full snow gear, but I thought I managed it just fine.

"Where are you going?" Peter shouted after me.

Away. Far away from here, you and everything else.

"Freddie, for God's sake, will you wait?" Peter caught my arm and spun me around to face him. "What is going on?"

"Nothing, just—"

"So what's changed? Why don't you want to be friends with me?"

I folded my arms across my chest. "Friends don't try to kiss other friends."

Peter's eyebrows shot up. "Excuse me? I was just reading your signals last night. You seemed interested—like the night of the dance. Was I wrong?"

No, he wasn't wrong…I'd just remembered what an awful mistake it would be. "Yes."

"You're lying. Why?"

"I'm not lying!"

Peter snorted. "You bloody are. Either to yourself or to me, but you are lying. Why all the back and forth, Freddie? Why do you act like you want more from me then treat me as though I'm the last person in the world you want to be around? Why all the games?"

"Oh, that's rich, coming from you," I said with a huff. "*All* of this is just a game to you! Is it an Upton thing? A boy thing? Or do you just like trying to get girls to fall for you when you have no true feelings for them whatsoever?"

"What?" Peter asked with a blink.

"I was willing to try and be friends with you, but I realised even that is impossible."

"Why?"

"One word. Jemima."

"Jemima?" Peter repeated. "Who's Jemima?"

I rolled my eyes and resisted the urge to whack him with my skis. "Are there so many girls in your life you have trouble keeping them straight?"

"I do if I have no idea who they are!" Peter said with exasperation. "Freddie, I don't have a clue what you're on about."

I chuckled quietly and shook my head. "This just makes it even worse. Did you not bother to even get her name?"

"*Who?*"

"Jemima's!" I cried. "Jemima! My friend, Jemima! Jemima, the girl I found you with *minutes* after I left you at the dance! Jemima, Jemima, Jemima!" *Good Lord, I'm having a nervous breakdown…*

Peter blinked again, processing my outburst. He held his hand out. "Okay, I'm not really sure where to start with all of that. This 'Jemima' from the dance…if she's who I'm thinking of, no, I never did get her name. I was standing by myself when a girl approached me and asked me to dance. As I was politely declining, she got this sad look on her face and said no one had wanted to dance with her all night, so I agreed to be a nice guy. She was a little on the clingy side, but nice enough. I told her that I was waiting for someone and she smiled and said that was fine, she would disappear as soon she returned." Peter's face softened and he took a step towards me. "But you never did, Freddie. The lights came up and I couldn't find you. I made my friend wait until every single other bus and car had left before I finally got in the car, just to make sure I hadn't missed you."

The anger began to dissipate. "But," I said quietly, "you both looked really happy together. You were smiling, she was smiling. Later, she couldn't stop bragging about the fitty that she pulled."

Peter snorted a laugh. "Trust me, there was no pulling of any kind. The second the song ended, I make my excuses and left."

Why would Jemima lie? She was a gorgeous girl and I knew that she had the pick of the Stonebridge boys that night. Which again begged the question...why would Jemima lie?

"When you told her you were waiting for someone, did you tell her who?" I asked.

"Yes, I did."

The breath was punched out of me by his confirmation. So it turned out I really had been betrayed...I just hadn't realised by who. One of my best friends.

"Freddie, are you all right?" Peter asked, taking another step towards me. "You look like you've had a shock."

"I think I have," I breathed. "I can't believe her."

"Who? I'm sorry, I'm so lost it's unbelievable."

I scrubbed at my eyes that stung with unshed tears. I refused to cry. This year alone had proved what things were worth crying over, and Jemima and her selfish, vindictive nature were not one of them. "That girl— Jemima—is one of my best friends. If you told her it was me you were waiting for, then that means she orchestrated the whole thing to hurt me. To get one up on me. To *beat* me." I laughed ruefully. "The ironic thing is, when I saw the two of you together and she looked so happy, I decided to pretend I had no idea who you were so our friends wouldn't think badly of her. So she could have you. I'm an idiot."

"You're not an idiot, Freddie," Peter said, quietly. "You're amazing, and a true friend...even to those who don't deserve it."

"How can you even say that to me? I've been so horrible and unfair to you," I whispered. God, I felt awful. I wouldn't be surprised if Peter never wanted to see me again.

He closed the small distance between us and clasped my chin, tipping my face up so I would meet his eyes. "Frederica, you are the most interesting, loyal, funny person I have ever met. You reacted to what you thought you knew, and I can't blame you for that. If anything, it makes you a strong character to stand up for what you believe in and not let a boy you thought was a love rat sway you."

A laugh bubbled in my throat. "I'm so glad you're not a love rat."

"Me too. It sounds extremely complicated."

I clutched his wrists. "I really am sorry. And I wish I had just asked you to, save all this hassle."

"Then let this be a lesson on not making assumptions on what you *think* you see. And if you ever want to know something, just ask me. I promise I'll always be honest with you."

A light flurry of snow began to fall. I tilted my face up to the sky to watch the white flakes fall. I laughed, in part marvelling at the beauty, and also in relief. A huge weight had been lifted from my shoulders. What I had felt yesterday on the slopes wasn't freedom — *this* was.

Peter brushed away the flakes that melted on my skin. Snow clung to his thick eyelashes and a soft smile was playing on his lips. "I'm going to ask a direct question, now. Freddie...may I kiss you?"

I grinned and nodded, all but grabbing him and pulling his face down. Peter dipped his head, fitting his mouth over mine.

My stomach fizzed with excitement. I clutched his shoulders as he pressed against me. I thought I would combust. The heat inside my snow gear would surely set my outer layers on fire.

Peter slid his hands into my hair as he deepened the kiss. I sighed and kissed him back with everything I had. The reality of kissing Peter was so much better than the fantasies I'd scolded myself for having. The feel of his body, the natural scent of him combined with his heady aftershave, his delicious kisses all drove me to a state of excited bliss.

I never wanted it to end.

I wanted to stay on that mountain and kiss him forever.

I woke on Christmas morning and was all at once hit with a barrage of emotions. Athena practically fell out of the bunk above me and threw herself onto my bed.

"Come on, lazy bones! Don't you want to see what Santa brought you?" She grinned.

I smiled at her enthusiasm. "Go on without me, I'll just be a second."

Athena nodded and a moment later I was alone.

The sounds beyond the door weren't ones I associated with Christmas.

There was no Louisa screeching for Augustus and I to hurry up so she could start opening her presents. There was no Mummy humming Christmas carols under her breath.

There was no Daddy...his deep voice resonating through the house as he voiced his good cheer.

This year, there was no Daddy at all.

There would be no feast created by Aimee—but then there would also be no poultry heads, so there was that at least—and for the first time ever, there was no stocking at the bottom of my bed.

I rubbed my eyes quickly, forcing away the melancholy that grew in my heart.

This year there would be so many unfamiliar things, but that wasn't necessarily a bad thing. I was spending the holidays with my friends, and that was sure to be anything but dull.

Taking a deep breath, I shoved back the covers and climbed out of bed. I made a quick stop to the bathroom to brush my teeth before joining the others in the great room. Before I rounded the corner into the room, a hand curled around my wrist and tugged me into a doorway.

Peter gripped my hip and pulled me into his body. He smelled fresh and warm and so very, very delicious.

Nope.

This Christmas would certainly not be dull. Not by a mile.

"Merry Christmas," he murmured.

"Merry Christmas."

"Look what I found." Peter lifted his hand, and I followed the movement up to see him holding a plant cutting.

"Is that...?"

"Mistletoe?" he finished with a wolfish grin. "Shall we find out?"

A giggle bubbled up in my throat and I grasped the sides of his face before pulling him down to kiss me. A smile curved my lips and I sank deeper into his embrace.

"Is Freddie still not up yet?" I heard Cassandra ask.

"She said she was just coming," Athena said. "I'll go check on her."

Peter groaned and squeezed my hips.

I pressed one last soft kiss against his lips before breaking away. "Later?"

"Absolutely," he purred.

I floated on a cloud of unrelenting happiness for the rest of the day. Peter made all my apprehension, all my uncertainty about being away from my family fall away like melting ice.

Later didn't really happen. We hardly got a moment to ourselves on Christmas day, but it didn't matter. Stolen glances and discreet hand-brushing got us through the day.

I hadn't told my friends yet about me and Peter.

I wasn't even really sure why.

I found myself stealing moments with him when no one was looking—enjoying breaks from skiing heating up instead of cooling off. Steamy kisses were now my norm and I craved each and every one like they were concentrated sugar.

On New Year's Eve, there was a big party at the main lodge. They were throwing a Hogmanay ceilidh and all my friends were excited to go. We got ready together like always, and this time I knew the dance would end in my favour. There would be no other girl to claim the dance meant for me.

"I'm so excited for tonight, I can hardly believe our holiday is almost over," Harriet said as she applied her mascara in the mirror.

"Me, too," Annie agreed. "We're going to be so busy when we get back to Mapleton Manor with studying for exams and stuff. No life for the next few months...*woo hoo*."

Athena giggled. "I'm sure we'll manage to find fun somewhere, Annie. But it's Freddie who will be the saddest to leave here, I'm sure."

My cheeks warmed but I tried not to give anything else away. "Me? Why would that be? I will miss the skiing, I suppose. Wouldn't it be good if we had mountains closer to school and we could ski all the time?"

"I bet you would love it if the mountains were closer. You could visit all the time then, and never have to miss them," Athena's lips twitched with amusement. "Will you keep in touch when you leave?"

Harriet laughed. "Athena, how on earth can she keep in touch with a *mountain*?"

"I think our friend is using the mountain as a euphemism for something else," Annie said, sliding her eyes over to Athena and me with a knowing smile.

"Really? For what?" Harriet asked.

It had occurred to me a few times over the last few days that perhaps Harriet wouldn't be happy at the prospect of her friend and her brother going out with each other. She was a wonderful person with a big heart, so part of me knew that she would be absolutely fine with it. But I couldn't quiet the tiny voice that said she would object.

Harriet gasped and flew her hand out to grab my arm. "It's a boy, isn't it? You met a boy and now you don't want to leave because you're going to miss him! When did you find the time to meet a boy? All you do is ski and then hang around here. Was it on the slopes? Did Pan introduce you to someone? *Oh my God!* Is it Pan? Are you seeing my brother? Are you in love? Freddie, we're going to be sisters!"

No one moved, didn't even utter a breath once Harriet had finished her excited ramble. I blinked as I let it all sink in, and gave a small nod of confirmation.

Harriet shrieked and threw her arms around me, pulling me into a fierce hug. "Oh, I'm so happy, Freddie."

Well, at least I didn't have to worry about upsetting her.

Harriet released me and turned to face Annie and Athena. "Did you two already know?"

Athena shook her head. "Once I realised what was going on, it became pretty obvious."

Harriet turned back to me. "Why did you want to keep it a secret?"

"I suppose...I didn't want to turn the holiday into being all about me. And I wasn't sure how you would react," I said.

She grinned. "Don't be silly! I'm so happy, honestly. This is all so exciting!"

We laughed at Harriet's enthusiasm, and I felt more than a little relieved she had taken the news so well. The mood was light and carefree as we finished getting ready.

The ceilidh was in full swing when we arrived, the band playing traditional folk music with people doing set dances. There was a table reserved for us but my friends and I wasted no time in storming the dance floor.

It had been ages since I'd laughed so hard. We barely knew any of the steps and tried to keep up as best as we could, but it turned into a bit of a calamity.

Peter was my partner for most of the dances, and he was considerably better than I was. A fact, I knew, he would never forget. I might be the better tree climber, but he was by far the better dancer.

The night passed far too quickly, with the hours slipping away like sand through my fingers. We all gathered on the dance floor for the countdown to midnight.

Peter cradled my face, smiling before dipping his head to kiss me at the stroke of midnight. "Happy New Year," he whispered.

I closed my eyes and wondered if this was what complete and utter happiness felt like.

Later that night, when we were all tucked up in bed, Athena whispered a question in the dark. "Did you ask Peter what had gone on with him and Jemima?" Truthfully, I had wondered when she would. My friend was sharp as a tack and didn't miss details.

"Yes," I replied. "I did."

"And?" she prodded. "He was the guy, wasn't he? The guy you were walking on cloud nine over? I still can't believe you let Jemima have him when you were, are, clearly mad over him."

I sighed, also wondering why I had been so gracious. If I hadn't, then all this heartache and trouble would never have happened. "I won't make the same mistake twice, trust me. He only danced with her. Everything else she told us was a lie."

Athena swore under her breath. "Why would Jemima lie? It's not like she can't really pull a guy."

"That's exactly what I thought. But it was for my benefit. Promise you won't tell anyone this? The last thing I want is to divide our group."

"Of course, I promise."

"He told her he was waiting for another girl. Peter made it clear he was only being polite and when his girl showed up, he would be leaving Jemima for her." I let out a breath, the pinch of pain flaring in my chest again as I thought about her betrayal. "He told her my name, Athena. She knew he was waiting for me."

Athena was quiet for a moment as she let that information sink in. Then she swore a tad more colourfully than she had a moment ago. "What are you going to do back at school?"

"I have no idea." But I would have to figure it out...and soon.

I stood outside the chalet and watched with a heavy heart as Peter and his dad packed up the people carrier to take us back home. The holiday, especially the second half, had sped by entirely too fast for my liking.

Annie kissed my cheek as she dashed past me, yelling for me to get my behind on board before they left without me. With one last glance at the chalet and the mountains surrounding it, I climbed inside the vehicle.

Peter had finished helping his dad and was already inside, lounging in the seat he had occupied on the journey up to Aviemore. He looked at the empty space beside him then cocked his eyebrow at me. I giggled and manoeuvred my way over to him.

"I thought you got travel sick back there, Freddie?" Athena asked in an innocent voice.

"Oh, er…I found some sickness pills in my travel bag so I'm sure I'll be fine."

Athena's eyes flickered to Peter then back to mine. She smiled, like she was genuinely happy we were together. "I'm sure you'll be more than fine, Freddie." She gave us a wink then turned back around in her chair.

Peter laced his fingers through mine as Glen started the car and we put the chalet in the rear-view mirror.

Every minute that passed brought us closer to Mapleton Manor until it felt like it had only been yesterday we'd first driven through the gatehouse. As our luggage was being unloaded, Peter caught my hand and tugged me around the people carrier, out of sight from everyone else.

"What's wrong?" I asked, studying his face carefully. My heart sank — was this when he told me it had been lovely, but now that we were back home nothing else would happen?

Peter shook his head and gave me a small smile. "Nothing. I just wanted a proper goodbye without my parents and all your friends watching."

"Oh," I said, giggling.

He kissed me, quick and dry. "When can I see you again?"

"Anytime. I could come and see you?"

Peter grinned. "Absolutely. But it's a long way for you to travel, wouldn't you rather I came here?"

"It's virtually impossible to sneak into Mapleton Manor. But I can always find my way in places."

He laughed. "My girlfriend, the master of break-ins. I like it."

And I like the sound of girlfriend... "Is that what I am, then?"

"What? The master of breaking in? I don't know, I'll have to see you in action first before I let you have that title."

I huffed and rolled my eyes.

"Oh, you mean *girlfriend*? Of course—what else would you be?"

"I don't know…but I like it." I smiled.

Peter grinned and kissed me quickly again. "You know what this means, don't you? You're going to be inundated with letters from me."

"Good, I can't wait."

After a quick glance around and confirming there wasn't anyone within peeping Tom distance, Peter pulled me closer for a deeper, proper goodbye kiss.

When we all trudged upstairs to dump our luggage, Jemima appeared from the common room. "Thank God you're all back. I've been on my own for a few hours and it's deathly boring being here by yourself."

Cassandra yawned and pushed past Jemima. "Bummer. I'm going to bed — travelling exhausts me."

"And me," Annie agreed as she headed into her own room.

Jemima caught my eye and paused. She scanned me from head to toe, frowning as she met my gaze again. "Why does Freddie look like the cat that got the cream?"

"Maybe because she did. Only instead of cream, she got Harriet's brother." Athena gave Jemima a broad, fake smile. "You remember him, right, Jemima? Peter Davenport?"

Jemima frowned. "I've never heard of him before. Harriet never introduced us to her brother."

"Maybe not, but you met him at the dance last year." Athena held her hand a foot above her head. "About this tall, lovely green eyes, handsome? I think you had the last dance with him..."

Jemima's eyes widened as realisation sank in. "That...was your brother?" she asked Harriet.

"I guess so," Harriet said with a shrug. "I hope you two won't fight over him!" She laughed.

"Don't worry, it wouldn't be much of a fight," I said, smiling at Jemima. "Would it, Jemima?"

She opened and closed her mouth for a moment, looking like a fish out of water. Jemima knew she had been caught out in her lie, and the heated anger in her eyes said she probably realised that I knew her dancing with Peter had been to intentionally upset me.

I gave her a wide smile as I brushed past her to get to my room. Only time would tell how Jemima reacted to the news about me and Peter. While I was still hurt and upset over her actions, I wasn't about to ostracize her. For all intents and purposes, our friendship was over. But for the sake of our group of friends, I could fake it for a few months.

17

The new term at school saw me busier than ever. A-Level exam pressure was amped up and it set my nerves on edge. All my free time was spent pretending to study while really I was anxiously contemplating my future, writing to Peter, or daydreaming about him.

I managed to squeeze in a trip to Upton the week after the Christmas holidays. I got the train — well, two trains and an underground, technically — up to see him and he met me at Upton station where we kissed and acted like love-struck teenagers.

Upton was ridiculously easy to sneak into — I literally just walked into the place. I had to hide in Peter's room the entire time, which I didn't mind at all. His desk was neat and tidy, with sheets of writing paper and an assortment of fancy pens. His shelves were crammed with books, and his tuck box was full of sherbet sweets. I had a feeling he'd stocked them just for me.

We curled up together on his bed and talked late into the night about absolutely everything — books, films, music, friends. Peter in particular seemed to like my anecdotes and tales of mischief and never got tired of hearing them. Which was good, because I seemed to have an unlimited supply of them.

He laughed so hard tears rolled down his cheeks when I told him about the time I got into a huge fight with my friend Daisy and I threw her new leather briefcase down the stairs and it ripped. Peter called me a hothead and when I threw him a dirty look, he appeared stricken and asked me to please not throw any of his things down the stairs.

Sneaking out was a touch harder as the place was busier when I had to leave, but I rolled my hair up to hide it under a cap. I wore Peter's school uniform and pretended to be an Upton boy. No one suspected a thing.

I couldn't decide if that was a good thing or not...

It would be a few weeks before we got the chance to see each other again because of my history trip to China.

Where a plane on an internal flight had just crashed.

Honestly.

Everyone went mad with worry until the school decided that we would take the train during our trip instead.

It couldn't be that much longer on the train, surely.

Cassandra was the only one of my friends in my history class, and it would be fun to go with her.

We flew from Heathrow and it took twice as long to get to the airport as the silly Tour de France was starting in Kent, so half the roads were closed and the other half were clogged with cycling enthusiasts and their ruddy camper vans. It took around three hours to fly to Tel Aviv, then a further six and a half to get to Beijing.

I felt dead on my feet as we trudged to the hotel. Although once there, I soon perked up. We were staying in the Beijing Kunlun Hotel in the Chaoyang District. The hotel was fairly new, and an absolutely stunning piece of architecture. It soared skyward, easily the tallest building in the immediate area.

Cassandra and I were sharing a room with two other girls and it was like being back in a dorm again. The first night we tore through the supply of snacks we had brought, leaving next to nothing for the rest of the trip. I couldn't wait to get my hands on the sherbet that our school friend Venetia, who lived in Hong Kong, would bring in her tuck box.

She hadn't been able to come on this trip because she wasn't in the class, but Venetia had given us a list of treats we just had to try.

That was the problem with going to school with a bunch of girls who came from all over the world – they gave you a taste for yummy sweets you could hardly ever get.

Our trip schedule was jam-packed and our first day in China we visited The Forbidden City and the Temple of Heaven. We also headed to Tiananmen Square – the fourth largest city square in the world.

And crikey...was it ever.

The place teemed with people, and huge, intricately built architecture rose up from the ground. Mausoleums and monuments that looked like nothing I had ever seen before attracted thousands of visitors.

Armed soldiers patrolled the area, and we school girls snuck glances at them. We'd found out there had recently been shootings in the area and it made me more than a little nervous. We stayed close together in our group, never straying from each other. I scanned the crowds, the buildings and the people, completely enraptured with this city.

A leaflet was shoved into my hand and I whirled around to see a bunch of other people sneakily handing them out. It was obviously in Chinese, but it looked like some kind of propaganda. One of the armed guards spotted them, and started shouting. He ripped the leaflets out of tourists' hands, shouting as he did.

On a whim, I shoved mine up my jumper.

It could make a good souvenir.

We left shortly after, and that evening, we boarded a sleeper train to Xi'an.

Our teacher assured us it was the nicest train China had, which was good because apparently we were in for a long journey. We had our own cabin that had bunk beds attached to the walls and I could see the tracks below when I went to the toilet. Which was really weird. And disconcerting when I had to use it.

At some point during the journey, there was a knock on our cabin door.

Cassandra opened the door to a small boy whose entire hand was covered in blood.

I gasped and rushed forward. "Oh my gosh, what happened?"

His mother stood behind him and gestured to the boy's hand. "He trapped finger — you have bandage?" she asked in poor English.

Cassandra glanced at me. "Mr Richards will have a first-aid kit — I'll be right back." She rushed out to fetch our teacher.

I nodded and gestured for the mother and son to come into the cabin. Cassandra returned a moment later with Mr Richards who quickly cleaned up the boy's finger and wrapped a bandage around the cut.

The woman nodded her thanks as they left.

"Why did they ask us?" Cassandra wondered aloud.

"They probably realised with us being on a school trip we would have a first-aid kit," Mr Richards said. "Hopefully there won't be any more excitement on the trip." He left the cabin, and Cassandra pulled a face at me.

"Was that weird?"

"What was weird was that the boy didn't make a sound—Louisa who would have screamed bloody murder."

The China not written about in guidebooks whizzed past our window. China was like a whole other world to me, and really…it was. There were hardly any cars. At all. Everyone cycled everywhere and all I had seen were bicycles and yet more bicycles.

People lay outside on their metal beds, making the place look bleak and desolate.

I also found out exactly how much longer it was to get a train to Xi'an than it was to fly.

A day. That was how long it took to get a train from Beijing to Xi'an.

We arrived in the afternoon and I trudged off the train stiff, tired and feeling grimy. There was no time to rest, and after dropping our things at the hotel we visited the Big Wild Goose Pagoda—a seventh century Buddhist pagoda that housed ancient scriptures.

"Just think…a hot shower, some dinner and bed…" Cassandra murmured as we walked behind the teacher who was busy telling us all about the pagoda. He sounded like he had memorised everything from a history textbook. Which he probably had.

I groaned and examined my fingernails. "I can't wait. I've never wanted to wash my hair more in my entire life." Now, I was no stranger to travel. But there was something about this mode of transport, a confined and stifling hot mode of transport, that left a layer of filth on my skin.

"Rock, paper, scissors for who gets the first turn in the bathroom?" Cassandra asked.

I grinned. "You're on."

We fisted our hands and pumped them three times.

"Girls, are you paying attention?"

Cassandra and I shared an amused look before chorusing, "Yes, sir."

The next afternoon, Cassandra and I were in better spirits thanks to long showers and the ginormous McDonalds lit up like Disneyland that we had found near the hotel.

"What's the deal with this place again?" Cassandra asked as we headed to the museum entrance.

"Honestly, didn't you look at what we would be seeing on this trip?" I asked with a laugh.

Cassandra rolled her eyes. "Yes, cheeky. But I forget. There's only so much China I can absorb."

I sighed. "This is the museum of the Terracotta Army."

"Which are?"

"An army made of terracotta," I said, smothering a smile. "Some farmers discovered the pits and called in proper archaeologists. It turned out the pits contained funeral art that was buried with Qin Shi Huangdi and there's over eight thousand soldiers."

"Wow. That's pretty cool. This place must be huge."

It turned out that Cassandra was right. The museum that was built around the pits where the Army was discovered was colossal. It attracted thousands of visitors and I was humbled to be one of them.

The next day of our trip we visited the Great Wall and the Free Market. I was charmed by the market and all the different wares on sale, and I found a couple of wristbands to take home. But then we found the food, and all the live animals being sold to eat. Rabbits, chickens, turtles, snakes...baskets and crates full of them, and people were eyeing them up like they were a delicious cheeseburger!

I had never craved English food so much in my entire life.

The last thing I wanted to do was board the train to take us back to Beijing. I loved the trip to Xi'an...but I never wanted to do that journey again.

The train was hot and stuffy, with tons of bodies crammed into such a tiny space. We girls had a cabin again, but we all got cabin fever at being trapped in such a small space. We all complained of numb bums and stiff legs—especially me, being the tallest and therefore having the least legroom.

"Remind me to never do this again," I mumbled to Cassandra as I rested my head against the clammy glass window.

Cassandra sighed. "Me, too. But, I can't wait to come back. I'm definitely seeing more of the Far East in my gap year."

I turned around to face my friend. "What gap year?"

She nodded. "Yeah, didn't I tell you? I talked about it with my folks over Christmas. I'm blowing off college for a year and travelling the world."

My eyes widened. "I had no idea. By yourself?"

"I guess so. I have friends everywhere, so it's not like I'll be in isolation for twelve months. I'm meeting people in Australia, India, and I'm definitely going to hook up with Venetia in Hong Kong. Maybe Thailand, too."

"That sounds amazing," I murmured.

"Mmm. I can't wait. Only a few more months and then I'm out of here, so to speak. Just imagine — you'll be in another classroom, living in another dorm with loads of other girls again, and I'll be skipping across the continents with the world as my classroom."

It felt like someone was laying a heavy slab of concrete on my chest. She hadn't been intentionally cruel, but her words hurt all the same. I pictured our two different paths in my head, and couldn't help but see Cassandra's as a bird soaring through the sky...and mine as a shackle.

"Have you thought about it?" Cassandra asked, snapping me out of my reverie.

"What? Doing a gap year?" I asked. I shook my head. "No way. Mummy would kill me."

"Uni won't go anywhere. It's not like you wouldn't ever go, you're only delaying it for a little while." Cassandra shrugged and opened her magazine. "Besides, wouldn't it be a blast if we spent some of it together?"

"The Mapleton Manor girls take on the world," I said with a chuckle.

Cassandra laughed. "Exactly. And think how many wristbands you could collect."

My mind swam. It sounded incredible and so, so tempting. But I couldn't...could I?

Shaking my head again, I pulled out the postcard I had bought of the Terracotta Army to send to Peter.

Dear Peter,
Right now I am (not) enjoying the longest train journey of my entire life.
China is pretty cool – the Great Wall is really long and bendy and the Terracotta Army is massive. Did you know there are over 8,000? Mad! I've bought you some seaweed to try – it's actually really nice. It's one of the nicer local treats to eat – I didn't think you would enjoy the chicken foetus. I'm looking forward to getting off this train and stretching my legs! It takes an entire day to get to Xi'an.
I can't wait to

The train jerked and clattered, making me scratch a long, sharp line through my words. It almost felt as though we had run someone over.

"What was that?" Cassandra asked, sitting up straighter in her seat. She leaned over me, smacking me in the face with her ponytail as she tried to see what was going on out of the window.

The train shuddered to a stop, earning many complaints I couldn't understand from the other passengers outside our cabin.

Mr Richards poked his head inside our cabin. "Stay in your seats, girls! I'll find out what's going on!"

Twenty minutes later, an announcement was made over the train speaker system in Chinese. I didn't understand a word of it. The grumbling passengers cleared the aisle, seemingly unperturbed by the news.

Mr Richards came back, seeming flustered and his face an alarming shade of grey. "We'll be moving along in a few minutes girls, just be patient, please."

"What happened, Mr Richards?" Cassandra asked.

"We seem to have gone over a body," Mr Richards said. He let out a high-pitched giggle. "They're getting him moved out of the way now, it won't be long." He giggled nervously again and started heading back down the aisle.

Cassandra turned around to face me, her eyes as wide as saucers. "No way."

"Look around—no one even cares. This is so weird," I whispered as we glanced through the window and into the aisle.

"Maybe it happens all the time," she wondered.

"That's comforting." I sighed as I looked at the mess of the postcard. Well, there was nothing I could do about it—I was hardly going to ask if we could make the journey again so I could buy another one.

Sorry about the scribble…we just ran over a body.
Can't wait to see you!
Freddie x

There was a reply from Peter waiting for me at school when I returned.

Dear Freddie,

I hope you have recovered from your visit to China, it sounds like you had a lot of fun. Bit concerned about the running over of a body by the train though...

Can't wait to hear all about your adventures when I see you next weekend. My days have been like wilted flowers waiting for your return – void of life, drooping under my sorrow. I need my Freddie Sunshine to put a bit of life back in me. (How was that – romantic? Or too much?)

Peter x

I wrote him back immediately.

Dear Peter,
Perfect.
Just like always.
Freddie x

The train couldn't go fast enough for my liking. I had been waiting with my backpack at the doors for well over fifteen minutes so that I could be first off when the train finally stopped at Upton.

It was strange how time played tricks on you. The train in China had literally taken more than a day to reach its destination. But I would swear down dead that this train took longer.

We slowed down as we approached the station, and I scanned the people waiting on the platform, desperately trying to see the one face I looked for.

I hopped on the balls of my feet as I waited for the doors to unlock, mumbling under my breath for them to hurry up. They finally slid open, and I leapt from the train. I tried to spot Peter, but couldn't see him.

"Freddie!"

Whipping around at the sound of his voice, I grinned when he came into view. I sprinted towards him and threw my arms around his neck when I reached him. Peter lifted me off my feet and pressed his face into my throat.

"I missed you," he murmured.

"Not as much as me."

He set me back on my feet and lowered his head to press his lips to mine. "Come on, I've got a surprise for you."

Peter led me to the car park and gestured for me to get into a little red hatchback. The back seat was crammed with camping equipment—tents, a kettle, barbeque and cool box.

"What's all this?" I asked him with a grin.

"Your surprise," he answered, with his own smile. "My friend is covering for me. I thought tonight would be nice to get away from everyone, everything."

"Are we camping?"

Peter reached over to squeeze my knee. "Yes, but be prepared to do most of the heavy lifting. I've never made a campfire in my life."

A laugh bubbled in my throat. "I'll look after you, I promise. I'm a pro at camping—we did it all the time at Bourne Park, and we used to make campfires with flint."

He drove us to a woodland area and parked the car. After ignoring his protests, I helped carry some of the gear to our little camping ground. I sat in a folding chair for an hour as I watched Peter wrestle with the little two-man tent. When he whacked himself with a pole for the third time, he admitted defeat and allowed me to take over.

In no time at all, the tent was up, the campfire was crackling nicely, the barbeque was heating up and the sleeping bags were unrolled. It was a lot cooler in the woods, especially with the day fading, and Peter gave me his jumper to put over mine.

We cooked beef burgers on the barbeque and for pudding there were some Dip Dabs.

I think I fell a little bit more in love with Peter for that gesture. He already knew me so well.

Technically, we had known each other for a year. But it had only been a couple of months, really. Peter knew me better than a lot of people. He knew what made me laugh, what made me happy, sad and everything in between. We were so similar in a lot of ways, and yet at the same time, vastly different. I had an adventurous heart—I loved climbing trees and scraping my knees and zooming all over the world on my school trips. Peter preferred the slower pace, the company of his books and familiar settings.

He was by no means boring. Whenever we saw each other, Peter told me about some of the parties he had gone to and what mischief he and his friends had got up to.

One of my favourite things about him was that he had the ability to make me slow down. Usually I was scurrying around at a million miles an hour, rushing to some sports practice, hurrying to class, dashing off to London to see Fenella. But with Peter, I could pause and catch my breath. We could stand still and talk and enjoy the moment we were living in.

Every time I saw him, my feelings grew more intense. The more I saw him, the more I wanted to see him.

Peter was also ever so patient with me. The first time I'd visited him at school, I had worried he would expect certain things from me. But he'd been the perfect gentleman—aside from kissing the life right out of me—and had never pushed anything I wasn't ready for.

"I can't believe it's almost Easter," Peter said. We were sprawled out on top of the sleeping bags inside the tent. The door was zipped shut to keep out the bugs and it was quiet, like we were the only two people in the world.

"Mmm," I murmured sleepily. I was tucked into his chest with his arm loosely draped over me. With his other hand, Peter slid his fingers through my hair, sending delicious shivers down my spine.

"After Easter it'll be exams, then finally summer. Then uni." Peter chuckled. "Time is flying."

Why does it feel like time is running out?

My eyes flew open, the now familiar dread settling low in my stomach whenever I thought about university.

"I've never even asked," Peter said, giving me a small nudge. "Where are you planning on going?"

I imagined myself standing at the airport, playing eenie meenie miney mo with the departure board. "St Finbars."

Peter didn't reply, and for a second I thought he hadn't heard me. Then he sat bolt upright, jolting my body with his sudden movement. "Are you serious?"

With a frown, I replied, "Yes, why?"

Peter grinned. "Freddie, that's where I'm going."

"What?" I laughed. "Really?"

He nodded, his eyes sparkling with delight. "Yes. This is amazing. We're going to be together next year."

My smile wasn't at all forced. It would be amazing to be at St Finbars with Peter, to see him every day and not have to sneak out to visit him. Knowing Peter would be there too would give me something positive to focus on, instead of all this worry that had been gnawing in my gut.

So why, instead of relief, did the dread turn to a heavy stone?

The day after I flew home to Monaco, we flew to Courchevel in the Alps for our annual Easter skiing holiday. It was a welcome distraction. I was so busy every day and exhausting myself so that by night time I slipped into comas rather than sleep. It gave me a welcome break from all the thinking I had been doing recently.

We had lessons in the day to brush up our techniques. Louisa had got so good it wouldn't be long until she was out on the harder slopes with me and Augustus.

There was a bittersweet feeling to the holiday, because Daddy wasn't with us. It awoke the familiar grief that weighed heavy in my heart. I missed him so much. More than anything, I wanted to curl up on his lap and tell him the secret wishes I kept, and ask for his guidance on what to do.

But deep down, I already knew.

Mummy and Daddy had both always told me my place was at St Finbars, getting a good education so I could be anything I wanted.

What if what I wanted was to be free to make my own path?

My last night in Monaco, I tossed and turned in my bed for hours. In the end I gave up and went to the kitchen to get a drink.

A single light burned in the room, casting a soft glow on Mummy, who sat at the table nursing a mug of cocoa. She smiled when she spotted me, and fastened her dressing gown more tightly around her slim body. "Hello, darling. What's the matter, can't you sleep?"

I smiled and shook my head.

Mummy rose from the table and patted my shoulder. "Have a seat, I'll get you a hot cocoa."

I took the chair beside Mummy's, and drew my knees up to my chest.

"It's not like you to be nervous about going back to school. Are you thinking about your exams?"

"A little. My head just feels really full these days."

"There's a lot to think about. But once your exams are over, you have the whole summer to relax before going back for university."

My stomach churned. "Peter will be there, did I tell you?" I asked her quietly.

"No," Mummy said with a smile. "How exciting. You must be delighted."

I nodded. When I had spoken to Mummy after the Christmas holidays, I had told her all about Peter. Well, as much as I'd dared with ten other girls listening in to the conversation. She was happy for me that I had met someone I really liked. And it turned out she knew his grandparents, which didn't surprise me at all, as Mummy and Daddy always seemed to know somebody who knew somebody.

"Cassandra isn't going to university right away. She's doing a gap year first. Isn't that exciting?" My heart picked up speed as I wondered how she would react. Mummy, while so kind and gentle, was also super strict, especially when it came to formal matters and doing what was right and expected of someone.

Mummy pursed her lips. "Hmm. I've always thought people who did gap years lack motivation."

"Why? She's still going to university, she's just delaying it for a little while," I said, parroting Cassandra's own words back to Mummy.

"If she doesn't go now, I doubt she will ever go." Mummy gave me a sharp look. "I hope she hasn't been filling your head with nonsense, Frederica."

I swallowed the rising emotion in my throat. My hesitation was all the confirmation Mummy needed.

She sighed. "Oh, Frederica, what on earth are you thinking? Do you know how disappointed Daddy would be if he knew you were considering upsetting the family like this?"

"Why would I upset everyone, though? Mummy, I've been in boarding school for ten years, I feel like I've already *been* to university. I'm sick of living with other girls and having a cramped bedroom and living by a schedule made up for me by someone else. I want to just *live* for a little while." I sucked in a deep breath, my pulse rocketing.

The idea of a gap year had been whirling around in my mind for months now, but until I'd spoken about it out loud, I hadn't realised just how passionately I *didn't* want to go to university.

Mummy stood up and rinsed her mug out in the sink. She looked out of the window and kept her back to me. "It's only another four years. Once you graduate from university we can talk about you possibly taking a month or two to travel before you get your first job. In the meantime, I want you to forget about this silly notion. For goodness's sake, you're the oldest, Frederica. Think about the example you are setting for your brother and sister."

Sadness and fury welled up inside me.

Why did it fall to *me* to be the example? Why couldn't *I* be the child for once, and play and have fun and not think about the consequences? I bet Louisa, when the time came, would never even ask Mummy for permission to do a gap year. She would just go. But that was Louisa's motto — better to beg forgiveness than ask permission.

"Now off to bed, or you'll be exhausted in the morning."

I nodded then hurried out of the kitchen before Mummy could see the tears streaking down my face.

18

At the beginning of term, my friends and I decided we wanted to leave something behind at Mapleton Manor. A legacy of sorts, something physical to say that we had been there. And that we were awesome.

There was loads of scrap wood in the craft shed, and after getting some sketchy plans from a book in the library, we set about building a boat. Our idea was that it could be used to row around the lake on warm spring days, enjoying the weather and getting some exercise. But we also thought the girls could use it for Polly Pearl night, and really make it something worth remembering.

A few weeks after we'd returned to Mapleton Manor after Easter, it was ready. Our exams were about to start and we decided to have one last fun outing with all of us together before we had to buckle down and study our butts off.

We carried the boat across the grounds from the craft shed to the lake.

After all, we had to make sure she was seaworthy.

"This is brilliant," Annie said, squealing with delight.

"I know!" Cassandra agreed. "I can't believe we actually built a boat. They are so going to remember us forever."

"This thing had better float," Jemima grumbled.

Athena caught my eye and we pulled a face before giggling.

"What are you two laughing at?" Jemima asked.

"Why, nothing at all, Jemima, dear," Athena said with mock innocence.

At the lake, we eased the boat into the water and let it bob for a few minutes. When no leaks appeared and she stayed afloat fine, we clamoured inside, shrieking and yelping when it swayed from side to side.

The last thing any of us wanted was to fall into the lake. Green pond scum floated on the surface of the water, and the water itself was a murky, muddy brown.

Yes, we wanted to leave a boat so the younger girls could enjoy a spot of rowing...but no one would ever, *ever* want to risk putting a single toe in the water.

We settled down, taking seats and huddling together. Alicia and Harriet rowed, each taking an oar. For a while we went around in circles until they found their rhythm. When we reached the middle of the lake, the girls stopped rowing so we could just bob and float and relax.

"This is the life," Annie said as she tipped her face towards the sun.

"I think I'd rather be on the *Poseidon* and enjoy real sunshine," I teased.

"That sounds like heaven," Athena murmured.

"My foot is wet," Harriet said in a curious voice. "Why is my foot wet?"

We all dropped our eyes to the floor of the boat and saw a little water seeping in and gathering at the bottom.

Glancing around at each other, it was clear we were all trying not to panic. "I'm sure it's nothing. But perhaps we should..." Cassandra started.

"Head back?" Jemima finished.

Harriet and Alicia started their rowing again, taking it slow and easy...just in case.

Annie shrieked. "There's a leak back here!"

"And here!" Athena yelped.

"She's sinking!" Jemima screamed.

I held my hands out, trying to calm the girls down. "Stop, nobody panic! It's going to be —"

An ominous crack halted my words. There was a split second where we all looked horrified at one another then accepted our fate.

The boat seemed to break and split at every possible place it could. It came apart and unceremoniously dumped us all in the lake. I surfaced, and one by one, so did everyone else. Coughs and splutters filled the air, along with shrieks.

"*Oh my god!*" Someone screamed.

"Urgh...something touched my leg!"

"I'm going to be sick... I'm going to be sick..."

"This water *stinks!*"

We scrambled for shore so quickly we could have broken the land-speed record. The second we were on dry land, we made a run for Crosby.

Housemistress gasped when she saw us race in, her face turning to disgust when she caught a whiff of us. "Don't tell me you girls have been swimming in the lake?"

"Not intentionally!" Athena called to her.

There was a fight for the showers, all of us squirming beneath the lake muck and needing to wash it off. But soon we were clean and sparkly again, and only the phantom grossness remained.

So much for leaving a legacy, but I doubted any of us would forget that afternoon.

At last the exams were over. I felt the way I usually did after them — a little on the frazzled side but more or less optimistic. Annie and I had gone our traditional route of studying by cramming the night before, listening to music and staying up all night with the help of Pro Plus.

The afternoon of my last exam, I caught the train to Upton to see Peter. I hadn't seen him since before Easter, and it had been far too long. He sneaked me in to his room again, and like all the other times, no one was any the wiser.

We stayed up all night talking, kissing…being young and foolish. The room began to lighten as the sun rose lazily in the sky. Before I knew it, it was almost time to leave again.

I lay wrapped up in Peter's arms, breathing in the scent of him, which did crazy dangerous things to my heart. His bright green eyes studied my face, sweeping over every plane, every dip and curve as though he wanted to commit me to memory.

"I really hate saying goodbye to you," Peter murmured quietly. He gripped my hip and tugged me closer to him, drawing me into his body.

"So do I," I whispered. "Do you ever feel like we wasted time?"

"Because of the dance last year?" Peter shrugged. "Sometimes, but not really. Yeah, I guess we missed out on a few months together because of the misunderstanding. I don't know about you, but I'm not planning on this relationship ending anytime soon."

My heart gave an uneven thump. I smiled and burrowed deeper into the crook of his neck. Peter felt safe and constant but at the same time exhilarating, like I was standing on the edge of a cliff.

Peter released a long breath. "I just can't wait for uni. No more sneaking out to see each other, no more disappearing for weeks at a time on school trips. Just you and me. In the same place. For years."

A cold chill swept down my spine.

He meant his words to be a comfort—something to look forward to. A part of me was excited by what he'd said, couldn't wait for that future he talked about. But the other, more dominant part, was terrified.

"What's the matter?" Peter asked. "You've gone as stiff as a board."

I forced myself to take a steadying breath. Leaning back, I peered up at his handsome face. How could I tell him the secrets I held in my heart? That the prospect of going to university now felt like a prison sentence?

Giving my head a quick shake, I reached up to kiss him briefly. "Nothing, I was just thinking about the horrors of fresher dorms."

Peter chuckled. "I bet it won't be so terrible. Who knows—maybe we'll get sick of dorm life and get a place together, just you and me."

Despite my bleak mood, I smiled. "You would get sick of me for sure."

He kissed me. "I think I could see you every day of my life and never get sick of you."

"Peter," I started, "do you ever feel like you're doing things just to please other people?"

Peter was quiet for a moment as he considered my question. "Like when I attempted to climb that tree to please you?"

A laugh bubbled in my throat and I swatted his chest. "No, silly. I mean...important decisions. Like, was it your choice to go to St Finbars?"

"A bit of both, really. My dad went there, and so did my grandfather. It was always presumed that's where I would go too. But I *want* to go there, I like being part of a legacy." Peter stroked my cheek. "Are you feeling pressured by your family?"

I shrugged. "Sometimes...sometimes I think I want to run away."

"Well, if you do, promise you'll take me with you."

"I will," I said with a giggle. "We'll pack our belongings in handkerchiefs tied to sticks and face the big wide world."

Peter laughed and kissed me again, longer this time. "Sounds perfect."

"A girl ran away from my prep school once. She didn't get far, and all she had taken was a slice of bread and her hamster," I said, thinking back to a girl at Bourne Park.

"Well," Peter said thoughtfully, "I'm glad she got back before she ended up having to eat her hamster."

I snorted a laugh, taken completely by surprise at his words. "No one more so than the hamster!"

Peter stroked his fingertip across my bottom lip. "It's almost time to leave."

Like Peter, I was beginning to really hate saying goodbye too. It felt like I was being split in two — there was the person I was, the good girl who did everything she was supposed to and never upset anyone, and also this other girl who wanted to brush off all her responsibility and just go and have fun.

Peter fell somewhere in the middle of this dilemma.

Both girls wanted him, but it was clear only one would get to keep him.

There was a new temptation that went along with accepting my fate and following the path that had been chosen for me years ago, and that was unbridled access to Peter.

I could hardly imagine a life without him in it anymore. It was like he had become a part of me, and me of him. Resigning myself to the inevitable came with great rewards, but also great sacrifices. Could I even do it? Could I break my mother's heart, and Peter's?

Could I be that selfish?

My chest ached under the pressure. Part of me wanted to close my eyes and wake up to find the decision had been made for me and this dilemma was all over. But…that was the problem, wasn't it?

The choice had already been made for me.

I gazed up into Peter's beautiful green eyes. I felt like I knew every inch of that face now. From his strong Roman nose to his wide, infectious smile. His eyebrows which could be so expressive. The tiny scar on his forehead from when Harriet had thrown a building block at him when they were children.

Everything about Peter made my head spin and my heart thump erratically. Like the way he looked at me, as though he couldn't believe that he was with me. Like he was the luckiest boy in the world when really, I was the lucky one.

Peter moved his finger from my mouth to my eyebrows, where he smoothed them out from what must have been a considerable frown. "They look like serious thoughts."

I tried to smile, but couldn't quite make it reach my eyes. "I was just thinking about the future."

He grinned. "Was I in it?"

Pressing my hand to his cheek, I smiled more genuinely. "Of course you were. I can't even imagine a future without you."

"I'm glad," Peter said, turning more sombre. "It makes saying goodbye a little easier, knowing it's not for long. And you know I feel the same way, don't you?"

"I do now."

Peter swallowed. "I'm thankful every day that I found you. And shocked that I get to keep you."

I was saved from answering by Peter lowering his head to kiss me. Soft, sweeping brushes of his mouth against mine at first, before he applied a more heady pressure.

My head swam, my blood roared and all that mattered was the feel of him against my body. Peter nudged me onto my back and I went willingly, relishing in the sensation of the weight of his body. He kissed me deeper, making the world around me fade to a distant whisper.

I loved kissing Peter. I could do it all day, every day for the rest of my life and it still wouldn't be enough.

The alarm on Peter's bedside table bleeped, breaking the spell that had coated us like a blanket. Peter groaned as he broke the kiss, breathing hard as he rested his forehead against mine.

"I hate that bloody alarm."

"Me, too," I agreed.

"So let's ignore it. They'll never notice you're gone from Mapleton Manor, right? You've already finished your exams, you could stay here and pretend to be an Upton boy for a few weeks."

A laugh rose in my throat. "As tempting as that sounds, I don't want to explain it all to Mummy when I inevitably get caught."

He sighed. "Fair enough." Peter kissed me one last time then pulled himself away from me.

I pulled on a layer of Peter's clothes, my usual disguise, then gathered the rest of my things together.

The late Samantha sun had already begun its rise when I left Upton at an ungodly time in the morning. It was set to be a beautiful day, and no doubt my friends would take full advantage. I predicted an afternoon of sunbathing on the lawn, all of us in a neat row as we baked ourselves, making our skin a lovely golden brown for the leavers' ball in a few weeks.

At the station, Peter kept me tucked into his body as we waited for the train to arrive. My heart sank when I heard the first rumblings of it on the rails, signalling the end of another wonderful weekend with Peter.

I turned and pressed my face into his throat, breathing in the intoxicating scent of his skin. "I'll see you in a few weeks?"

"Of course," Peter answered, hugging me tightly. "I wouldn't miss your ball for the world."

"Good." I chuckled. "I'm sure this dance will go a little better than the last one."

"So long as you don't trick me into climbing any more trees," he mumbled, pressing his nose into my hair. "Do you think you could sneak away that night?"

I pulled back so I could see his face. "The night of the ball? I should be able to, why?"

He smiled. "I have a surprise lined up for you, so you'll have to wait and see."

The train stopped and Peter let me go. I gave him one last kiss goodbye then climbed aboard. I took the first seat available, and waved to him out of the window. Peter blew me a kiss, and as the train began to move out of the station, he turned and headed back for the car park.

My chest ached watching him leave.

I hated saying goodbye to him when I knew I would see him again in a week or so...so how on earth was I considering a future where I would have to say goodbye to him for months?

Unless...

Unless I could convince him to go with me.

The last production of the school year was a big deal at Mapleton Manor. Lots of parents would come to watch, as well as other friends and family members. It was always packed, and it was always chaos. Almost every leaver was involved with the production in some way or another, and my friends and I were no exception.

We all had a part in the show, mostly minor roles, but Athena had the lead. She was a natural actress, and quite the chameleon. She could transform herself into any role, and I loved watching her perform.

This year, we all looked forward to the very last performance. Not for the show's sake, but for the fact it was going to help us with a mass breakout. Exams were over, the leavers' ball was next week and after that...school was finished. We were done. And to celebrate, we were all sneaking out to go clubbing in London.

The plan was simple, but hopefully effective.

We took to the stage for the final bow, grinning like maniacs and buzzing with excitement. The moment the curtain closed, we dashed backstage to one of the dressing rooms where we had stashed clothes for us all to change into.

"Has anyone seen my —"

"*Ouch!* That was my foot!"

"Hurry up, hurry up!"

When we were finally dressed in our clubbing clothes, we sneaked out of a back door to scurry across the grounds while the rest of the school was in chaos over the end of the show.

"Someone should have brought a torch," Jemima grumbled.

"Why didn't you, if it's such a good idea?" Athena threw back.

"Are we almost at the road?" Harriet asked.

"Almost," I answered.

We cleared the school grounds and made it onto the narrow country lane. We peered around in the darkness, trying in vain to spot our lift. A short way down the lane, a sudden flash of headlights illuminated us.

"There he is," Annie said. "Come on."

We all piled into Annie's friend's car and we headed into the big city. Cassandra had smuggled a bottle of vodka with her and she passed it around. The journey was spent with us squirming in our seats as we impatiently waited to get to London.

When we arrived at the club, Liquid, we clambered out of the car. I smoothed down my outfit and we took turns double-checking our hair in the glassy reflection of the car window. Annie's friend promised to be back for us by the time the club closed to drive us back to Mapleton Manor.

The night was spent dancing and getting tipsy, enjoying life and loving being young. For me, dancing away in Liquid was a welcome distraction. I didn't have to think about university, disappointing or hurting people, sacrifices or my own happiness. I could just be me with my friends and have a great night.

We staggered out of the club close to four in the morning. Athena hung off my neck as she sang so badly and out of tune that I had no idea what song it was she was butchering.

"Uh, Annie?" Cassandra said. "Where's your friend?"

There was no sign of the friend or his car. I bounced on the balls of my feet as I spun the wristband I'd got inside the club around my wrist. The sky was turning a greyish pink as dawn approached. We *had* to get back to Mapleton Manor.

After waiting twenty minutes and there was still no sign of him, we headed down to the payphone so Annie could try to call him.

He finally picked up the third time she called and promised to be there in a few minutes.

It was closer to forty-five minutes before he finally showed up, looking half asleep and scruffy. But by that point we were all shattered, Athena was feeling ill and all I wanted was my own bed. He dropped us off near the gatehouse and we cut through the wood to get to the school.

We slipped off our shoes so we could tiptoe inside the Sixth Form Centre hopefully unnoticed.

But alas, this was not meant to be.

"Did you have a good night, girls?"

We all jumped about a foot in the air at the sound of Housemistress's voice. She sat in a corner, obscured by shadows. Housemistress stood and crossed the foyer to us. She folded her arms under her chest and gave each and every one of us an ominous look.

"It was a brilliant night," Athena said with a hiccup. "You should have come."

Housemistress's lips twitched with amusement, though she schooled her features back quickly. "Next time, perhaps. Now, off to bed. You had best get a few hours' sleep before you need to be up for Sunday service."

My friends and I exchanged glances. That couldn't be it...surely?

Housemistress smiled. "You're all eighteen, you're young and school is virtually over. There isn't much point in punishing you all when you will be leaving in a week anyway."

We laughed and hugged Housemistress before trudging upstairs and falling into our beds.

After we returned from Sunday service, I headed back to my room for a much-needed nap. It felt like my head had only just hit the pillow when there was a tap on the door and Housemistress poked her head into the room.

"Freddie, there's a phone call for you downstairs. It's your mother."

I yawned and mumbled my thanks before stumbling back out of bed. Downstairs, I picked up the receiver and settled into the little chair beside the phone.

"Hi, Mummy."

"Hello, darling," Mummy said. Her voice was different, strained somehow. As though she was trying very hard not to cry.

I sat bolt upright in the chair and gripped the receiver so tightly my knuckles turned white. "Mummy? What's the matter?"

Mummy laughed, a sad sounding noise. "Nothing gets past you, does it sweetheart? I'm fine, there's nothing to worry about, I promise."

"Then why do you sound like that?"

She sighed. "Because I feel like I owe you a rather big apology. Since you left for school, I haven't stopped thinking about our row. I feel awful."

I frowned. "Whatever for?"

"I wasn't fair to you. I should have listened to what you had to say instead of snapping at you." Mummy took a deep breath. "Now, I want to make myself perfectly clear. The right thing to do is attend St Finbars after the summer so you can begin your studies. It's the right thing to do because it means you will get your degree sooner, get a career started and make your whole family proud of you, including setting a wonderful example for your siblings."

My heart sank. It wasn't anything I didn't already know, but hearing the words again felt like sealing my fate. I was heavy and resigned and full of sorrow.

"But," Mummy said, "if you choose to...delay it for a short while, I won't object. I won't be happy about it, but I won't stand in your way, either."

"What?" I gasped. "Mummy, are you serious?"

Mummy chuckled. "Yes, darling. But I am holding out hope that you will make the right decision. Just promise me you will think long and hard about what you really want, and what you should do."

"Okay, I promise," I said. The only thing was, what I really wanted, and what I should do, were two entirely different things.

I hung up and bit my lip, unable to keep the smile from spreading across my face.

"Freddie, you missed your post yesterday," Matron said as she spotted me. She handed me a single envelope.

Looking at the familiar scrawling handwriting, I smiled and thanked her before skipping back to my room. I tore open Peter's letter and flopped down on my bed. As well as a short letter, there was also a sketch of a tree with what looked like a boy at the very top cheering in victory.

I laughed at his silliness and reminded myself to put the sketch somewhere I wouldn't lose it. More than likely with all Peter's other letters, which I carefully hoarded out of sight of nosey girls.

Dear Freddie,

I am counting down the days until I see you again. I can't wait to see you in your beautiful ball gown and I just know you will look amazing. You'll be impressed with my tux — I look like James Bond, only far better looking.

You might not believe me, but I have spent my free time over the last few weeks perfecting my tree-climbing abilities.

I am now as good as you, if not better, and because of this I thought it better to send you proof of my new skills, rather than embarrass you in person. I wouldn't want your pride to get hurt.

Until I see you again, beautiful.

Peter

Tears pricked my eyes as I lowered Peter's letter to the bed. I had just been given the greatest gift my mother could have ever given me — the freedom to make my own choices, even if she didn't agree with them, and now it felt like that choice had been taken away again.

With all my heart I knew what I felt for Peter was real, and I didn't want to think of him as an obligation or a burden. If I stayed, it would only be for him. Could I live with that decision while never knowing what could have been?

19

Mapleton Manor had rolling, expansive grounds that were the perfect setting for the Masters Leavers' Ball. A pristine white marquee had been set up on the principal lawn and all day we had all been trying to sneak a peek inside, but all our efforts had been thwarted.

My friends and I rode our bicycles to the Ville to get our hair and makeup done for the ball. I went for an elegant but loose chignon that left a few strands free.

We spent hours getting ready. Thanks to the wonderful weather, we were all indeed a gorgeous golden brown and our beautiful dresses showed off our tans. Athena and Annie both wore blood-red gowns, Jemima went for a sea green and Cassandra and Harriet wore different shades of a paler blue. I was the only one who had a champagne-coloured dress, and I was thankful I seemed to be an individual.

Mummy had had the dress specially made for me by our childhood dressmaker, Jackie, and it was simply stunning. It was an A-line dress with a princess scoop neck and tiny, short sleeves that flattered my delicate shoulders and collarbone. It nipped in at the waist, which gave me a wonderful silhouette, and the bodice was decorated with intricate stitched patterns. The skirt was floor length and made of wispy organza. I felt fragile and effortlessly feminine.

Peter was going to love it.

When we were finally ready, we headed downstairs. Housemistress's eyes welled up when she saw us, and she hugged us each in turn, whimpering about us growing up so fast.

Outside, the evening summer sun was still warm and bright, crickets chirped in the long grass and swallows swooped and dived in the air. Athena and I linked arms as we made our way round to the front of the school where our dates would meet us. She had invited a boy from Stonebridge, as had Annie and Cassandra. Harriet was meeting her boy from Minster College and Jemima…was dateless. He had cancelled on her at the last minute and we suspected it was because he got a better offer.

Somehow I managed to resist the urge to gloat that it was her 'just desserts'.

A crowd of boys lingered near the front steps as they waited for their dates. I spotted Peter in an instant, standing tall and gorgeous in his tailored black tux. He looked amazing, and my heart stuttered at the thought that he was there for me. Me.

He looked up and spotted me, an easy smile falling from his face.

Peter broke apart from the crowd as he walked towards me, his eyes locked with mine. I stepped away from my friends and met him, suddenly feeling almost shy.

"Hi," I said as we reached each other.

Peter took my hand and raised it so he could kiss the back of it. "Hi, gorgeous."

My cheeks flushed at his compliment. "I like your tux."

With a grin, Peter grasped his lapel and spun in a circle. "Not bad, eh? Well, I had to scrub up nice, seeing as I was going to be with the most beautiful girl in the world."

"Stop teasing," I said, grabbing his hand and giving it a light squeeze.

All humour bled from Peter's face. "Who's teasing? Certainly not me."

I ducked my head, but Peter clasped my chin to raise my face back up.

He pressed a light kiss to my lips. "Never hide this face from me," he whispered. "It's far too beautiful to be kept hidden."

Once all the girls had arrived, we posed on the front steps for photographs, then again with all our dates. After that, Mrs Macpherson led everyone down the lawn to the marquee.

Peter loosely clasped my hand in his as we entered the tents, and I couldn't help but gasp when we did. I had known Mapleton Manor would throw an amazing Masters Leavers' Ball, but they had seriously outdone themselves.

The theme was black and gold. Balloons were tied to the centrepieces — large glass vases with lit candles held in place with black sand. Each round table had white linens and were surrounded by chairs wrapped in black fabric with elaborate gold ribbon. The most eye-catching part of the ball was the parachute ceiling, made of glittering gold fabric with twinkling lights strewn across it.

It looked like something out of a fairy tale.

Peter and I found our seats, and I was pleased that Annie and her date would also be sitting with us, together with another couple from a different Masters House.

Mrs Macpherson stood on the stage in front of the band and gave a moving speech about leaving childhood behind as we embarked on the first steps of our adulthood.

It made a lump form in my throat and a dull ache throb in my head.

After the speech, we were served a delicious four-course meal. Peter pulled my chair closer to his so he could murmur in my ear, sending shivers down my spine.

Once dinner was over and the plates had been cleared away, the band started playing up on the stage. Peter wasted no time in grabbing my hand and hauling me onto the dance floor. My friends soon joined us with their dates and we made a tight group.

For the rest of the night, Peter won my friends over — even more than he had at Christmas — letting them see exactly why I was falling for him. He was polite and courteous, asked questions about them and really listened to their answers.

When I felt like my feet were about to fall off from overuse, I headed back to the table for a sit down. I left Peter on the dance floor having a weird dance-off with Harriet, earning many laughs and smiles from the people who watched them.

I had been sitting alone for a few minutes when Annie and Athena found me.

"Everything okay?" Athena asked as she sat beside me.

"Yes, just hot and tired," I answered with a smile. "Are you both having fun?"

"I'm having a ball," Annie said with a grin. "This night has been amazing, don't you think we'll remember it forever?"

Athena and I nodded our agreement.

"It feels like the end of things now, doesn't it?" I asked quietly.

Annie leaned her head on my shoulder. "Maybe it's the start of something new."

"I like the sound of that," Athena said. "One thing ends and another begins. I for one am looking forward to whatever comes next. Aren't you, Freddie?"

For the last few weeks it had been on the tip of my tongue to unload my concerns on my friends. They would listen, and they would give advice. But I knew this was a decision I had to make on my own. "I am excited. Nervous and excited."

Athena chuckled. "Whatever comes next for you, Freddie, you'll kick butt."

I laughed and nudged her with my elbow.

"Peter looks gorgeous in his tux, doesn't he?" Annie asked.

"Scrumptious," I agreed with a giggle.

"Has he told you what this surprise tonight is yet?"

I shook my head.

Athena leaned closer towards me. "Do you think he expects…something?"

My cheeks flushed. It had crossed my mind once or twice — okay, five thousand times — that perhaps Peter was taking me somewhere with the intention of taking our relationship to the next step. "I've thought about it. But, you know, he really isn't like that. I don't think he would presume anything without at least talking to me about it first. So he's probably just got a romantic night planned, but with no expectations."

"What are your expectations?" Annie asked. "Have you decided if you want to or not yet?"

That was the question of the hour—was I ready? A part of me was absolutely ready, but there was a tiny voice in my head that I couldn't quiet, whispering that maybe I wasn't. "I think I am. I trust Peter, you know? I trust him to take that step with him. And...I do want my first time to be with him. I can't even imagine it being with someone else. I care about him so much."

Athena hugged me. "Trust me, darling, when you're in the situation, you'll know if you're ready or not. Peter is a good guy and won't care if you aren't ready yet."

I nodded, knowing this to be true. Blowing out a long breath, I scanned the room, taking in teachers and students I had known for years. How was it I was sitting with my two best friends at our leavers' ball, discussing my virginity already? It felt like I had only blinked since my arrival and now...now it was almost over. "It definitely feels like the end of an era."

Annie giggled. "I bet they won't forget us in a hurry!"

"Of course not!" Athena cried. "We have been the best Masters class in the history of Mapleton Manor!"

"I wonder if any other girls will find our spot in the woods," I said.

"I hope so. This school needs some mischief makers." Athena laughed.

"On that note, why don't we mischief makers get back to our dates and enjoy a good dance?" Annie suggested as she stood.

"No way," Athena said, also rising. "This one belongs to the girls. Come on, Freddie."

I followed Athena and Annie onto the dance floor where we grabbed the other girls to shake our hips to the song the band played. The night was drawing to a close, and soon it would really be over.

Who knew when I would see these girls again once school was officially over in a few days? It could be months...years? I hoped not. We were as close as friends could be—probably closer than most people ever get to others, but life was sure to get in the way.

"Let's make a promise," I said to the girls. "Let's promise that we'll never be the sort of people who only say they'll meet up after school. Let's promise that we'll never fall out of touch and we won't be strangers at school reunions."

Annie swiped a tear that fell from her eye. "I promise. I'll love you girls forever."

"I promise to always write to you girls from wherever I am in the world." Cassandra vowed.

"Like you could ever forget about me," Athena said with a laugh. "But I promise, too."

"So do I," said Jemima.

"Friends forever," Harriet agreed.

"And ever and ever," Alicia concurred.

We laughed and dabbed our eyes as the emotion swelled, then bundled together for a group hug.

I loved those girls.

I had a feeling I always would.

The boys grew impatient at being ignored, and soon cut in to steal us away. Peter pulled me close as the music slowed for a romantic dance. "It's hot in here," he whispered in my ear. "Do you want to get some air?"

"Absolutely," I said. Cool night air sounded like heaven. I let him lead me out of the marquee and away from the bustle of the ball.

Peter held my hand as we strolled across the lawn, the light from the marquee stretching out like long fingers over the grass, casting strange and peculiar shadows.

"You're quiet tonight," Peter commented. He stroked the back of my hand with his thumb.

"I got a little nostalgic with the girls," I said, leaning into him. "I think it only just hit me that I won't live with them anymore. I won't see them every day and wake up to having all my best friends in one place."

Peter leaned over to press a kiss to my temple. "You may not see them every day, but your relationship won't change. I bet if you don't see them for sixth months, when you do finally meet up, it will be like no time at all has passed."

"Do you really think so?"

"Of course I do."

It meant everything to me that he got how important my friends were to me. He didn't brush aside my fears, instead he comforted and reassured me. Peter had made everything about this night special. He was incredible.

And I didn't deserve him.

Especially not with the dark secrets in my heart.

"What are your friends' plans for next year? Will any be close to you up at St Finbars?"

My chest ached, like it always did when I thought about uni. "Annie is going to Edinburgh for uni. Everyone else is closer to London." I glanced at him. "Except Cassandra. She's doing a gap year and is travelling all over the world."

Peter didn't respond for a few minutes. He wasn't stupid and I knew just by saying that one innocent sentence he would hear the underlying query. "Are you thinking about going with her?" His voice, normally smooth and rich, was gravelly.

I let out a breath. "I have to admit I've been thinking about it."

"Just thinking?" he asked quietly.

"There is a lot to consider," I admitted.

"What does your mother think about it?"

"Mummy doesn't want me to go. I think I would disappoint her." My stomach twisted. "I don't want to disappoint her."

Peter cleared his throat. "Are you feeling pressured because I'll be there? Is it too much, the thought of us going to university together?"

"No!" I cried. "Of course not." Peter being there was the only thing that made the idea of going tolerable. "You're everything to me, Peter. Absolutely everything. I don't want to be apart from you."

He was quiet for a few moments. Peter stopped walking and tugged me back so I stood in front of him. "Will you dance with me, Lady Frederica?"

I giggled. "Here?"

"Where better place than under the stars?" His face showed no humour as he gathered me in his arms. He held me tightly, as though any moment I would disappear. The music from the ball reached us like a soft whisper and we swayed in time.

I rested my head against Peter's shoulder and closed my eyes. I was determined to remember every moment of this night for the rest of my life. I wanted to remember with perfect clarity how it felt to be held by him, to be in his arms and to feel his heart beating through his shirt.

My heart was full of turmoil and doubts, but this…this I was sure of.

Peter tilted my chin up and lowered his head so he could meet my lips. He cupped my cheek and held me all the closer to his body.

It became clear to me then, as I danced under the stars with Peter and as he kissed me like I was the only thing in the world that he wanted, that I was in love with him.

In the bustle of guests leaving Mapleton Manor grounds, Peter smuggled me into his car. I lay on the back seat until we were clear of the gatehouse, when I climbed over into the passenger seat.

"Where are we going?" I asked with a giggle.

"To your surprise," Peter said, giving me a saucy wink.

I pretended to huff and stare out of the window, but I lasted all of four seconds before I forgot myself. "Tonight has been amazing, I can't think of anything else that could make it even better." I scooted over in my seat until I could rest my head on his shoulder.

Peter found my hand and gave it a squeeze. "Hopefully you will like it, then."

A little while later, we pulled in to a small hotel car park. The hotel looked like a converted farmhouse, with dark bricks and creeping ivy trailing up the sides. Peter led us inside, bypassing reception but giving the desk clerk a nod, and headed straight for the lift.

On the second floor, we alighted from the lift and Peter fished a key out from the breast pocket of his jacket. He opened a door into a magnificent room, with tall windows framed with thick, heavy gold curtains. Red and gold leaf wallpaper decorated the walls and a few armchairs were placed around the room. An open door revealed a large en suite bathroom with a massive corner bath.

But all of this faded into the distance because of the absolutely enormous four-poster bed that completely dominated the room.

"Whoa," I mumbled, turning in a circle to view the entire room. I came back to the bed and was awed all over again. "Whoa."

Peter quietly closed the door behind him. "What do you think?"

"I think it's beautiful," I said, letting out a breath.

"Apparently, royalty used this room when they visited Dambrook," Peter said.

A laugh bubbled in my throat. "Really? No way."

Peter nodded. He crossed the room to where I stood and wrapped his arms around me. Dipping his head, he brushed his mouth against mine. "Only the best for my lady. Do you like it?"

"I think it's incredible," I said quietly. Reaching up, I threw my arms around his shoulders and kissed him briefly. "Did you get this room for us?"

He nodded but a small crease formed between his eyebrows. "Not because I expect anything, because I don't. But so we can spend a proper night together, not cramped in my tiny room at Upton. Just the two of us, before I don't get to see you for most of the summer."

Emotion rose in my throat at his thoughtfulness. It really was a beautiful gesture, and it made me love him all the more for it. Especially because he'd done it with pure intentions.

Athena had told me that when I was ready, I would know. At the time a part of me had doubted her words...until now.

I wanted to be connected to Peter in every way I could possibly be. I wanted to somehow repay him for all his kindness, to give him a gift—the most important gift I had. I wanted this with him before...before whatever happened next actually happened.

"What if I expected something?" I asked, searching his eyes.

Peter's eyebrows drew together. "Freddie?"

"Yes, Peter?"

He cleared his throat. "I really didn't bring you here for that, you understand that, don't you? Please don't feel like this is an obligation or anything."

I smiled. "I don't."

Peter swallowed.

There were no nerves present. I wasn't afraid or apprehensive.

I trusted him.

I loved him.

"Kiss me, Peter."

Pale sunlight drifted into the room. It couldn't be too late in the morning. Beside me, Peter still slept soundly, his breath blowing past his lips in a soft snore. I pulled out of his embrace, mourning the loss of his body the second I was away from it.

I grabbed the bag that Annie had packed for me and given to Peter. How on earth the girl had kept the secret I had no idea, as she was far too excitable most of the time to keep anything to herself.

After a quick shower, I dressed in a floaty yellow sundress and left my hair hanging loose to dry naturally. Peter was still asleep when I left the bathroom. I curled up in one of the armchairs by the window, and watched the world begin to wake up.

My heart was heavy.

I had thought last night would change my perspective, in all regards. I had thought the prospect of saying goodbye to my friends and the life I had known for ten years would dispel any and all remaining doubt about doing a gap year. I had thought being intimate with Peter would cement my feelings for him to the point that the notion of leaving him would be ridiculous.

But as I sat in that armchair, my mind was still drawn back to a life of freedom.

If anything, it was now abundantly clear not just what I wanted, but what I *had* to do. I didn't think I would ever forgive myself if I didn't. Nothing else stopped me now, except myself. And I would always wonder. I feared that wonder could easily turn to resentment. Especially if I stayed for all the wrong reasons.

I loved Peter, more than I'd ever thought possible. I hadn't been prepared for the overwhelming feeling of caring so much for another person. It felt like my heart had been cleaved in two and the other part was in the hands of someone else. Part of me did still want to stay with him. He was worth staying for...but at what cost?

If I left, did that mean we were over?

We didn't have to be.

He could always come and see me, wherever I was.

We could have little holidays together.

Or he could —

Could he?

Would he?

I slid my gaze over to his sleeping frame, his gorgeous face relaxed in sleep. I didn't want to say goodbye to him. I wanted him to come with me. Surely if he felt as strongly about me as I did him, he would at least consider it?

The sheets rustled as Peter turned over. He stretched and reached for me, but when all he found was an empty space he sat up and scanned the room. When he spotted me, a sleepy, contented smile stretched across his face. "Morning, beautiful. What are you doing all the way over there?"

"Thinking," I said as I smiled. Rising from the chair, I practically skipped over to the bed. Sitting cross-legged, I said, "I have something I want to talk to you about."

Peter chuckled and sat up, leaning back against the pillows. "This sounds interesting."

"Okay, but before I start, I know it will sound a little mad, but just hear me out, okay?"

Peter nodded.

Taking a deep breath, I decided to just blurt it out and get it over and done with. "How do you fancy taking a gap year with me?"

Peter blinked. "Are you being serious?" he asked, deadpan.

"Of course! Just think how amazing it would be! A new location whenever we feel like, seeing the world together, visiting all the places we've ever dreamed of. I could take you to China and show you the Terracotta Army, though we would definitely by flying, no way would I ever get on that train again! And we can go to America, you can see where all your favourite authors are from—Poe's house, Hemingway's, Steinbeck's...we can see them all!" I sucked in a breath and laughed, caught up in my excitement.

Peter scrubbed a hand over his face. "Freddie...I don't know what to say."

"What is there to say?" I asked, giggling. "It will be amazing, won't it?"

He shook his head. "No, because I'm not going."

I deflated like a party balloon, all the adrenaline and excitement draining from me. "You don't want to go?"

Peter sat up straighter. "It's a foolish dream, Freddie. One for children. We aren't children anymore."

"How can you say that?" I whispered. "It doesn't have to be a dream— What's stopping us?"

"Everything," Peter said with a humourless laugh. "We have responsibilities."

"I'm sick of responsibilities!" I cried, rising from the bed. "All I ever hear is how I have to be *responsible*! How my brother and sister need me as their *responsible* example for someone to look up to. How I have to be *responsible* and knuckle down at school so I get good grades. How going to St Finbars is the *responsible* thing to do!"

Peter moved to the side of the bed and pulled on his trousers from the night before. "This is the real world, Freddie! Like I said, you aren't a child anymore. You can't act like a flake and expect people to think it's cute. You're an adult, now. Act like it."

I reared back as though he had struck me.

He sighed and reached for me. "I'm sorry, I didn't mean for it to come out like that. But, bloody hell, Freddie... I'm speechless right now."

Swiping away a stray tear, I took a step towards him. "Please, please consider it, Peter. It would be amazing, *we* would be amazing. And it's not like we wouldn't come back. It's only one year."

Peter shook his head. "I have a plan, Freddie. And messing around for a year isn't part of it. Look, why don't we go get ready and have some breakfast? We can talk about planning it for after uni, maybe."

Another tear slid down my cheek. "No."

"No? No to what—no to breakfast?" he asked, puzzled. Peter scanned my face, and I felt myself break apart piece by piece.

"No to after uni. I know how these things work, Peter. If you keep saying 'one day' then one day never comes. It's like chasing the end of a rainbow."

Peter took a step back. "What exactly are you saying, Freddie?"

I sucked in a deep breath. "I'm saying that if you don't come with me...I'll go alone."

The breath rushed out of Peter. Shock was all over his face, pain lanced his fierce green eyes. "Are you serious? You would just leave? But, what about us at St Finbars together? What about...Christ, what about *us*?"

"Please understand, this is something I feel like I have to do. Otherwise I'll always wonder." I took a step towards him. "All my life I've tried to make my family proud. I've always been the good girl. I've always done exactly what was expected of me. But now it's time to do something for myself. Daddy dying last year has only made me believe in that even more. Life is short, no matter what age you live to. And I don't want to look back on my life and wish I had done things differently."

"Like me, you mean?" Peter asked in a cold voice. "You don't want to look back and wish you had faffed around the world instead of going with me?"

I shook my head as more tears rolled down my face. "No, you aren't listening to me. Peter, I—I love you. I love you so much that this is killing me right now. But I can't stay for you."

"That's great, it really is," he muttered. "So what was last night? Your special goodbye?" he asked, flinging his hand in the direction of the bed. "How considerate of you, Freddie."

I gasped and flew my hand to my mouth. "How can you even think that?"

"I don't know what to think anymore!" Peter bellowed. "Last night, I thought I knew everything and it turns out I was nothing more than a delusional, romantic idiot! I thought last night was perfect, from the ball to coming back here. I fell asleep with you in my arms last night, and I actually thought that I was the luckiest man in the world because I was holding you. I couldn't believe you chose me, out of every person on the planet, that we were together and we wouldn't be separated next year." Peter laughed ruefully. "Little did I know you've been thinking about how you can't wait to get away from me."

"Peter, please," I whispered. "*Please* understand that this has nothing to do with you."

"Yeah, I'm beginning to get that."

"Are you forgetting that I asked you to come with me? I don't want us to be apart!"

Peter shook his head. "Admit it, Freddie. You knew I would say no."

"I hoped you would say yes."

"Well, I didn't, and I won't. So here we are."

I wrapped my arms around my waist to hold myself together. "Here we are."

We didn't go for breakfast.

I gathered my things together as Peter finished getting dressed. He drove me back to Mapleton Manor with both of us in silence. Peter pulled in at the gatehouse so I could walk up the drive to school.

Neither of us was particularly concerned with getting caught. I was leaving the next day. I doubted the Mrs Macpherson would make me scrub the red staircase in Hemston.

Peter let the engine idle. He stared out of the front windscreen. "I'm sorry it ended this way," he said quietly.

"So am I," I whispered. A thick lump lodged in my throat. "We said a lot of things in the heat of the moment."

"We did."

I cleared my throat. "I'm going to leave this open, Peter. If you decide you want to see me, then I will always say yes. A weekend, half term, anything. Wherever I am."

There was a heavy pause before Peter answered. "I...I'm sorry, Freddie, but I don't think I can. This year has been hard enough only seeing you at weekends. How can you expect me to go months at a time without seeing you? It will be too hard."

A tear streaked down my face and I scrubbed it away. "I understand. But the offer is always there. Always."

Peter nodded.

"I'll be off then."

He looked down but made no further move.

I could delay the inevitable no longer. It took all my strength to wrench open the car door and climb out. I closed it behind me and started the long walk up the drive. A few minutes later, I heard the squeal of the car as Peter threw it along the road.

I hugged myself and didn't bother to wipe away the tears running rivulets down my face.

All I could think about was that I had lost the best thing that had ever happened to me.

And he hadn't told me he loved me back.

Epilogue

Masters House was quiet.

The usual shrieking, banging, heavy footsteps running across the floorboards and complaints of missing tuck box items were all absent. All the doors were flung open, letting in a flood of bright sunlight across the silent halls.

I stood in my room, peering round at the blank, empty walls that only yesterday had held so much life. Clothes had been packed, posters taken down from the walls and wristbands carefully stowed away in my trunk.

On my return to Masters, Annie and Athena had been waiting in my room, eager for the juicy details on my night with Peter.

I'd taken one look at their familiar faces, faces I wouldn't be able to see every day anymore, and had burst into body-wracking sobs. I mourned the loss of Peter, but in that moment, the loss of my friends had been a hundred times fiercer.

We'd spent the rest of the day lounging around, half-heartedly packing up our rooms and eating the scraps at the bottom of our tuck boxes. I'd found a multipack of Fruit Pastilles in a shoe, so we'd torn into them and made another pledge to never forget about each other.

They'd listened as I'd poured my heart out about the argument with Peter. They'd offered their condolences, but then they'd whooped and cheered me on for making such a difficult decision. Both of them had made me swear that I would either fly them out to wherever I was, or that I would drop in and visit them at university.

A year was simply far too long a time to go without seeing your friends, we'd decided.

For our last night in Mapleton Manor, all of us— Athena, Jemima, Harriet, Cassandra, Alicia and myself—had bunked down in Annie's room. We'd lain on our quilts, cramped together on the floor as we'd giggled and cried until the sun had come up.

I pressed my hand to the doorframe as I took one last look around my empty room. Masters, and Crosby before it, was as much my home as our house in Monaco.

Picking up my heavy trunk and light tuck box, I carried them down the familiar stairs.

I was leaving a different girl than the one who had arrived. I wasn't the gangly mischief-maker that had first walked these halls. I was a confident, beautiful young woman about to embark on the next stage of my life.

I had broken bones here. I had climbed trees and scraped my knees and torn so many uniforms that Mummy had threatened to make me wear them with patches. I'd got into trouble, and scrubbed the red staircase more times than I could count.

I had made the best friends in the world here.

I had grown up here.

"Freddie dear, thank goodness I caught you," Housemistress said as I met her at the bottom of the stairs.

"What's the matter?" I asked her.

"This was delivered for you this morning. I was dreadfully afraid I wouldn't find you to give it to you. The young man who brought it said it was most important," Housemistress said.

My heart pounded as I accepted the letter from her with a shaking hand.

"Are you all set?" she asked.

I nodded.

Housemistress sighed and pulled me in for a quick hug. "I'm so proud of you, Freddie. You've turned into a remarkable young woman. I can't wait to see what you become."

With a wobbly grin, I thanked her and stepped outside into the warm July day.

The Mapleton Manor grounds were alive with people. Girls ran about, shrieking and giggling. I passed more than a few groups of friends who sobbed in each other's arms. Parents tried to herd their children into cars, but failed in the face of someone else they just *had* to say goodbye to.

Jessica, my shadow from last year, stood with a large group of her friends, talking and gesturing animatedly. She had come so far in just two years, and was now a far cry from the shy young girl I had met on her first day of school.

She caught my eye and gave me a huge wave, a massive smile on her pretty face. I waved back and felt a rush of pride that she was now having the time of her life — just like I had promised.

I stood on the steps of the main house to keep an eye out for the car that had been sent for me to take me to their airport. The letter that I knew was from Peter burned a hole in my pocket.

As I reached to pull it out, Athena and Annie spotted me and rushed over.

"We're just about to leave," Athena said in a rush. She threw her arms around me. "I wanted one last goodbye."

We had been having 'one last goodbye' all morning.

Annie hugged me next, then Cassandra and Harriet also arrived.

Athena rubbed her eyes and I stilled her hand. "No more tears, girls. This isn't goodbye. Not really."

"Not for us at least," Cassandra said with a wink.

I grinned at her. After returning from the hotel, I'd sought out Cassandra and we'd starting planning. I would spend one week at home in Monaco so I could see my family, then I was flying out to California to stay with Cassandra for a week or two before we decided where to visit first.

"You're right," Annie said, grabbing my hand. "This is definitely not goodbye."

"Exactly. We're all far too fabulous not to be in each other's lives," Athena said with a laugh. She groaned as her mother called her again. Athena kissed my cheek then vaulted down the steps.

One by one, my friends left Mapleton Manor, taking with them pieces of the school that would live with them forever.

We'd each smuggled a brick from one of the more crumbly buildings on the grounds.

When I was alone again, I finally pulled the letter out of my pocket. My hands shook as I opened it and inched it free of the envelope.

Dear Freddie,

To my mad, adventurous and brave Lady...I want to say I'm sorry for the harsh things I said. I didn't mean them. Call it shock...injured pride...hurt that you would be leaving me.

I understand now why you have to leave. You aren't meant to be tied down, least of all to a person. So this is me 'letting you go', and hoping and praying that you one day come back to me.

Be safe, have fun and don't forget me.

I love you.

Peter

A vehicle drew up in front of the steps where I stood, and a driver got out of the black town car. He gave me a nod and moved around the car to open the boot.

A smile touched my face and I carefully tucked Peter's letter back into my pocket. I would add it to my substantial collection of others later.

I picked up my trunk and tuck box and squared my shoulders. Taking my last deep breath of crisp Mapleton Manor air, I took my first steps towards the greatest adventure of my life.

About the Author

Lady Victoria Hervey is known for being a model, socialite and aristocrat. Daughter of the 6th Marquess of Bristol, Lady Victoria led a privileged life until she chose to pursue her dream of becoming a model. In her career, she notably modelled for Christian Dior. Lady Victoria was the author of the popular party animal diary column, 'Victoria's Secrets' in The Sunday Times, which gave readers an insight into the life of a London socialite.

2016 sees Lady Victoria releasing her first fiction novel and embracing a new direction in her career as an author.

Lady Victoria loves to hear from readers. You can find her contact information, website details and author profile page at http://www.finch-books.com, and see her series website for The Wristband Diaries at:
https://www.finch-books.com/sites/lady-victoria/wristband-diaries/

More from Finch Books

A haunting romance story.

When destiny gets it wrong, a lifetime of true love hangs in the balance.

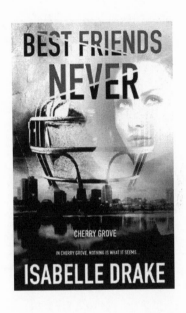

A tale of wicked truths.

Be careful who you keep secrets with, especially in picture-perfect Cherry Grove, a place where average isn't good enough, and nothing is what it seems.

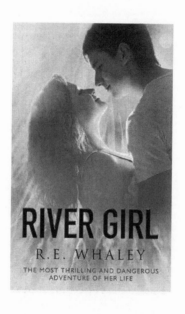

RIVER GIRL

R. E. WHALEY

THE MOST THRILLING AND DANGEROUS
ADVENTURE OF HER LIFE

Romance, danger and adventure. The perfect mix
for a thrilling read.

Pauline thinks she's going on an ordinary
vacation, but instead finds the most thrilling and
dangerous adventure of her life...and one very
handsome young Marine.

Spooky twists and paranormal sightings to capture your imagination.

When her Grandma Haley warns her to shake the spiders from her shoes, Kim comes to understand those words can also apply to all the unhappy things that life has brought her.